THE

STILL SILENT

PROPHET

By

Susan Davis Sandberg

Cover design by John Sandberg
Cover photo by Christin Lola, Shutterstock.com

To Ken, my very unique son-in-law, whose good common sense coupled with a wry sense of humor warms my soul

CHAPTER 1

On a quiet fall morning, on the outskirts of Willow Glen, forty-five minutes north and slightly west of Chicago, inside an apparently modest one story farm house, the chunky, middle-aged Praetzel housekeeper, Bertha Locke, was clearing the table while Gerard sat in his high chair trying to pick up the cheerios scattered on the tray.

Stanley and Aleta Praetzel had left early that morning so Aleta could make her statement at police headquarters before going to the office.

When the door opened and Jamara walked in, the baby lifted his arms and asked her to pick him up. The black nanny went over, kissed him, took off her coat, hung it up and then sat down next to the baby.

"They be gone?" Jamara asked.

"She shot a man dead last night," Bertha announced as she set Jamara's breakfast in front of her.

"Here?" Jamara asked.

"On the trail out back that leads to the Forest Preserves."

"They doesn't ride at night," Jamara declared.

As she said that, the side door opened and the ancient groomsman hobbled in.

"Sit down," Bertha said pleasantly. "If you don't want your eggs scrambled, you'll have to wait."

"Scrambled is fine," Hubbs said good-naturedly. "The vet's coming this morning."

"How badly was Minx hurt?" Bertha queried.

"Not bad," Hubbs grunted, accepting his plate of food.

"You called a vet," Bertha pointed out.

"Mr. Praetzel said to."

"Oh," Bertha said, relaxing. "So Minx will be okay?"

"Don't know," Hubbs said.

"What don't you know?" Bertha persisted.

"Don't think she's ever been shot before."

"You think she'll be skittish?"

"Maybe."

"How was she this morning?"

"Restless."

Jamara broke in.

"Why they be riding at night?"

"He went to meet somebody."

"Why?" Jamara asked.

"Don't know," Hubbs said. "The Missus followed on Shadow bareback. I called Chief Milani when I saw the rifle on her back."

"Then what happened?"

"There was three shots," Hubbs said.

He forked another spoonful of eggs in his mouth and swallowed before he went on.

"Shadow came home without her, so I went back for her."

"Where was Mr. Praetzel?" Jamara probed.

"Gone."

"Gone where?"

"Where Minx took him."

"The horse ran off with him?"

"Yep."

"I thought Minx didn't run," Jamara said.

"She run full out last night," Hubbs reported. "Guess she don't like being shot."

"Is Mr. Praetzel okay?" Jamara asked.

"He hung on. She brung him back."

"What about Mrs. Praetzel?"

"She weren't on Shadow when she fired her rifle."

"Didn't she tie him to something?" Jamara asked.

"Shadow brung that with him. Seems a little tree ain't no match for a big horse that's scared."

Bertha picked up the tale.

"From what I heard this morning, Mr. Praetzel got a call from the men who planted those twelve bombs and arranged to meet them on the road that runs past the Babcock estate," Bertha explained. "One of the men that was caught said there were two bombs in the barn. The dogs only found one. Mr. Praetzel wanted the location of the other one pretty bad. It would be one of the last two out there. He cleaned out his safe. He figured they'd go for the place he picked. It's a quiet road. And I guess he figured that being on horseback would keep him safe."

"Weren't a bad plan," Hubbs noted.

"Aleta followed him," Bertha continued. "The driver got out of the car and grabbed Minx's reins. Aleta shot him in the hand. He let go and got back in the car. Guess the men in the car asked Mr. Praetzel who was doing the shooting. He told them that it was one of the best marksmen on the police force. He told them to take the money and go."

"Then what?" Jamara pressed.

"It gets mixed up after that," Bertha said. "It seems that one of them pulled a gun on Stanley. Then someone inside the car shot Aleta. Nicked her ear. I think that's when Minx was shot."

"And?" Jamara urged.

"Aleta shot the man outside the car dead and Minx ran off. The car chased the horse. Then the sheriff came," Bertha finished. "That's as much as I could piece together from what Stanley said this morning. He was still upset about her following him."

"Is she talking?" Jamara asked.

"No," Bertha said. "But Mr. Praetzel got the location of one more of the bombs, so he's pretty pumped. But he's also angry. That I don't get at all."

"So she's still not speaking?" Jamara concluded.

"As long as there's still one voice-activated bomb hidden somewhere, she's silent."

"Still can't sign?" Jamara asked.

"Evidently that was a temporary gift meant to help her through the transition period."

"Can she write or type?" Jamara asked.

Bertha shook her head and then added, "Stanley and she accept this as a protective device. As long as she can't communicate, Stuart Fouts doesn't see her as a threat."

"He be enjoying her suffering," Jamara observed.

"Only two men in that gang left," Bertha surmised. "And one is the bomb maker."

"So there could be more coming?"

"Who have the police got?"

"Sergio Vannella's boys worked over Lennie Archer. He's unconscious in the Tri City Hospital. Butch Lennert drove him there and was arrested."

"Sergio Vannella? Isn't he the boss that works out of Cicero?" Hubbs asked.

"Aleta saved his life the same time she was saving Frank Catalano's," Bertha said, "You remember the stink about her saving the lives of mob bosses. Jamara almost quit until her son told her Aleta was saving the lives of the people who would be killed if there was a mob war."

"Innocent people," Jamara reiterated.

"Don't Butch know where all the bombs are?" Hubbs asked.

"He says he doesn't," Bertha replied. "And he won't say anything else until he talks to Lennie. And Lennie is in a coma.

Shortly after Aleta gave her statement at police headquarters, Stanley drove her to the office. He could tell she was still angry with him.

"I know you're still angry with me for being so foolhardy, but it seemed like such a clever idea at the time," Stanley explained. "No one kills the goose that lays the golden egg. It never dawned on me that they might want to capture that goose."

Aleta acknowledged his explanation with an almost imperceptible nod.

"You'll have to speak up if you want me to hear you."

Aleta pummeled his arm with her fist and burst into tears.

"Point made," Stanley said. "Now are you ready to go to work or do you want me to take you home?"

Aleta pointed in the direction of the office.

Once there, Stanley called for a five-minute emergency meeting in the library. The entire staff left their offices, their work and their clients. Only Alice stayed at the front desk.

Once the entire staff had gathered in his office, Stanley plunged right in.

"Last night the men, who are behind the bomb plot, tried to kidnap me. Aleta shot one in the hand and the other in the head. The first had grabbed the reins of my horse; the second had a gun pointed at my head. That was a mistake. There are still undiscovered bombs, so Aleta is not yet able to speak. Any questions?"

"You were riding at night?" Roland Chin asked.

"I was delivering a payment in exchange for information on the bombs, and I foolishly thought I would be safe. Aleta followed me, hid behind a small hill and shot from there. She is an excellent marksman."

"You couldn't just gallop away?" Chin pressed.

"My horse, Minx, is a calm horse. She is also a slow horse. She doesn't like to trot let alone gallop. Something spooked her and she ran off on her own with me on board."

"Maybe gunfire?" Chin suggested.

"She was one of four horses near an exploding grenade a couple of months ago and she didn't even step back."

Aleta clapped her hands.

Stanley turned at once and asked, "You think that the fact that the bullet grazed her spooked her?"

Aleta nodded and then stretched out her hands as if pull taffy. Then she pantomimed falling against someone.

"The dead man fell on her?" Stanley asked.

Aleta nodded.

Stanley continued. "The guards are here to protect Aleta and to keep me from any more escapades."

Aleta nodded, smiling.

Stanley's mother, former judge Lydia Davis, ended the meeting by saying, "Aleta, let me show you how we've set you up."

The meeting broke up and Lydia followed Aleta to her office. When they were in Aleta's office, Lydia shut the door and embraced Aleta.

After she released Aleta, she added, "I intend to scold Stanley soundly since I know you can't."

Aleta shook her head.

"He apologized?"

She nodded.

"Well, he's going to get a piece of my mind."

Aleta nodded, chuckling.

"Use the phone as an intercom. If any of us see a call from you, we will come at once."

Aleta's woebegone look prompted Lydia to add, "It's okay, Aleta. We are all hoping for a call or two from you. Please use us. Break up our day. Make us feel important. Most of us are working on contracts today. You can call us in to meet a client. We'd like that."

Aleta nodded.

The first client was a thin woman in her fifties. Her paperwork was neatly filled out.

Aleta handed her a card on which was typed, "I can't speak."

The woman handed Aleta a card that read, "I am deaf."

Aleta laughed and gestured to the woman to be seated. The woman signed a short query.

"Do you sign?"

Aleta shook her head and she found herself signing the reply, "I used to be able to."

The woman gazed at her bewildered.

Aleta signed again.

"God sometimes gives me special communication skills when I need them. Right now I can sign. Let me call my husband. If he can understand our signing, he can translate your needs to one of our staff.

"Will that person be my lawyer instead of you?"

Aleta nodded. She punched two intercom buttons. Stanley and his mother both appeared.

Aleta looked at Stanley and signed, "Can you understand me?"

Stanley turned to his mother and said, "She's asking if I understand her."

"Do you?" Lydia asked.

"Yes, I do."

Aleta signed. "I want you to translate my interview with Mrs. Herman. She is able to write, but right now this method will be more productive."

"Go ahead," Stanley said.

Mrs. Herman signed, "My mother is being conned. I need help."

Lydia began asking questions which Aleta signed to Mrs. Herman. Stanley translated Mrs. Herman's responses.

It was almost an hour before the four were done and Lydia finished outlining what she planned to do and all Mrs. Herman's questions were answered.

"I can pay," Mrs. Herman signed. "I know that you, Mr. Praetzel charge three hundred dollars and hour. Do I pay for each of you?"

Aleta shook her head as Stanley translated her question for his mother.

"My husband is a proud man," Mrs. Herman signed. "He will not allow me to take charity. We don't want my mother's money. What we want is for her not to suffer the shame that will be hers if she'd conned out of her nest egg. We are willing to pay to prevent that."

Aleta signed. "A tabulation of the time each of us spends on your case will be kept and you will be billed accordingly."

"Thank you," Mrs. Herman signed, smiling.

Lydia rose and shook her hand, telling her she would see her later. Lydia guessed correctly that Mrs. Herman could read lips when it came to simple, expected exchanges.

Mrs. Herman nodded. The closing remark was merely a courtesy. The plan had been hammered out in detail using sign language.

The next client Tim ushered in was a short, plump man with an unkempt beard. Other than that he as neatly attired. He handed Aleta the form he had been told to fill out. Aleta recognized the scrawl of someone who had suffered a recent stroke.

"Nobody understands me and I can't write," he complained and when Aleta nodded with apparent understanding, he went on to explain what he needed.

As he talked, Aleta pressed the intercom buttons that brought Stanley and their newest associate, Nigel Oliver to their side.

Stanley heard the incoherent jumble of words and realized that while Aleta could understand him, the tall black lawyer standing beside him couldn't. Nigel Oliver was completely confused.

Then Aleta signed and Stanley translated her signing. Mr. Krantz nodded happily.

Nigel Oliver stumbled backwards and sat down hard. He was then introduced to Mr. Krantz as his lawyer.

Nigel stammered that he wouldn't know where to begin.

Aleta glared at him. Then she signed and Stanley translated her words, "I know what Mr. Krantz needs and I can translate his needs to you."

She handed him a pad.

"Take notes," she ordered through Stanley. "Mr. Krantz needs a final will, a trust set up for his youngest daughter, a change in the ownership of his house, a financial power of attorney and a letter to his barber."

An hour later Aleta was satisfied that Nigel could complete the tasks before him. He had learned how to communicate in a simple fashion with his client. Both were now happy. They went to Nigel's office to finish.

Stanley leaned over and kissed his wife.

"I'm proud of you," he said. "You helped two desperate people today."

She shrugged off his praise. She felt as if she were a mere translator, unable to interact.

Stanley was puzzled by her attitude.

"We have more people waiting, but I can have your police guard take you home if you like."

Aleta burst into tears. Stanley pulled her into his arms.

"Your emotions are running away with you. Don't let them. You are failing no one, least of all God."

Aleta pushed him away, wiped her eyes, blew her nose and sat back down.

"Don't forget there are still several lawyers whose day hasn't been interrupted. I don't think you should leave until you send each of them a difficult case."

Aleta smiled and nodded and pointed at him.

"Not me!" he exclaimed. "I can get my own cases, thank you very much."

He left her chuckling and told Alice she was prepared for the next interview.

Wilson Metzger had waited over three hours to see Aleta Praetzel, so when she handed him the card informing him that she couldn't speak, he sand into the nearest chair and fingering the card, said, "What do I do. I need a really sharp lawyer."

He looked at Aleta and she cocked her head and raised an eyebrow in query.

"I need you," he said.

She held up a preprinted card. It read "discrimination?"

"Of a sort," he responded. "I haven't been fired yet, but it's coming. Worse than that is the fact that the treatment is so abusive, I'm not sure I can hang on long enough to get the pension I've worked all my life for."

The second card said "basis?"

"I'm a heart transplant recipient," Wilson Metzger said. "I'm only fifty-four. I can take early retirement in a year. I will also receive a sizeable bonus if I can make it to the end of this fiscal year."

Aleta pushed a button. Hubert appeared a minute later.

She handed her father-in-law Metzger's file. The men shook hands and Hubert introduced himself.

"You're a criminal attorney," Metzger commented. "I've read about you over the years. You head a law firm in Chicago on the north side."

Hubert smiled.

"Not any more. I'm one of the associates of this firm now."

"What happened?"

"I wanted to represent honest people for a change."

Metzger laughed. "Are any of those left?"

"You're one," Hubert said. "Otherwise Aleta wouldn't have accepted your case."

"I don't know how much of a case I have. The acts are so subtle."

"Just my speed," Hubert said warmly. "Come to my office and let's see what we can do for you."

The next prospective client was a slovenly dressed young man. He told Aleta he had information to sell.

She held up a card that said, "not interested".

"Your boss will be," he charged.

Aleta pressed the intercom. Stanley appeared within a matter of seconds. She held up the card that said "not interested".

"That ain't so," the young man said. "Word on the street is that you pay good."

"We don't buy information," Stanley stated flatly.

"I know where one of them bombs is," he blurted out.

"How do you know?" Stanley asked.

"I seen it put where it is."

"Aleta, do you have your cuffs?"

"How old are you?" Stanley asked as he reached for the cuffs.

"I ain't no juvenile," the kid said, backing away. "I come here because the guy said you paid good. I didn't plant the bomb nor nothing. You ain't got no reason to arrest me."

"You're under arrest," Stanley said, grabbing a wrist and snapping on a cuff. He pulled the other arm around the kid's back and cuffed it. Then he read him his rights.

Finally, he opened his cell and called Tom.

"Got a present for you. Aleta wants her cuffs back. He says he knows where another bomb is."

"Where are you?" Chief Milani asked.

"Office," Stanley replied. "I didn't want to send him to you. It could be a ploy to pull off one of the guards."

CHAPTER 2

Before Stanley left her office, Aleta pointed to the boy with a streak of purple hair who had gold rings in his nose and ears, studs above his eyebrows, and whose pants barely clung to his hips when he stood up.

"Mine?" Stanley asked.

The boy shook his head.

"I want her," the boy said.

"Why?" Stanley asked.

"I need a really smart lawyer."

Aleta put three Scrabble tiles on the holder to spell one short word: "him".

"I need someone that's not afraid of people with money."

Aleta pointed to Stanley.

"You know anything about investments?" the kid charged.

Stanley chuckled.

Aleta put more tiles together and spelled: "richer than you".

"That isn't rich at all," the boy said and then offered his hand to Stanley. "Wendell..."

"Alexander Kingston the third," Stanley finished. "Come into my office and let's see if we can work together."

When Wendell saw the fish, he exclaimed, "Wow! You own the building, don't you?"

"An astute observation," Stanley said. "How did you come to that conclusion?"

"These tanks hold a lot of water. This is an old building. You had to do some major structural changes to hold up these tanks."

"Yes, I did," Stanley said. "You're the first to notice."

"Maybe you can help me after all."

"You plan to build something?"

"Yeh. My future," Wendell said. "Right now it's in the hands of my father and he's not letting me have any say."

"He's the trustee of your trust fund, isn't he?"

"Yeh. Grandpa set it up when I was little. And Dad invests in CD's and Treasury Bonds and stuff like that."

"That's a wise way to invest Trust money. I would do the same."

"But I know how to invest. Grandpa taught me. And he gave me a hundred thousand dollars to invest and I have my own brokerage account and I invest in the stock market, and my father buys whenever I buy and sells whenever I sell, and still he won't give me access to my trust even though I've almost doubled the hundred thousand in three year's time."

"So, what brought you here?"

"I want to break the Trust and take over," Wendell said. "I want to invest in property."

"Have you told him this?"

"Yes.

"And?"

"It has a business on it."

"You want to go into business?"

"It's a tree farm," Wendell said. "It's for sale and I want to buy it."

"What do you plan to do with it?"

"Grow trees."

"There's not much money in that."

"There's enough," Wendell said. "I want to live there."

"On a tree farm?"

"I like trees. I like growing them. There's land nearby so I can expand. I need my trust money to do that."

"What does your father want?"

"He wants me to go to college."

"And you don't want to?"

"I'd go if I could major in forestry."

"And he put thumbs down on that idea."

"Way down," Wendell said. "I think it's because I said I planned to live there."

"Why?"

"So people don't steal my trees."

"People steal trees?"

"People steal everything."

"Are those rings removable?"

"Yes, why?"

"Go into the bathroom and wash that stuff out of your hair and remove the rings. I'm going to call your grandfather."

"He doesn't mind the way I dress."

"You need to look less like a rebellious kid and more like a young man with a vision."

"What about my clothes?"

"There's a clothier in the block of stores on this street," Stanley answered. "I will have him bring you appropriate clothing."

"Grandpa…"

"Your grandfather needs to see the young man I see."

"It won't work with Dad."

"I already know that," Stanley said. "But I have a plan. The first part of it is for you to have lunch here in my office with your grandfather. You tell him what you want. If you can convince him that your plan is a good one, I will make it happen."

"You can do that?"

"Yes, but you need to convince your grandfather that yours is a good idea."

"Will you eat lunch with us?"

"I have a doctor's appointment at eleven thirty. It's a short one. I will be back at noon, but I will eat with my staff. My secretary will show in the clothier. At one o'clock we will finish."

Immediately after he sent Wendell to the restroom to wash his hair and remove his rings, he asked Alice to request that his mother come to his office at her convenience. She showed up one minute later.

"Mother," he said as soon as she closed the door. "I have a doctor's appointment. I don't want Aleta to come with me."

"What's wrong?"

"When I was in the hospital after the dumpster incident, Dr. Cook gave me a full physical," Stanley began.

"I heard about that," his mother said.

"He did blood work and Dr. Cook wants to discuss something with me," Stanley said. "I think my cholesterol may be a little high, but I don't want Aleta to put me on a diet before I talk with Dr. Cook."

"She does tend to go overboard sometimes," Lydia chuckled.

"I will be back in time for lunch," Stanley said. "He said he wanted to check something."

"Are you sure it's your cholesterol?" Lydia asked, a trace of suspicion in her tone.

"No Mother, I'm not," Stanley said. "Results can be handled over the phone. Drawing blood for a second lab test cannot. I believe I have another lab test in my immediate future and I'm not happy about it."

His answer satisfied his mother.

Closed up in her office, Aleta didn't see Stanley or his police bodyguard leave.

He came back just before noon. He was limping slightly.

The entire staff broke for lunch at noon.

"Thanks for the Metzger case," Hubert said as everyone gathered in the library. "It's a humdinger."

Chin spoke up. "Did you know that Mrs. Cherrystone's sister is a millionaire?"

Aleta nodded.

"The only basis for the suit I can perceive is fraud," Chin said. "Is that what you had in mind?"

Aleta nodded.

"Glad you asked that," Tim said. "I promised her that Aleta would be working with you. She looked so worried."

"No wonder she was so eager to get to work," Chin said. "She thinks Aleta is her lawyer."

Aleta shook her head.

Stanley clarified the situation. "Aleta will guide you as she just did. It's your case. She has no intention of taking over."

Aleta nodded her agreement.

Chin's disbelief was almost undetectable, but Stanley spotted it.

"Aleta would have handed Tim her card with yours if she planned to be lead counsel," Stanley said.

Aleta nodded her affirmation.

"I'm sure she remembered the great job you did with you part on the Van Horne case. You were one of the reasons we came away with such a big fee," Stanley said, his smile broadening. "We never forget details involving money."

Everyone chuckled.

"Oh, and just to prove it, my latest client, who by the way, is lunching in my office with his grandfather, pegged my hourly rate at less than Aleta's and I had to return fifty bucks."

This time the entire group laughed.

"I want a raise," Stanley declared in response.

More laughter ensued.

"You need to raise Aleta's rate," Lydia said. "Then you can move up to mine and Hubert's level and we can move up with her."

"You mean Alice is charging our clients that much for your services?" Stanley asked, aghast.

Lydia smiled as she responded, "I'm a sitting judge, after all. You didn't think that the city council would expect that I would be lower on the scale than Aleta?"

Hubert quickly added, "And I'm her husband. What she gets, I get."

"I'm the Senior Partner," Stanley groused. "How come I'm lower?"

"Because you consider you wife and your mother valuable assets," his mother answered.

"Or you're a realist," his father said. "We all have a reputation in legal circles. You can command more for our services. And perhaps this is the time to mention that none of us is outrageously high-priced."

"We don't want to be out of reach for the average man," Stanley said.

"We aren't," several chorused strongly.

"You all think I should raise Aleta's rate, don't you?"

"Considering the miracle I witnessed today," Lydia said. "Definitely!"

"Considering what I was privy to," Nigel Oliver said. "I agree wholeheartedly."

"Okay, Alice, Aleta's rate is now four hundred dollars and hour."

"And mine?" Lydia asked.

"You're only going to be here one more week," Stanley pointed out, slightly nettled.

"I want a promotion. I'm worth it."

"I'm not even paying you," Stanley protested.

"Heavens! I know that!"

The group chuckled at the exchange.

"Alice, Judge Davis's rate is raised as well."

"And your father's?" Lydia asked.

Alice spoke up.

"His will be equal to yours, Judge Davis. Goodness knows he's worth it."

"Did I get a raise too, Alice?" Stanley asked facetiously.

"Of course. That's what this is all about. You get a fifty dollar raise."

"They each got one hundred," Stanley blurted out.

"You're a child advocate. The county won't pay that much."

"I work at half-rate now," Stanley declared.

"And they count every cent," Alice countered.

"Raise Robert's rate too or they'll send him all the cases."

"Well, that's one way to get a promotion," Robert commented tongue-in-cheek.

"Promotion?" Stanley shot back. "Robert, you're a partner. I'm only changing our fee schedule, not our salaries."

"It's a step up," Robert said. "Bertha will see it as a promotion."

"Why aren't you home eating with her?" Stanley asked querulously.

"I didn't want to miss the fun," Robert said. "Beside she said she had lots of baking to do for your party tomorrow night."

"Well, miss the fun from now on. I won't have a disgruntled housekeeper on my hands."

"It was her idea," Robert returned.

"She didn't expect you to take her up on it," Stanley pronounced with certainty. "Take an hour and go home."

Robert glanced at his daughter who nodded almost imperceptibly.

"I will take you up on that offer," he said cheerfully. "I'm dying to tell her about my promotion."

"It's not a…" Stanley started when he felt the touch of Aleta's hand. "It's not a regular promotion, but it is a raise in how you're valued."

"On second thought, I will call her," Robert said. "I can't possibly stuff down a second lunch and she'll be upset if I leave a crumb."

This time Stanley joined the laughter.

A little before one, Stanley left the group and entered his office. He smiled at the grandfather and grandson and asked, "Where are we?"

"Grandpa is going to live with me on the tree farm," Wendell said. "I'm going to Willow Glen College for the first couple of years. That's the deal."

"Wendell wants me to buy the tree farm," the elderly man said.

"You can't. You have too large a family. You've divided up as much as you could and still keep enough for a comfortable old age," Stanley said. "Your grandson needs to do this on his own."

"So you'll get me my trust money?" Wendell said.

"Not exactly," Stanley said. "We're going to take out a loan with your trust fund as collateral."

"The banks won't do that," Wendell said. "I tried."

"You're a minor," Stanley stated flatly.

"Dad wouldn't co-sign," Wendell complained.

Stanley grew thoughtful.

"Did you say that you and your grandfather planned to live together on the tree farm?"

"Yes. Grandpa likes trees too," Wendell said. "And we aren't going to cut them down. We're going to replant them."

"Then you can buy the farm as a joint venture. Your grandfather will save money on taxes if he reinvests his gains from his house sale in a new place that's his primary residence," Stanley said. "This is going to be complicated. You need to talk with our tax expert first."

"Why is it complicated?" the grandfather asked.

"You need to protect your grandson's future should anything happen to you."

"I agree," the old man said.

Stanley picked up his phone.

"Robert, we have a client who needs tax advice. Have him sign a contract... Yes, Robert, I have been dispensing legal advice... Yes, he can pay."

A knock on the door was followed by the entrance of a tall man closer in age to Kingston Senior than Stanley Praetzel. He handed Stanley a contract.

"Mr. Kingston, may I present Robert Locke, our resident tax expert," Stanley said. "Mr. Kingston and his grandson plan to buy the tree farm west of Catalpa Grove."

"It'll be years before Willow Glen expands that far out," Robert said.

"That's what they're hoping," Stanley said. "They want to live there and grow trees."

"You'll have to learn to fly a chopper," Robert said.

"Why?" Stanley asked.

"That's how they deliver the trees."

"They don't truck them?"

"I guess they could, but it's easier to bring them in by chopper."

"Wendell, did you know that?" Stanley asked.

His grandfather's eyes grew merry.

"He knew," he said. "That's why he put me in charge of the baby trees."

"Gramps, we hire a chopper when we sell one of the big trees," Wendell explained. "Otherwise we truck them."

"Does anyone buy the big trees?" his grandfather asked.

"Mr. Praetzel might," Wendell said. "He wants a tree outside his children's wing to block the view of the garage."

"Did the owner tell you that?" Stanley asked.

"Yes," Wendell said. "You're his best customer. And you talked the Tontine Lake subdivision into buying a tree for every lot and you bought the first two for the lots you bought on spec."

"That's why I knew about the chopper," Robert said. "I watched them plant the two. It was a big production."

"Must have cost a fortune," the Senior Kingston said.

"It did," Stanley said. "The price of the lots went up significantly and are now considered choice."

Robert cleared his throat.

"Oh, yes," Stanley said. "After you discuss the tax advantages when Mr. Kingston sells his house and buys the farm where he plans to live, we need to complete the contracts to protect this plan in the offing. Mr. Kingston plans to loan his grandson enough money to own sixty percent of the tree farm. Wendell is using his trust fund as collateral. We will be trustees for Wendell in this transaction. His father is the trustee of his trust fund, but we aren't touching it."

"This will entail a lot of contract work," Robert said.

"Give it to Aleta. That's her bailiwick. Mother can help her," Stanley said.

Stanley turned back to Mr. Kingston.

"Your house is on the market?"

"I have an offer, but it's a little low."

"If it's above two million five, take it," Stanley said.

"I was hoping for two seventy-five."

"They want it furnished," Stanley said. "Take the grand piano and your desk. Charge them three hundred thousand for the furniture and appliances except for those two items."

"That's too little," Kingston said.

"I suggest you let your children pick out what they want to remember their mother and anything else they fancy. They each get to choose three items. After those items are chosen, they can buy anything else they want. They'll pick out the valuable items, believe me."

"I guess," Kingston said hesitantly.

"You don't need to sort through memories at this time. You don't need to fret over whom to give what to. Let Wendell pick out several items for you and for himself. Then pack your clothes and leave."

"What else?"

"Tell your cook to pack her favorite pots and pans and move them to the new house. You are planning to keep her, aren't you?"

"I hadn't thought about the staff."

"You need a cook and a housekeeper," Stanley said. "You need someone around should you have another stroke."

"Is there anything you don't know?" Kingston asked, nettled.

"You still have less use of your left arm than your right," Stanley said. "Stress is one of the causes of strokes. I'm suggesting a path through this transition that will cause the least stress. Don't be in the house when your children make their choices. Wendell can monitor the transactions and log in what each one took."

"I don't know what to charge."

"Wendell will set the price," Stanley said. "Give him some guidelines."

"Suppose they won't listen to him?" Kingston asked.

"Call me, Wendell. I will charge whoever is giving you trouble my hourly rate to adjudicate. I am your grandfather's legal representative, so don't be afraid to call me. Believe me, I know the value of things and I will respect your opinion as your grandfather's representative."

"Maybe you should just be there," Wendell said.

"Let's give your father and your uncles and aunts a chance to work things out first." Stanley said. "I will tell them what they can and can't do before they arrive. I will set the day and time."

"What do I do?" Kingston asked a trifle facetiously.

"You make an offer on the tree farm. If the price is under three million, take it as is."

"Without haggling?" Kingston asked, suddenly engaged in his future plans.

"You need to act quickly," Stanley said. "Once someone realizes a man as rich as you is interested, he'll grab it up and you'll pay more."

"Is it worth more?"

"You know it is. That's why you're interested," Stanley said knowingly. "I can tell from the look on your face that the price is close to three million. Make a straight offer to buy at the price listed. You'll take the property as is."

"Isn't that foolish?"

"Don't quibble over fifty thousand dollars in house repairs on a three million dollar deal, Stanley advised. "That's like fussing over sixteen cents on a ten dollar purchase."

"I understand what you're saying, but…"

"If a bidding war starts, you'll lose," Stanley said.

"I will pay for the repairs, Grandpa," Wendell offered. "It's going to be my house too."

""Where are you going to get fifty thousand dollars?" Kingston snapped.

"I'm going to sell Mr. Praetzel trees," Wendell said. "Of course, we can't fix everything all at once, but if you loan me a bit extra on my trust fund, I can pay for us moving the piano and the desk and my stuff and fix the roof so nothing gets ruined."

"You know about the roof?" Kingston asked his grandson.

"That's the biggest expense. I asked the handyman."

"I will match everything you spend," Kingston said.

"Hey, we'll be rich!" Wendell exclaimed.

"I'm looking forward to that," Wendell's grandfather said, smiling.

"Let's talk in my office," Robert said.

"Once in Robert Locke's office, Wendell Kingston Senior asked, "Does Mr. Praetzel know anything about property?"

"He owns Main Street, Second Street and Third Street," Robert said. "He is already drawing up plans to renovate Second Street. The Third Street renovation is still in the thinking stage. Second Street is going to have a restaurant. I'm looking forward to that."

"He's not the person buying my house, is he?" Wendell Kingston asked.

"He doesn't invest in high-end residential," Robert said. "He will buy land and build, however. He did that in the Tontine subdivision I'm living in."

"I'm surprised that subdivision is growing so slowly."

"My mother is particular about her neighbors. She can afford to be. She owned the original parcel of land."

"And she sold some to Mr. Praetzel on spec?"

"Yes, she did," Robert said. "How much are you going to realize from your house sale?"

"Practically all of it."

"Grandpa needs to put most of it in the tree farm and we need a contract so I can buy shares from him," Wendell interjected. "I want to make small payments for four years and a balloon payment when I'm twenty one. I want to own sixty percent."

"You need to draw up a new will," Robert told the grandfather.

"Yes," Wendell cut in. "Otherwise, Dad will sell the farm right out from under me. I need a will too, so Grandpa will be able to stay on the farm if I get killed or something. That's our new home. We need to protect it.

Wendell Kingston, Senior nodded happily.

CHAPTER 3

While Stanley was busy with the Kingstons, the line began forming on the staircase. When Aleta looked at the line at one o'clock, she recognized several from the morning line. Tim went to work as Alice made a new flash card for Aleta stating her new hourly rate.

"It was decided at lunch," Alice stated.

Aleta spelled out, "tomorrow".

"No," Alice responded firmly. "We finished with this morning's group. This is the beginning of tomorrow's group."

Aleta sighed and took the new card and handed Alice the old one.

She sent the first two elderly gentlemen to Nigel and dismissed a tax case.

The next prospective client was a young girl. The name on the folder was Brittany Watson.

"Paige sent me," She said. "I can't pay all the money at once, but I will pay. I get a hundred dollars a month allowance, so here's my first payment."

Her blonde curls bounced when she spoke.

Aleta nodded and then spelled out, "half for teens".

"The lady out front said you charge four hundred dollars an hour"

The curls made her appear coquettish, but her voice was serious.

Aleta nodded.

"I'm pregnant. I'm a senior. I'm farther along than Paige. I have to decide right now if I should get an abortion or not."

Aleta shook her head.

"No abortion?" the girl questioned.

Aleta nodded.

"Can you get the School board to let me stay in regular classes?"

Aleta spelled out: "pregnancy leave".

"You mean like in business?"

Aleta nodded.

"Well, why not," Brittany said. "They keep telling us they're preparing us for the real world."

"Home school," Aleta spelled out.

"You mean at the end when I'm really big?"

Aleta shook her head and swung an imaginary baby in her arms.

"After the baby comes?"

Aleta nodded.

"You think they will let me go to the end?"

Aleta fluttered her hand.

"Give or take a few days?"

Aleta nodded.

"I'm for that," the girl said.

Aleta spelled out the word, "doctor".

Brittany shook her head. The curls bounced.

Aleta opened her the drawer in her desk, took out two cards and handed them to Brittany. One was her business card; the other, Dr. Chesney's.

"He won't tell my parents?"

Aleta used her letters to spell out, "you will".

"They will want me to get an abortion," Brittany said.

Aleta handed her another card.

"Who is this?" Brittany asked.

Aleta pressed a button on the intercom and Stanley appeared. She handed him the folder and he scanned it.

"You took the case?" he asked.

She nodded and pointed at him and then at herself.

"We are taking the case?"

Aleta nodded.

"Do we have a plan of action?" Stanley asked.

Aleta gestured and Brittany spoke up.

"Pregnancy leave like in business only after the baby is born, except maybe a bit during the end of the pregnancy so I don't drop it in school. And I'm not to get an abortion. I'm supposed to go to Dr. Chesney, so the baby will be healthy. I need to tell my parents. They will want me to get an abortion. I don't want one. I read an article about that. Women never get over that. I need help with that."

Aleta pointed to Stanley.

"You can help me with that?" Brittany asked Stanley.

"I'm a child advocate," he said warmly. "That's what I do."

Aleta turned the holder around. She had spelled out one word: "expert".

"I have to pay in payments," Brittany said. "I paid half of the two hundred to Mrs. Praetzel. She said teenagers get a special rate."

"I'm even cheaper," Stanley said. "That's because Aleta is the best lawyer in the firm. I will go with you to speak with your parents."

"Now?" Brittany asked.

Her tone told Stanley it was a request.

"I don't want to miss more than a half day of school," she explained.

"Is your father available now?"

Brittany took out her cell phone and punched in a number on her speed dial.

"Dad, I've got something dreadfully important... no, it can't wait... I have a lawyer. He's on the clock and he's expensive... We'll be right there."

"Is your father a lawyer?" Stanley asked, a slight smile tickling the corner of his mouth.

"Dull stuff," Brittany said. "Taxes."

"Maybe Robert should go?" Stanley ventured.

"Is he better than you?" Brittany asked.

Aleta shook her head.

"I will drive," Brittany said.

Stanley grinned.

"We'll go in a patrol car. I'm being guarded."

"Wow!" Brittany squealed. "Dad will flip."

"The guard will come to the door of the office with us."

"Whoa! What a ride this is going to be."

Stanley smiled. "We like to give our clients full value for their dollar."

"Can you please not tell him that you're cheaper than your wife?"

"I'm not much cheaper," Stanley said.

"Oh, okay. It'll blow his mind that I've got two lawyers."

After they left, Hubert entered Aleta's office.

Aleta looked at her father-in-law, questioningly.

"I want you to know that you can send me easy cases too."

Aleta smiled and waved him into a chair.

The next person to walk into the room was a dark-haired, dark-eyed teenager whose first words were, "Brittany and I were together. We have the same problem. Wherever she's going with that handsome man, I want to go to."

Aleta chuckled and Hubert couldn't repress a smile.

"It's not funny. We were supposed to split the cost," the girl went on.

She handed the folder to Aleta. The name Sophia Antonopolous was written on the folder.

"You'll see. It's the same problem," Sophia insisted.

Aleta shook her head as she scanned the contents.

"Yes, it is. We're both seniors. We're both pregnant. We both want to stay in school;"

Aleta pushed the fee sign in front of the girl.

"Four hundred dollars!" she gasped. "Brittany agreed to pay that."

Aleta nodded.

"An abortion's cheaper."

Aleta shrugged.

"Did you talk to Brittany at all? She's dead set against one."

Aleta nodded.

"Paige said you can't speak. How can you be a lawyer if you can't speak?"

Aleta spelled out, "can advise".

"You haven't advised me."

Aleta spelled out, "you need to pay".

"Wait until I get hold of Brittany. She was supposed to handle this. My parents will be furious."

She placed four hundreds on the desk.

Aleta spelled out, "allowance?"

"Hell no!" Sophia sputtered. "I need my allowance."

"Source?" Aleta spelled out, grateful that Lydia had made one of the blank tiles a question mark.

"I borrowed," Sophia said.

"From?"

"My mother."

"Does she know?"

"Not yet," Sophia hedged.

Aleta handed back the money and spelled out, "put it back".

"Are you free then?"

"You pay".

"What difference does it make where the money comes from?"

Aleta looked at Hubert.

"Stealing is a crime. Lawyers can't participate in a criminal activity which includes receiving stolen goods," Hubert explained. "How much allowance do you get?"

"One hundred fifty a month," Sophia said. "But I have to pay for my clothes."

"We'll take a hundred a month for four months," Hubert said.

"But she'll just use the same arguments in my case as in Brittany's," Sophia protested, as she dug two fifties out of her purse and took back the four hundred dollar bills.

Aleta spelled out, "case by case".

"What's that mean?"

Hubert again explained. "It means the cases are separate. Mrs. Praetzel is planning to appeal on a single case basis. She will argue for Brittany as an exception."

"But our cases are alike. It was the same boy. And the rubbers broke both times. It was just our luck that it was the wrong time of the month."

Aleta spelled out her question, "right time?"

"Only if he wanted to get us pregnant... You aren't saying... But, why?"

Aleta shrugged.

She spelled out, "name of boy?"

"We can't do that. We promised each other."

Aleta offered, "half price for name"

"Carlton Brockbank," Sophia said instantly.

Aleta looked at Hubert.

"Pass," he said.

She smiled as she spelled out her next query, "abortion?"

"I was thinking about it," Sophia said. "I'm not ready to raise a baby, but letting someone adopt it might be okay, only they would have to be Greek Orthodox. My parents would insist."

Aleta spelled out, "no abortion".

"I guess I don't believe in it either."

Aleta spelled out her first piece of advice, "tell parents".

"They'll kill me!"

Aleta went on, "doctor?"

Sophia shook her head.

Aleta handed her two cards and spelled out, "to verify".

"He won't tell them?"

Aleta shook her head.

"Can I wait until I know for sure?"

Aleta nodded.

"I took the test, you know."

Aleta nodded.

"You want to be sure I'm healthy?"

Aleta nodded.

"Why wouldn't I be?"

Aleta shrugged.

Slowly she spelled out, "my advice is costing you a lot".

Sophia laughed.

"You bet it is! But you will keep me in school so I can graduate, won't you?"

Aleta nodded.

"Okay, then, you're worth the money."

Aleta spelled out an order, "apt w parents one wk".

Hubert translated the shorthand. "You are to bring you parents to see Mrs. Praetzel in one week."

Tim opened the door for the next man who entered in a wheelchair. Tim handed Aleta the folder and introduced both Aleta and Hubert. Aleta scanned the contents quickly and handed the folder to Hubert.

"I come for the Senior Citizens man who doesn't charge a lot," Mitch Fowler said, nervously.

Aleta pointed to her father-in-law.

"I'm your man," Hubert said cheerfully. "In this firm, we all help our Senior Citizen's lawyer who's pretty busy right now. No charge unless we sue someone. Then we get a percentage."

"That's fair enough," Mitch Fowler said. "If you decide to sue the damned insurance company, then you should get paid. All I want is what's mine."

"Tim, please escort Mr. Fowler to my office. I will be right there," Hubert said.

After Tim left with the client, Hubert eyed Aleta askance.

"You handed me another big case, didn't you?"

Aleta smiled and blew him a kiss.

"I will send Tim back to help you since Stanley's gone," Hubert said.

Aleta nodded.

Although having someone with her was helpful, she was upset that she needed help.

Tim came in bubbling enthusiastically, "Mr. Praetzel said you wanted me to help you."

Aleta smiled and nodded.

"This is a great learning experience for me," he said. "We've got quite a few left. People keep coming."

Aleta spelled out, "weed".

"Now?" Tim asked.

Aleta nodded, got up and stretched. She walked to the door, telling Tim to give her ten minutes. She forgot her guard was supposed to follow her everywhere. As she entered the restroom, he positioned himself outside the door.

She wanted to tell him she didn't need to be watched so closely, that Chief Milani was upset with Stanley and, well, maybe a little bit with her, but, mostly with Stanley.

Both of the men should be guarding Stanley, she reasoned. She wasn't in any danger of being kidnapped, just blown up.

As far as she was concerned, there was no longer any real danger of her being blown up. Her house and the office had been searched repeatedly and cleared each time.

Wherever the last bomb was, it wasn't in the two places she spent most of her time in.

Then she remembered her talk with her grandmother in which Harriet had quoted the next to the last verse in Ecclesiastes that stated that the whole duty of man was to obey God. Her grandmother had gone on to say that God wanted her not to speak a word anywhere.

This admonition had come shortly after she had told Stanley that he was to pillow her as soon as she said the word "mother". ,

She had had a few moments to tell him that this might be forever and then she added. "If I speak, I will die."

Stanley's resolve had been solidified by that single prediction. It wasn't long after that he deduced that a voice-activated bomb had been placed somewhere that Aleta frequented.

She recalled that at the beginning how certain everyone was that a bomb had been planted in her car. It was that certainty that spurred Hawk, the county's chief forensic scientist, into searching until he found it imbedded in the steering wheel.

Willow Glen Chief Tom Milani's men then searched the house thoroughly and found nothing. He believed that the bomb in the car was the only one there was.

She couldn't remember when Stanley had been called and offered the location one of the bombs for fifty thousand dollars. Stanley had goaded the man into revealing that twelve bombs had been planted. He had paid the whole fifty thousand for the location of one bomb because Hawk had said he needed a second bomb to understand the mind-set of the bomber and be able to figure out how the others were disguised. Stanley had been given the location of the bomb.

He and Chief West had decided to see if Hawk could discover it if he was told what room it was located in. Hawk immediately zeroed in on the mobile above the baby's crib. He told the Praetzels that that was an easy one.

Aleta continued to reminisce. She remembered she had asked Hawk for a bit of the C-4 to use in training the dogs to sniff out the bombs. Scooby and Tank had had their first lesson at the Tontine Lodge at Clipper Lake in Minnesota the following day. She remembered thinking that the lodge was a safe place because neither she nor Stanley were really connected with it unless you counted the fact that her grandmother was the head of the Tontine.

She recalled that she had decided not to speak out of deference to her grandmother's charge that she wasn't to utter a word anywhere. That had proven to be more difficult to do than she had imagined. She remembered swimming in the middle of the lake with her grandmother's husband, Claude, and thinking how safe she felt there. Then Claude had taken her to task over her silence when the two of them were treading water in the middle of the lake.

"There's just the two of us in our swimming suits," he had argued.

Aleta had looked around. His reasoning was sound. There was just the two of them, and, of course, Stanley's Irish Wolfhound, Tank, who was swimming circles around them. Aleta remembered thinking that they were too far away for any voice-activated device to even pick up the sound of her voice. Still she hesitated. The order she had been given had been absolute. She wasn't to speak anywhere.

The training of Scooby and Tank had begun that first day.

After their first lesson, the two dogs had been confined to the RV to think about the lesson. They had both laid down and fallen asleep. When they emerged from the RV after their naps, Scooby was carrying Tank's collar in his mouth. Aleta remembered laughing at this unexpected sight. So delighted had she been, she gave each of the dogs a biscuit when they both sat in front of her expectantly. They repeated this new trick on cue. She remembered that she had ignored her grandmother's warning about teaching them a trick that wasn't useful and rewarding them each time they did it.

Now as she reminisced, she was glad she had followed her impulse to let the dogs know that they had delighted her. Shortly after that, Hawk zeroed in on the possibility that the bombs might be tiny. Two days later, the bomb imbedded in Tank's collar was discovered. Claude wasn't the only one who was shocked over the find. Aleta had been shocked as well. She had had no sense of danger out in the middle of the lake. None at all!

Meanwhile, Hawk's dog Topper had started dragging around the suitcase that Paige had borrowed from Aleta. It had been then that Hawk's other theory—that the bombs were scattered—proved to be as viable as his theory that they varied in size.

It was after that that Tank and Scooby had pointed to the bomb planted in the RV. That had happened after Butch and Lennie had robbed the RV for the second time. Aleta had been hiding in the shower when Butch had asked Lennie to point out the bomb. Aleta hadn't seen where Lennie had pointed. She only knew was that there was a bomb in their RV. When the dogs found it, Aleta had become even more frightened. She remembered feeling that nowhere was safe.

Sergio Vannella's men caught Lennie and Butch when they tried to pawn a second necklace. Lennie gave up the location of most of the bombs that had been found plus one new one. It was hidden in the rafters above the kitchen table. He also said there were two in the barn.

Armed with that information, Hawk had taken Paige and Topper with him to the Praetzel house on the Monday after the dog show. Topper pointed out the bomb in the rafters in the barn, the one in the wall in the bedroom and the small one inside the brass top of the coat rack. He also pointed out the one above the kitchen table that they knew about.

After Hawk had finished searching the house, he had taken Topper to the office of Praetzel, Locke and Praetzel and found another bomb in Aleta's briefcase.

When Stanley and Aleta had arrived home after Hawk had completed his search of their house, Stanley had received another call offering to give him the location of another bomb. He had bargained for the two in the barn and paid double because there were two. That had been the reason for the meeting with the remaining three of the bomb group.

As Aleta finished her reminiscing, she realized for the first time that if she had been riding bareback on Shadow, there was a good possibility she would have spoken to him. That morning's encounter in Chief Milani's office had shaken her. She never dreamed that Shadow's bridle would hold a bomb. It would have blown his head off as well as hers because when she talked to him, she would have leaned over. The man who did all this planning was exceedingly clever.

She had chafed under Chief Milani's scolding that she was taking this absolute silence thing too far. That very morning he had berated her for not giving her statement verbally. He knew that she could neither type nor write. God had taken both those abilities from her. She had been reduced to communicating via the use of Scrabble tiles, hand gestures and head shakes. Occasionally when God wanted her to prophesy, she found that she could type on her computer, which is why she took it everywhere. When Chief Milani found that she couldn't use the computer, he became impatient. He wanted the details of the shooting death of Lukas Kvidahl, and he wanted them quickly. His office was absolutely safe. Of that he was certain. Aleta had, however, held fast to her promise not to speak.

Even though Stanley thought Milani's office was safe, he backed Aleta when she refused to speak. So did Hawk. Both were shocked when Tom Milani pulled Shadow's bridle out of his bottom drawer. Both thought it was in the evidence room, which was in the basement. Everyone in the room realized how close to death they had all come.

There was still one bomb still out there.

That was her last thought as she finished washing her hands and dried them and left the office restroom. She returned to her office, her reminiscing reminding her that no place was safe. No place at all. And she wasn't going to be warned when in the presence of a bomb. In fact she might even feel safe as she did in Chief Milani's office. She vowed not to forget that. Or the fact that if she spoke to others, she might kill or maim them as well. That thought shook her anew.

CHAPTER 4

Stanley returned while Tim was still checking those in line. Aleta saw her husband enter his office and hurried in after him. She pressed the intercom buttons connecting him to both his parents. Both answered simultaneously.

"Aleta wants to see you in my office," Stanley said.

When they arrived, Aleta found she had no way to communicate. She gestured at them all to stay and went into her office.

"It must be important," Stanley commented.

She reentered her husband's office carrying a small wooden Scrabble tray holding the letters that spelled out, "tell him".

She pointed at Hubert.

"Tell him what?" Hubert asked, seemingly baffled.

His eyes, however, twinkled.

"Let's go to your office," Stanley proposed. "We will wait until you spell it out."

The three followed her into her office where they found her frantically searching for letters. The first to appear were "Sophia said wherever she…"

She looked at Hubert who smiled and said. "The 'she' refers to Brittany. Go on, Aleta, you're doing great."

"is going with that…"

"You'll have to steal an 'h'," Hubert said.

Aleta spelled out the next word, "handsome…"

"Man," Hubert finished, "meaning Stanley…"

Aleta beamed.

"You called us all in here because a young girl called me handsome?" Stanley asked, obviously irritated.

Aleta nodded. She knew he was embarrassed, but she also knew he was inwardly pleased.

"It's a comment every parent wants to hear," his mother observed.

"I guess I understand that," Stanley said, slightly mollified.

"It surprised us," Hubert said. "Rather pleasantly, I must admit.'

"My looks have no place in this office," Stanley declared.

"You do want us to report favorable client reactions, don't you?" his father said evenly.

"Not with respect to personal appearance," Stanley shot back.

"But that's important," his mother said. "That's why we all dress in suits instead of jeans. Come on, Stanley, give your wife a break. She wanted to share a comment with us that pleased her. She expected Hubert to repeat it. But, being the tease that he is, he didn't, and the whole incident got blown up. I, for one, am delighted that she charged ahead and didn't leave me hanging."

"There is that," Stanley admitted reluctantly. "But I didn't need to be present."

"Sure you did," his mother argued. "But I must admit your reaction leaves something to be desired."

"I'm reacting perfectly normally," Stanley insisted.

"For a toad," his mother quipped.

Aleta laughed and Hubert and Lydia left.

"She really said that?" Stanley asked.

Aleta nodded, grinning. He was pleased. Shocked, but pleased.

"I didn't do the surgery as a way to improve my looks, you know."

Aleta nodded.

"Just to keep from looking worse," he finished.

Again she agreed.

"But you're pleased, aren't you?"

This time she laughed. Then she hugged him.

"Now can I go back to work?" he asked.

She kissed him lightly. She let go as Tim entered.

"Am I interrupting something?" Tim asked.

"Your timing is perfect. My wife was just having a bit of fun at my expense."

"Oh," he murmured, confused.

"Just forget I said anything. Mrs. Praetzel is ready to begin interviewing again."

Tim ushered in a woman in her early thirties. Aleta glanced at her paperwork, waved her into a seat and pressed the intercom to call Lydia. As they were waiting Aleta began spelling out words on four different trays.

Aleta turned the first tray toward Lydia as she entered. It read, "not taking case".

She handed Lydia the folder as she finished the word on the second tray, "precedent ca".

Lydia shook her head. Aleta left the room and hurried to the firm's law library. Lydia meanwhile had extracted the details of the proposed suit the woman wanted to bring against the trustees of a trust her father had set up for her before he died. She wanted to direct investments into areas with a greater rate of return. Her father had specified that the money was to remain invested in bonds.

The income had been steady over the years but the dollars didn't stretch as far. Her husband wanted to use the trust funds to purchase a house.

Aleta returned and placed the law book on the desk. Lydia read the case in California.

Aleta turned the third row of tiles which read, "Please explain".

Lydia began by quoting the California case and telling the woman that it was much like her own. She then told her that an Illinois judge would probably rule with the trustees and she would be out a substantial legal fee.

"So you advise against it?" the prospective client asked.

Aleta nodded and Lydia said, "We do indeed. I know that if your father were alive, he probably would give you the down payment; however, he didn't allow for trust monies to be used that way and I'm sure he thought about it. His investment is conservative, but the court is not allowed to second-guess financial arrangements of the person setting up the trust, which, while conservative, are reasonable. His intention was that you should have a steady income. That is happening."

The woman smiled, "Thank you very much."

Aleta turned the final tray of letters which read, "no fee".

Dismay erased gratitude.

"Oh, but I must pay. And I must have a receipt," she said. "What is your normal fee for an hour? And since there are two of you, I will pay for each of you."

"Four hundred dollars," Lydia said. "And tell your husband that you not only were counseled by Aleta Praetzel herself who remembered a California case like your own, but that the second person in the room was Judge Lydia Davis in whose court you case is likely to wind up."

"Oh, thank you!" the woman said with genuine enthusiasm. "Thank you both. Thank you for taking the time to explain."

"Alice will make out the invoice and give you a receipt," Lydia said.

Tim escorted the woman out. Lydia turned to Aleta.

"That was beautifully handled. Call me anytime. You interruptions are not a bother. I like them."

Aleta had not ever seen the sensitive side of her mother-in-law as she had since she hadn't been able to speak.

She realized that Stanley was a lot like his mother as well as his father. She hadn't raised her son carelessly. She had paid attention to him, but she had let him develop in his own way. Her unwavering faith in him was the cornerstone of his self-confidence.

Several prospective clients later, Aleta had another man arrested when he wouldn't leave after she had refused to take his case.

When a frail elderly gentleman was escorted past the handcuffed man waiting for transport, Tim made a joke that fell flat.

"The man in the hall unsettled Mr. Hanson," Tim told Aleta. "I made a bad joke. I'm sorry."

Aleta held up a card with the words printed on it: "are you prejudiced?"

The man nodded.

She spelled out: "against whom?"

"You mean who do I hate right off?" the old man asked.

Aleta nodded.

"Members of the Ku Klux Klan, members of the Aryan Nation, used car salesmen and atheists."

Aleta smiled and pressed Nigel Oliver's button.

She spelled out new words on the tile holder in the time it took Nigel to arrive. She turned the tray toward Nigel. The words were: "take good care of him".

She handed Tim the folder and Tim introduced the gentleman to Nigel.

"He's prejudiced," Tim said. "But you and I aren't on the list."

"Mr. Hanson, please come with me to my office where you can tell me how I can help you."

"By not sitting me in the corner with handcuffs for starters," Hanson said.

Tim laughed and nodded toward Stanley's office. "Second one today."

Nigel smiled. "We never arrest senior citizens, only blustery, middle-aged jerks."

"And maybe used car salesmen?"

"If ever one chose to enter this office," Nigel said. "I guarantee he'd be arrested. So you hate them?"

"That's why I'm here."

One after another Tim presented the people lined up for Aleta's services. Stanley was interrupted repeatedly. By the end of the day, his leg ached and he was frustrated.

The following morning, Stanley held a staff meeting.

"Yesterday for two hours, Aleta could sign and I could understand her signing. It was a gift from God," Stanley explained. "A temporary one. Please do not promise anyone with a speech impairment that we can help them."

He looked around and saw a response indicating acceptance. He went on.

"Today, I want to talk about our case load," Stanley said. "We now have four large cases and a multitude of smaller ones. I do believe we are at our limit. After today we will take no new cases for a month."

"What about the Senior Citizen's Program?" Nigel Oliver asked.

"That goes on as does the child advocacy work that Robert and I do."

After that meeting broke up, Aleta took care of numerous prospective clients smoothly. Stanley left his office after a couple of hours had passed to check on his wife.

Tim was about to usher in the next client when Stanley pointed at Aleta. She was busy forming words on the tile holder. Tim stood hesitantly, uncertain what to do.

Stanley introduced himself to the prospective client and escorted him to his mother's office.

Aleta turned the tile holder around so Tim read what she had spelled out: "man stroke now with gift".

Tim nodded and left.

He stopped at the next person waiting in line and said, "There's a special client that made arrangements who is next, but you will be right after him."

Tim then walked down the stairs past the people waiting in line until he saw an old man leaning on a cane. He stopped and asked him if he had had a stroke recently. The old man shook his head. He walked further down the line and found an old man leaning on a cane with a prettily wrapped box in his hand.

"You're next," Tim said. "Please follow me."

The old man left the line and followed Tim to the elevator. Once he was on the second floor, he was ushered into Aleta's office.

As soon as he entered, Aleta pressed a button on her cell phone. A few seconds later, Stanley received a call from Chief Lyle West on his cell.

"Aleta called," West said.

"Hold on," Stanley said. "I'm only a few steps from her office."

Holding his open cell in his hand, Stanley burst into Aleta's office.

"Aleta, did you call Chief West?"

She nodded and turned around the tile holder.

It read "call hawk too".

She simultaneously pressed two buttons on her intercom.

Meanwhile, Stanley spotted the prettily wrapped package on her desk. He put his cell phone back to his ear.

"Lyle, we have a situation here. Aleta has just received what she believes is a voice-activated bomb. She is in her office... Yes, I will do that."

He turned to Tim.

"As quietly as you can, clear the building, downstairs shops as well."

Tim left at once.

The office door opened and Stanley's parents rushed in.

"Mother, Dad, what are you doing here?" Stanley asked, surprised.

Aleta waved them in.

"Aleta called us on the intercom," Hubert replied.

"We all need to leave," Stanley said.

Aleta shook her head and pointed to the tiles that spelled the word: "danger".

"That's why we must leave," Stanley argued.

Aleta shook her head violently.

"Mother, Dad, you two go," Stanley said. "I will stay here with Aleta. Lyle is on his way."

The two turned to leave.

Aleta picked up a handful of tiles and threw them at her father-in-law. He turned, surprised.

Aleta shook her head. She scooted around the desk, grabbed his arm, took him to a chair and pointed at it.

"She wants us to stay," Lydia concluded.

Aleta nodded and Lydia sat down.

"Are we in danger if we leave?" Hubert asked.

Aleta nodded.

"I don't understand," Hubert said.

Aleta took Stanley's hand and moved him next to his father. She stepped back and opened both hands and spread them as if to ask Lydia what she saw.

Lydia burst out, "You two look alike."

Aleta nodded.

"Are you saying that whoever is out there is waiting to take out Stanley might take out Hubert by mistake?' Lydia asked.

Aleta nodded vigorously.

"Hubert, we're staying here!" Lydia proclaimed.

"Someone is outside waiting for me?" Stanley asked.

Aleta nodded and pointed to him and then herself.

"Both of us?

Aleta nodded, then realizing her tiles were scattered on the floor, opened her laptop and placed her hands in position to type.   Suddenly, her fingers typed out the name Roger Brennan, then added that he brought the package.

The old man began to mumble angrily.   No one understood him.

Aleta began typing his words, "Why do you think it's a bomb? I wouldn't deliver no bomb."

"Who sent you?" Stanley asked.

"Stuart Fouts," he mumbled. His words appeared on the computer screen.

Seeing his words on the screen prompted him to continue.

"Fouts said there was an important message inside, and if Mrs. Praetzel didn't open it, I was to open it for her.   I didn't know it was a bomb.   He said if I did this, he wouldn't rape my wife again.   He knows I can't talk so anyone can understand.   Will it go off?"

Aleta shook her head.

Then she typed, "It won't go off unless I speak.   It is meant to force us to leave the building.   It is important that none of us leave, including Mr. Brennan."

Stanley read every word she typed aloud.

"Are you seeing something?" Hubert asked.

"Yes," Aleta typed. "Death."

"Then we stay," Hubert declared.

Mr. Brennan mumbled something and Aleta typed it.

"I must get back to Emily."

Stanley put his hand on Mr. Brennan's shoulder to keep him from rising.   His voice was soft but firm.

"Aleta is a prophet of God.   We will do as she says.   I will send a police unit to take your wife to the hospital and guard her."

Roger Brennan mumbled again.

Aleta typed, "She needs me."

"She needs you to come back to her alive," Stanley asserted.   "Trust me."

Stanley called Lyle and told him that Emily Brennan had just been raped.

"Old lady Brennan? Roger's wife?" Lyle gasped.

"He thinks Fouts is still there, but Aleta is shaking her head," Stanley reported.

As he was speaking, Stanley glanced out the window.

"Lyle, we're moving to my office where the glass is bulletproof," Stanley finished, turning and spitting out an order, "Everyone, move now!"

Everyone left quickly and rushed past the two guards.

"We're to evacuate," one guard said.

"There's a sniper out there," Stanley explained. "We are to wait here for Chief West or Chief Milani. Let no one else in."

Once inside Stanley's office, Aleta handed him her laptop on which she'd typed, "Search police cars in back."

Stanley went to the door to his office and told the police guards that they were to tell the bomb squad to search the police cars in back.

"What about the bomb in Mrs. Praetzel's office?" one of the guards asked.

"Voice activated," Stanley told him. "Same perp."

When Chief West arrived, Aleta was typing Mr. Brennan's account of the invasion of his home and the rape of his wife. Even though no one but Aleta could understand a word he said, all could see how distraught he was as he recalled the attack. Tears streamed down his face and his whole body shook as a result of a combination of rage and grief. His inability to come to her aid was repeated in nearly every sentence. His helplessness visited such shame on him that those watching the words being formed on the computer screen wanted to stop the declaration in order to offer him comfort. They restrained themselves because they knew that the statement needed to be completed.

While none of them every whispered their greatest fear, it hung suspended in their silence—the fear that not only Aleta's gift of understanding might be taken from her, but also her ability to type.

And as she typed the last word, that's exactly what happened.

Chief Milani arrived shortly after Chief West and announced that the bomb squad had arrived.

"Krantz insists the whole building be evacuated," Chief Milani said. "It's protocol. And he's German. They go by the rules."

A few minutes later, Karl Krantz burst into the room and shouted, "Everyone out! Now!"

No one moved.

"One of my patrol cars out back has a bomb in it," Chief Milani declared. "There's a sniper out front waiting for these people to exit."

"How do you know?" Krantz charged.

"I got a tip," Milani said. "Now go find the bomb."

Krantz stomped down the stairs as Hawkins Monroe arrived.

"Did you diffuse the bomb?" the forensic chief asked as he started up the stairs.

"They won't leave the building," Krantz spat out angrily.

"Who won't?" Hawk pressed.

"West, Milani and a group of lawyers."

Hawk paused.

"You're not leaving?"

"Chief Milani claims there's a bomb in one of his units out back," Krantz grouched.

"You could remove the bomb in the office and diffuse it elsewhere," Hawk suggested.

"That's how I work," Krantz snapped. "But I want them gone when I remove it. It's procedure."

"Chances are that it's voice activated," Hawk said. "The others all were."

"We don't take chances," Krantz proclaimed arrogantly.

"Mind if I take a look?" Hawk asked.

"Yes, I mind. This is my case. Leave it alone."

When the extremely tall forensic chief arrived on the second floor, Chief West and Chief Milani greeted him warmly.

"Stuart Fouts had someone hand carry this one," Chief West said. "It might not be the same as the others."

"Let me talk to Aleta," Hawk said.

He was immediately ushered into Stanley's office. He stared at the two walls of water where giant Koi were swimming back and forth lazily. He gazed at them for a moment before addressing Aleta.

"Aleta, can I safely touch the bomb?"

She shrugged.

"That's good enough for me," Hawk said.

"What are you going to do?" Tom Milani asked.

"Diffuse the bomb."

"We have a bomb squad downstairs," Tom pointed out.

"Idiots!" Hawk said. "Aleta would never keep everyone here if it were dangerous."

Lyle and Tom exchanged glances. Of course she wouldn't. Why hadn't they thought of that?

Both chiefs followed Hawk into Aleta's office where Hawk picked up the package sitting on the top of the desk and carried it out. He walked to the new addition, which was still a work in progress, set the package down on a table holding the building plans and studied it.

When he removed the lid, he removed a note and handed it to Chief West who read the note aloud.

"Hawkins Monroe, you think you are so clever, but that big black dog can't go everywhere. You found the one in the plane because I wanted you to find it. There are five more—all voice activated."

Chief West stopped and then read the second paragraph aloud.

"Aleta Praetzel, you are my prisoner. You and your husband will pay dearly for information. Retribution for my hand."

As Hawk lifted the lid to the music box for a closer look, Karl Krantz walked into the new addition and spotted the group crowded around Hawk..

"Stop!" he exploded. "Stop right now! You don't know what you are doing!"

"Oh, but I do," Hawk retorted, taking a tiny screwdriver out of his kit.

"I'm out of here!" Krantz shouted.

"Officer Krantz," Chief West said coldly, his voice bringing Krantz up short. "You may retire a safe distance while Mr. Monroe deactivates this bomb. Afterward, I expect you to return and find the bomb in the patrol car. That is your job, after all."

"I looked," Krantz protested.

"Look again," Chief West ordered.

"Here it is!" Hawk exclaimed, holding up what appeared to be a tiny metal button. "This is one made by our original bomb maker."

"So there are five more?" Chief Milani asked.

"Plus the one we haven't found," Chief West said.

"What bomb is he referring to in the note?" Milani asked. "You didn't tell me you found a bomb in Stanley's plane."

"This one is Doyle's. The one in the plane was a copy," Hawk explained. "That's why I didn't count it."

"Is it one of the five?" Chief Milani asked hopefully.

"No," Chief West replied. "He mentioned the one in the plane that we found and said there were five more. The one with the note doesn't count either. On top of that, there is still one of the original twelve that we haven't found yet."

"That makes six," Tom summarized.

"Doyle has changed his signature," Hawk said. "He was there when the bomb in the plane was made. He had a hand in it but he didn't make it."

"What do you mean he changed his signature?" West asked.

"He's sending a message," Hawk replied. "I need another letter. All I've got is an M and an O."

"You need to plug those holes in your head," Krantz snapped. "Your theories are leaking out and messing us all up."

"Go find the bomb in my patrol cars," Chief Milani ordered. "That's your job. Go do it!"

As Hawk slipped the note into a plastic bag and marked it, he remarked, "If Doyle is behind this, Krantz won't be able to find the bomb. We will need a dog."

Hawk handed West the note. West held it out to Milani.

"Guess you're off the hook, Krantz," Chief Milani said simultaneously shaking his head at West. "I'm not telling the Praetzels there are five more bombs out there."

Krantz interrupted him.

"Are you implying what I think you're implying?"

"You can go, Krantz," Chief West said. "Hawk will get his dog."

"We don't need a dog," Krantz declared.

"When the dog gets here, you're done," Chief West said.

Krantz rushed out grumbling.

As soon as Hawk had bagged the components of the bomb individually and packed them in his kit, the three entered Stanley's office.

Stanley read the letter and then passed it to Aleta who read it and handed it to Lydia who shared it with her husband.

"Five more?" Stanley questioned. "Plus the one we haven't found?"

The three chiefs nodded.

Everyone looked at Aleta who was crying. Her fingers lay motionless on the computer keyboard. It had been wonderful to be able to communicate. They all sensed her sorrow at the new twist her life had taken.

Stanley drew her from her chair and embraced her. He noticed all the worried faces surrounding them and said gently, "Aleta, if you don't stop, everyone in here will promise you the moon and we already have one baby, four dogs plus two guard dogs, three horses plus four guest horses and six empty rooms which between you and Bertha will be half filled before our second anniversary, so you see, we have no place for the moon.

Aleta, whose sobbing had lessened as her husband spoke, now managed a hiccupy laugh. She stuck her hand into his pocket and, not finding a handkerchief, yanked his shirttail from his trousers and wiped her eyes. Hubert rushed forward and gave Aleta a handkerchief. She used it to blow her nose while Stanley restored his shirttail to its proper place.

"Thanks, Dad," he said gratefully.

"Tell, Bertha, handkerchiefs in every pocket," Hubert said. "You have a pregnant wife."

"Can I safely take Mr. Brennan to see his wife?" Lyle asked.

Aleta nodded.

"Tom," Lyle said. "I will take the rape case. The bomb case is yours."

Hawk spoke up.

"Stanley, these guys like to plant several in one spot. If it's okay with you and Hubert, I'd like to fetch Paige and Topper, and after I go over the police cars in the back lot, go to the airfield and search both planes again."

Stanley handed him the keys.

"Any idea why Fouts gave us so much information?"

"He's rubbing our noses in it," Tom said. "That's why he's attacking old ladies in Arborville. He means to bring us all down."

CHAPTER 5

Unknown to Aleta, Stanley had asked his secretary to make reservations at Disney World for a couple of days. Now he checked back with her to see if everything he wanted had been arranged.

"Your father needs to see you," Alice said. "I didn't tell him anything, but it's about your plane."

Stanley entered his father's office.

"Did Hawk call?"

"My plane is clean. Topper found a smell he liked in yours," Hubert reported. "Hawk said he thinks it's in the control panel, but he didn't want to take it apart without asking. I told him to go ahead."

"Good!" Stanley said.

"I asked Alice if you were going anywhere and I could tell from her non-answer that you were. I told her about the plane. So where are you and Aleta flying?"

"Nowhere I guess," Stanley said. "I thought I'd surprise Aleta with a short trip to Disney World. I wanted to be sure she'd enjoy herself. Today has drained her."

"Lydia could use a trip. We could take my plane."

"I planned a private weekend," Stanley said forthrightly.

He never lied to his father.

"A mini-honeymoon?" his father asked.

"Something like that."

"We will leave you two alone the whole weekend," Hubert promised. "Both Lydia and Aleta need a bit of fun right now."

"I've only told Bertha where we will be," Stanley said. "And Alice, of course."

"We'll leave it that way," Hubert said. "I will surprise Lydia too. We'll leave tonight's party a little early to pack. What time shall we meet at the plane?"

"You're the pilot. You pick the time."

"Half an hour after Lydia and I leave the party."

"My biggest worry is that somehow Fouts will find out where we've gone," Stanley fretted.

"I will file the flight plan," Hubert offered.

"That may be enough," Stanley said hopefully.

There was no time before the party to have Scooby and Tank search the property as Hawk requested; however, since both dogs had been roaming free in the house all afternoon, Stanley and Aleta both assumed that the house didn't hold any hidden bombs. As soon as most of the guests arrived, Stanley ceremoniously cut the ribbon that was fastened across the door to the new wing and the guests entered the octagonal shaped single story addition to the main house— the children's wing.

Tank and Scooby followed the people inside. Glory, the little bulldog pup, had been plucked from her pen by Paige who carried her on a tour of the expansion.

"Which child gets a view of the garage?" Kurtz West asked.

"I guess which one has been naughty," Stanley joshed, than looked at Aleta. "That was a joke, Aleta. We'll move the garage and plant a tree. We'll get one from the new owner of the tree farm."

"Someone bought that place?" Kurtz West asked. "That's a hefty amount of money to invest in that business. Are the new owners planning to build?"

"They're planning to keep growing trees," Stanley said.'

"Who bought it?" Beatrice asked.

"Wendell Kingston the third," Stanley replied.

"He's younger than me," Jocelyn blurted out.

"And me too!" Paige exclaimed.

"His dream is to grow trees," Stanley explained. "His grandfather is going to live there and help him run the place until he finishes college."

"It's not a bad investment," Kurtz West commented. "The land will be more valuable in a decade or two. I hope he had a good lawyer broker the deal."

Hubert laughed and glanced meaningfully at his son.

"Stanley?" Kurtz West questioned and then answered himself. "Of course. Stanley is the only lawyer I know who wouldn't tell him to wait until he was an adult."

"Oh look!" Eloise Peets exclaimed. "Tank and Scooby already know which one is Gerard's room."

Paige, Hawk, Stanley and Aleta walked into the bare room. Scooby and Tank were sitting by the far wall, wagging their tails, their ears perked, their mouths open as if they were smiling.

Aleta immediately went over to both dogs and stroked them while Stanley made his way past his guests to the dog treat jar.

Hawk stood in the middle of the room and studied both dogs.

"I think it's in the wall between them," he guessed.

Aleta rewarded the dogs, and at Stanley's request, took them out of the room. Paige accompanied her, still carrying Glory, the Bulldog pup.

Stanley took Hawk aside.

"I'm taking Aleta on a trip tonight—a surprise," he said. "Bertha will be here. If you want to bring Topper and Paige to double check the entire place, that would be okay."

"If this is one, we've found three of the new ones. There was one in the back seat of one of the patrol cars and a second one in your plane. It was inside the control panel.

"I would guess there might be another on the property," Stanley said. "He likes to plant multiples."

"How about the office?" Hawk queried. "The gift was sent there."

"We've acquired new furniture. I will give you my spare key."

As the two walked into the study to get the office key, Stanley said, "I hate to do this to your weekend."

"Paige will love it. She'll get to spend the whole day with me. She finds that exciting."

"A busman's holiday, huh?"

"That's it," Hawk said. "My parents are coming next week. That weekend I can't work."

"I will try not to have any more bomb threats to be investigated," Stanley said.

"You know what I mean," Hawk returned. "What will I do if they bring up her age?"

"Bring it up first," Stanley said. "Talk about your own misgivings and what turned you around. Let them know you understand their feelings. You had reservations until you really got to know Paige."

"They are pretty straight-laced," Hawk said. "My grandmother has dementia, but Paige is prepared for that. I want them to see her as a woman. I didn't marry a child."

"Relax, Hawk," Stanley said. "Age is an arbitrary measure of maturity. That boy who bought the tree farm knew more about investing than most adults. On top of that, he knew what he wanted to spend his life doing. He's like Paige. Society doesn't allow for the exceptions. It can't function on the basis of the exceptional, but individuals can."

"Speaking of individuals, Paige will probably choose to sit with her schoolmates tonight," Hawk predicted.

Stanley eyed the taller man with amusement. "If I were a betting man..."

"There you are!" Paige exclaimed as the two came out of the house. "Lauren is going to let us sit together. Isn't that great!"

"Heck!" Stanley said. "Why do I always not bet when I know it's a sure thing?"

"Come on! Hurry! There are two seats left at Dr. Schwartzman's table," Paige said rushing ahead.

"I guess I'm supposed to sit and the food will magically appear," Hawk said with a tinge of sarcasm.

"Try it," Stanley chuckled. "Paige may have worked that out too."

Stanley was right. No sooner had Hawk seated himself than a plate was put in front of him. It was full.

"I told them how you liked your steak," Paige said. "And I said you liked every kind of food on the planet. You do, don't you?"

Hawk smiled at his exuberant wife.

"Pretty much. Everything on this plate looks good."

"You're working tomorrow, aren't you?" she asked.

"So are you and Topper."

"I thought you'd just take him. You don't need me."

"Oh, yes, I do. Topper only has a nose, but you have a brain. It thinks outside the box. I desperately need you."

"Really?"

"I will take you to lunch."

Paige looked around the table. Everyone was listening to their conversation.

"At the drive-thru hamburger place?"

"It's where you always want to go," Hawk replied, wondering why he was suddenly on the defensive.

Herve Schwartzman laughed. "Hawk, she's teasing you."

Paige grinned.

"He's right. I love hamburgers and fries."

"I will buy a bed," Hawk said.

Paige looked at Dr. Schwartzman and explained, "His parents are coming. Topper sleeps in our room in his own bed. Hawk knows if we camp on the floor, Topper will camp between us."

"You were planning to give his parents your bed?"

"His grandmother will be in the guest room," Paige explained.

"A double for the parents in the guest room. A single for his granny in what will be the baby's room," Herve said. "Let the single be your child's bed when he outgrows his crib. And if Granny is still visiting, the kid gets the couch."

"Okay, Hawk, I will work for you," Paige said. "For enough money to buy a single bed and bedding. And not out of our regular paycheck either."

Hawk's distress was immediate.

"Paige, I can't pay you—even though you're worth it. That's not legal"

"Stanley," Paige called.

"Paige, don't," Hawk begged as Stanley came over.

Paige told him what was being discussed.

"I don't know if what you propose is illegal, but it's not wise," Stanley said. "It would leave Hawk open to criticism. However, I can legally hire a consultant to work with the police, so, Paige, how does twenty dollars an hour sound?"

"Thirty," Paige declared. "You're hiring a brain, not a man to cut down your weeds."

"Paige!" Hawk scolded.

"Deal!" Stanley said. "Look, Hawk, a woman's perspective is something you just can't give. Aleta can't do it because it scares her to think of all the places a bomb could be. Paige, your first day's check will be waiting for you on the desk in my study in case I'm not here."

"It might not take eight hours," Paige said.

"I know you," Stanley said. "Your mind will stay engaged until all the bombs are found; therefore, the check will be for your first forty hour week."

"That's too much!" Hawk exclaimed.

"Deal," Paige said.

Herve Schwartzman leaned over when Stanley returned to his table and said, "Your mother had your brains. The chutzpah, however, is uniquely yours."

"Is that good—having chutzpah?"

"No!" Hawk declared before the aging psychiatrist could reply.

Dr. Schwartzman focused on Hawk.

"Do you think Stanley is a fool?"

"No, of course not," Hawk stammered.

"Do you think he can be taken advantage of in a business deal?"

"No, but he's charitable."

"Aleta is charitable. Aleta wasn't here. This was strictly a business arrangement. You wife has a superior brain. He bought a finite amount of its thinking. He got a real bargain if you ask me."

"But she asked for more than he offered," Hawk pointed out.

"Even then, she set her price a little low. Aleta gets four hundred dollars an hour. Given that two to three hundred of that is payment for education and experience, the rest is payment for her ability to think. Keep this in perspective, Hawk. Your wife showed spirit when it was called for. Be pleased. It means she is maturing under your wing."

Paige was hanging on Dr. Schwartzman's every word. She smiled at the last few sentences when he praised Hawk. She saw Hawk accepting Herve's entire argument.

Hawk turned to his wife. "This chutzpah is not bad. I was wrong."

"It means what—chutzpah?"

"Impudence, cheekiness, boldness, audacity."

"Those are not always good," Paige said.

"But at times they are essential," Hawk replied. "Follow your instincts. They don't lead you astray."

"But I'd rather please you."

Hawk gazed at his young wife thoughtfully. Sometimes he forgot how malleable she was.

"You please me most when you displease me rightly."

Herve chuckled.

"Paige, he just said a mouthful. Don't ask him to explain. When you are able, you will understand."

"But I do understand," Paige said. "Even when I displease him in one way, I may still be pleasing him in another."

"Your mother has taught you well," Herve said.

"Hawk taught me that just now," Paige responded.

"Stanley did indeed get a bargain!" Herve declared.

The entire group laughed with him.

That reaction dissolved Hawk's last feeling of shame. He smiled inwardly. His parents would be so impressed that she had been paid thirty dollars an hour as a consultant on a forensic case.

A short time later, Stanley asked Aleta to follow him. He led her to their bedroom, slipped the scarf over her eyes and drew the drapes. She heard him lock both doors to the bedroom.

She sat on the bed and waited for an explanation. It came immediately.

"You're exhausted, Aleta. It's beginning to show. So far I think only Bertha and I have noticed.

Aleta knew what was coming next. The scarf made protesting impossible. It demanded obedience. Silent obedience.

"You're going to bed. The scarf is so you won't have any choice but to sleep."

Buffaloed, she gave in. She let her shoulders droop.

"Don't worry about your guests. You've been with them for four hours. The party is winding down. You're not up to staying until the last person leaves. Better that you're the first. That way no one will take it personally."

Aleta nodded. Stanley had been undressing her while he talked. With her eyes closed, it was hard to stay awake.

She felt the smoothness of the satin as he slipped her gown over her head. She didn't remember raising her arms until the gown slipped down her torso.

I will just go to sleep, she thought, and not bother to wake up. I can't wake to another day like this one. Why did that one man's hate overcome all the love that had been directed toward her? Was evil so demanding that it seemed stronger than good? Or was it actually stronger? Right now it seemed like that to her.

I wonder if I will ever feel good again, she thought as she felt Stanley lift her and carry her to her side of the bed.

He kissed her gently and whispered, "I love you, Aleta, and I have a surprise for you when you wake up. Just think of what you want most and tomorrow you will have it."

Aleta was awake enough to hear all the words. Unable to ask him to promise, she merely nodded.

He left her then and she felt alone, but his words were the last she remembered when sleep grabbed hold of her. Its grip was tight. It was determined not to let go. She sank into a sleep beyond dreams.

When Stanley reappeared, Lauren asked him where Aleta was.

"I put her to bed. She was asleep before I left the room. I'm sorry to leave you in sole charge, Lauren."

"These are all her friends, Stanley. And by now everyone knows what a rough couple of days she's had.

"She would not have left had I not insisted."

"I know."

Lyle took Stanley aside.

"Your friendly police chiefs want a word with you. Peets and Milani are waiting in the barn."

"What's up?"

"You know what," Lyle said as they walked toward the barn. "You're planning to leave town without telling us."

"Are you still tapping Alice's phone?"

"That would be illegal without a warrant."

"Would that stop you?"

"Yes."

"So how did you find out? Who told you?"

"You did," Lyle said. "Here we are."

Peets and Milani were sitting on bales of hay. Lyle sat on another. Stanley remained standing.

"I wanted it to be a secret. I thought the fewer people who knew the less chance anyone would follow us. Aleta needs a stress-free weekend."

"Your plane's not been cleared," Tom said.

"Who said I'm flying?" Stanley challenged.

"Aren't you?" Lyle returned.

"Going south," Oakwood's Chief Alan Peets put in. "Orlando, I believe. Disney World?"

"Your father filed a flight plan," Tom explained.

"We're going to help," Lyle said.

"I don't need help," Stanley protested.

"Sure you do," Lyle declared. "First, I have a special cell phone for you. It's Lauren's. Our numbers are the first three. Your house is the fourth."

"What is Lauren going to use?"

"Yours."

"I will be answering calls all weekend," Stanley complained.

"Don't answer."

"Why are we doing this?"

"Doyle is an electronic whiz. Your phone will be here and active, hence, so are you."

"Okay, I can go along with that," Stanley conceded.

"Take your badges and guns."

"Why?"

"Because your chief is telling you to."

"I will take one," Stanley agreed. "One gun. One badge. Aleta will think I expect trouble otherwise. That will stress her out."

The three chiefs nodded their assent.

Stanley looked at the three who had gone to great lengths to protect him and Aleta and decided to explain.

"It was the note from Fouts," he said. "Fouts told her she was his prisoner. She took that hard. I could feel it. Granted she can't speak, but she needs to have some unfettered fun. I need to make that letter a lie."

"If we can successfully sneak you out of town, Fouts may trip himself up trying to find you," Lyle said.

"Bertha and Robert will be staying at the house. Paul has a show in October so he will use the weekend to finish a canvas or two. The girls will ride their horses. The dogs will all be active. The house will seem occupied."

"I won't pull the guards off," Milani said.

"Thanks," Stanley said. "That will help."

"I'm going to spend the weekend in jail with Butch," Alan Peets commented. "I think I have an idea how to get the information we need."

"I only wish you weren't registered in the hotel under your own name," Lyle remarked.

"Mother took care of that," Stanley informed the chiefs. "Her credit cards and driver's license are all in her professional name. Dad has been called Mr. Davis before."

"And you?"

"Won't matter. Mother is paying for everything. You're the only ones who know this. Even Alice and Bertha don't know. Mother cancelled my reservations and made her own. Dad was going to surprise her, but Mother got the whole story seconds after I left the office. She told me tonight."

Lyle nodded his approval. The plan was decent. It just might work.

"I'm driving you to the airport," Lyle said. "Tom is driving your parents. Your two cars in that tiny lot at the airport is too big a bread crumb."

"You aren't happy about this, are you?"

"Not at all. Stuart Fouts seems to be one step ahead of us. I never pegged him as being this clever."

"I think Doyle is the brains," Stanley said. "I don't like the fact that Fouts is taking lessons in bomb making."

"Do you think their falling out is the reason for the acceleration of the attacks on Aleta?" Lyle asked.

"So you're reading the change in attitude as I am?" Stanley asked.

"That's why Peets is spending the weekend in jail," Lyle said. "We need to know where the base of operations is."

"Hawk told you about the letters, didn't he?" Stanley asked.

"I'm his chief," Lyle said.

"The only one who could have scratched the letters on that metal button that was hidden inside the bomb was Doyle," Stanley said. "But he is still making the bombs we're finding, so that doesn't make sense."

CHAPTER 6

The next morning in Florida, when Stanley rolled the cart with the empty breakfast dishes into the hall, he met his father who was doing the same thing.

"I thought you two would sleep in," Hubert said.

"I woke Aleta so we could talk," Stanley said. "We're on our way to the Animal Kingdom. Care to join us?"

"Lydia," Hubert called back into his room. "They talked. We haven't done that yet. Or we could go to the Animal Kingdom with the kids."

Hubert turned back. "She nixed the talk idea."

When the four started for the elevator, Stanley walked backward. His father thought this strange until Stanley spoke.

"Mother, Aleta says she's sorry that she wasn't decent company last night."

"She can sign?" Hubert asked.

Aleta nodded. This time Stanley interpreted her words directly.

"We don't know how long this will last, but we've had a grand time communicating this morning."

Hubert addressed his son directly.

"So when you said you talked, you meant what you're doing now?"

Stanley nodded.

"Have you heard from anyone?" his mother asked.

"My cell!" Stanley exclaimed. "I turned it to vibrate, but I stuck it in the sock drawer when I woke up."

His father winked at his mother.

Stanley pulled it from his pocket and opened it up.

"Four messages from Lyle."

"Any texts?" Hubert asked.

"Not important... Not important... Will call later... Where are you?" Stanley recited. "I guess 'not important' got escalated over the last couple of hours."

"Let's stop here," Lydia said as they stood in front of the elevator. "See what he wants."

Stanley punched in Lyle's number.

"You called," he said simply.

Earlier that morning, Hawkins Monroe brought Paige and Topper to the Praetzel house. Bertha was serving breakfast to Aleta's younger sister, Jocelyn, and her first cousin Lettie, both classmates of Paige."

"There's an envelope on the desk in the study with your name on it," Bertha told Paige.

"My pay!" Paige exclaimed.

"Pay?" Jocelyn asked. "For what?"

"Stanley bought forty hours of my thinking," Paige replied.

"About what?"

Paige looked at her husband, but it was Bertha who answered. "Fouts planted five new bombs."

"Is that why Aleta and Stanley left?" Jocelyn asked.

"Pretty much."

"So you're the new bomb finder?" Jocelyn asked. "I thought Hawk did a good job last time."

Bertha spoke up.

"Sometimes two heads are better than one," she said. "Have you two had breakfast? There's plenty."

Hawk nodded and spoke for them both.

"No, thank you. We're anxious to start. Is it okay if we take Topper into the new wing?"

"Go ahead," Bertha said. "Go anywhere you want."

Jocelyn and Lettie followed Paige and Topper into the new wing. They watched her give her dog a signal and command from the doorway. Topper took off immediately and went straight into Gerard's new room and began pawing at the wall.

"He'll scratch the paint," Lettie cried.

Paige rushed forward with a biscuit and words of praise.

"I don't see a bomb," Lettie said.

"It's in the wall," Paige said. "Scooby and Tank found it last night. Same wall. Same spot."

"Good boy, Topper," Hawk said, ruffling the dog's ears and scratching his heavily coated chest.

"We'll come back after you've removed that one," Paige said, "to see if there are any more."

Hawk pulled on his gloves and opened his tool kit. He made a hole with his hammer half way up the wall and then sawed a large square piece of sheetrock and removed it.

"That's a big hole," Lettie said.

"I want to be sure I leave room around the bomb."

"Lettie, come on," Jocelyn called. "Let's ride."

Meanwhile Paige walked Topper through the garage. She hit the shed next. Topper and Paige arrived at the barn as Jocelyn and Lettie were saddling their horses. Hubbs was saddling a third horse.

"Who's going with you?" Paige asked.

"Mom rides," Jocelyn said. "She's able to handle Yudi. Not many people can. He's a handful."

Paige watched them saddle up while Topper roamed all through the barn. When Topper was near the rear door, Paige threw something into the stall Royal had just vacated.

"What did you throw in there?" Jocelyn asked.

"A bit of the substance the bomb is made of," Paige explained. "Topper searched the garage and shed and most of the barn. He needs to find something to keep him focused."

"But suppose there really is some of that stuff in here?" Jocelyn asked.

"Then he'll find it. Once I have this piece and he has his cookie, he'll start searching again."

The riders were only a few yards away when they heard Paige exclaim, "Good boy, Topper!"

"What next, Miss?" Hubbs asked.

"Now I have to think about where else to look," Paige said as she watched the riders go through the back gate. "Does the orchard have a swing?"

"No, Miss."

"Does Aleta ride around the inside of the ring where the jumps are?"

"Sometimes," Hubbs said. "She rides the trail most."

"Outside the property?" Paige asked.

"Past the gate," Hubbs said pointing to the gate the three riders had just gone through.

"Do the dogs always follow the horses?" Paige asked.

"Bertha don't let them go past the gate. They'll come away in a bit."

"They seem pretty excited." Paige noted.

"That don't figure."

"I will go see," Paige said, an idea forming as she walked.

"Why not the gate post?" she murmured.

She'd seen the riders stop and talk while one of them dismounted and opened the gate and held it open for the others to ride through.

Scooby and Tank saw her coming. Both their tails began to wag. Paige put her hand in her pocket and broke the dog biscuit into chunks with her fingers.

When they drew nearer, Topper ran on ahead and after sniffing the post began to wag his tail. He crowded next to the post between the other two dogs.

Paige couldn't see any sign of anything, but she gave each dog a piece of biscuit and patted each in turn and then gave each another piece of biscuit. She saw Hawk come out of the house and she waved at him.

Her excitement and the presence of all three dogs told him she'd found the fourth bomb. He never would have looked there.

He went to Hubbs first.

"I may need to take apart part of the gate. I need tools."

Using his cell, Hubbs called the house.

"Robert, we need help at the back gate."

"Robert?" Hawk questioned.

"He can fix it after you wreck it," Hubbs said. "He's the one what redid the barn. Him and Ed Ornstein."

Hawk decided to wait for Robert. He called Lyle. "Paige found the fourth one. On the back gate where the horses exit. All the dogs zeroed in on it."

Hawk walked up to his wife.

"Lyle says, 'Good going, Paige.'"

By the time Hawk was finished, Paige had been over the entire acreage with the three dogs. She told him how the dogs had ignored the training bumper and found the bomb in the trunk of Hawk's car.

"Harriet will be so pleased."

"You've earned your money today, Paige. There's no way I would have found the one in the gate post."

"Next the office and then the plane," Hawk said as they got into the car.

"After the office, can we have lunch?"

"Oh, Paige. I'm so sorry. You've been running around all morning," Hawk said. We will stop now. Whatever's at the office can wait while we eat."

With Topper drooling on their shoulders while they ate, Paige and Hawk finished in record time.

"I'm a mess," Paige said. "So are you. Maybe we should stop and change."

"Topper didn't need catsup on his fries," Hawk complained.

"He could smell it," Paige said. "I could tell he wanted it."

"I'm not sure a dog's stomach can handle fast food."

"We can't eat in front of him and not offer him any," Paige said.

"Can we skip the catsup?"

"We need to carry towels to drape over our shoulders when we eat."

"I guess we could always go inside," Hawk suggested.

"And leave Topper all by himself in the car?" Paige asked.

Hawk could tell he had suggested a bad thing.

"I guess we bring towels," Hawk said. "We got two more letters to add to the three I already have—M, O and F."

"What are the other letters?"

"An R and an A."

"M, O, F, R, A." Paige repeated and then fell silent for several minutes.

Hawk was about to say something when suddenly Paige said, "MOM FARM."

"How did you do that?"

"I'm good at anagrams."

"But you don't have all the letters," Hawk contended.

"I guessed at the two remaining letters," Paige said. "We have a finite number of letters. Every one must count."

"There must be other combinations," Hawk insisted.

"There are," Paige said. "But they made no sense."

Hawk punched in Lyle's number.

"Paige has figured out the message."

"Already?" Lyle whistled. "Stanley is getting his money's worth."

"We found the letter R on the bomb on the fence post. The wall bomb gave us an A. So the letters we have are M, O, F, R, A."

"Makes no sense to me. What did Paige come up with?"

"MOM FARM."

"That makes sense with Doyle sending us a message. Fouts may have imprisoned his mother on her farm, but what I still don't get is why Doyle isn't doing anything. Still I can use this."

"We're at the office now," Hawk reported. "Workers are putting in a new window of bulletproof glass in Aleta's office. They're almost done. We will wait until they clear out."

"I told Stanley about Paige's find—the gate post," Lyle said. "He told me to tell her, she's earned her whole week's salary. She's not to return a cent."

After Chief West hung up, he went down the stairs from his second floor office to the basement level where the Arborville Police jail currently held two prisoners, the others having been transferred to Oakwood's jail.

He opened Butch Lennert's cell door, told him to face the wall and then handcuffed him.

"Where are we off to?" Butch asked.

"Interrogation," West answered curtly.

"I ain't answering no questions. I done told you that," Butch reiterated.

"I have news for you." Lyle said. "Move out."

Butch was in the hall when Lyle's phone rang. Lyle pushed Butch back into his cell and locked it before he answered his phone. Only certain people had his number. He saw that the caller was Hawk.

"Now's not a good time," he said when he answered his phone.

"Stanley's office has been broken into," Hawk reported.

"Call dispatch and he'll send a unit."

"Whoever it was rifled Alice's desk," Hawk reported. "I'm surprised the alarm didn't go off."

"Stanley had to shut it off because the window was out."

"Do you want me to do a work-up? Paige is moving around the office with Topper."

"Print the desk. Call Milani. I will be right over."

He turned to go.

"Hey, Chief man," Butch yelled. "Come get your damn cuffs."

"Later," Lyle said. Doyle's mother is in trouble. Fouts has her at the farmhouse only we don't know where it is. You do, so a count of accessory to murder is going to be added to the charges."

"I don't believe you," Butch said.

"I don't give a damn! You've been no help at all so far. We're going to throw the book at you."

"Take off the damned cuffs," Butch repeated, his voice rising to a screech.

"Later. I've got an emergency."

"No one visits the prisoners," Lyle told the man on dispatch who was also watching the jail.

Because every available man was out searching for Fouts and checking on every elderly woman in Arborville, the dispatcher was doing double duty. Butch's yelling bothered him. After ten minutes of telling him to shut up, he locked the access door.

Dressed in street clothes, Oakwood's Police Chief Alan Peets grumbled at Butch when the door slammed shut.

"Didn't your mother teach you manners?" Peets growled, his dark features making his scowl more threatening. "You don't yell at a police chief. You ask politely."

"It's a trick," Butch said.

"Didn't seem like one to me."

"They want me to tell them stuff."

"Well, don't tell me!" Peets bellowed. "I don't want an accessory rap hung on me."

"They can't do that," Butch said.

"They can if you know anything, so keep your damned mouth shut."

"You think it's real--about Doyle's mom?"

"There you go, getting me involved."

"I just want to know so I can figure out what to do."

"Don't talk to me. That's what you do."

"But I didn't murder no one. I don't know nothing about it."

Peets sighed heavily. His face registered disgust.

"That's why they were taking you to interrogation, Dummy."

"Don't call me that. We ain't friends."

Peets did an about turn.

"You're right. You're not dumb. Cops are dumb. I don't know why they don't log onto driver's license records and find this Doyle's address."

"Doyle is his street name. It ain't his real name. I told Lennie it was a queer one and he said Doyle didn't want to be a junior. And Doyle was some author's name. It was a long one."

"Sir Arthur Conan Doyle," Peets murmured.

"Yeh, that sounds right. It had a Sir in it. I think that's a weird first name."

"It's a title."

"You mean like Chief?"

"Yeh, now be quiet. I've got to think."

"That's what Lennie did all the time. He was a great thinker. Geez, I miss him."

After ten minutes of silence, Butch burst out, "I don't want her dead. She was good to us. Who'd killer her? Lennie says to never believe a cop. They lie all the time."

"You're talking to me," Peets growled. "I told you not to."

"I can't snooze or nothing with these cuffs on."

Peets sat up.

"Okay, we can talk, but not about Doyle's mother. You got that?"

"Yeh, I got that. I ain't stupid."

"Besides even if the cops got to the Conan place out on Whisky Creek, they'll be too late."

"Why did you say that?"

"Say what?"

"The Conan place ain't on no Whiskey Creek."

"Okay, so it's near Whiskey Creek."

"It's nowhere near."

"Okay, so I don't know the name of the creek," Peets shrugged. "What I was trying to say was that cops usually don't know…"

Butch interrupted.

"A creek is next to the house, but there ain't no water in it. How come it's still a creek when it don't have water in it?"

"Because that's the way creeks are. They are sometimes dry."

"It don't make sense. They should call it something else when it ain't got water."

"Like what? What would you call that creek on the Conan place?"

"Ditch!" Butch exclaimed. "Dead Man's Ditch. That even sounds good. All scary."

Peets turned away and coughed. He pulled out his handkerchief and his cell with it. He punched in Lyle's number and sent him a text message: "Conan farm. Dead Man's Creek."

Five minutes later the guard appeared.

"It's your lucky day, Peters. Your lawyer got the charges dropped."

When they got back upstairs, Peets said, "You couldn't come up with a better line that that?"

"Chief West wants to talk to you right away," the officer said, handing him the phone.

"We need you to raid the farm house," West said. "We don't think Fouts is there. I'm on his trail. Doyle is either hurt or dead. Same for his mother."

Peets objected. "I need to shower, shave and kiss my wife."

"Put on your spare uniform and forget the niceties," West barked. "Good job, by the way."

CHAPTER 7

A little after one o'clock, the four Praetzels decided to stop for lunch in the theme park.

"I'm not sure that I'm up for a salad," Stanley said.

His mother looked at him quizzically.

"When did you start eating salads?"

"Aleta has me on a diet."

"Your weight looks good to me," his mother remarked.

"It's a diet for my health."

"You're sick?"

"Aleta wants me to live until I'm eighty."

Aleta shook her head and signed, "Longer."

"If you're going to be nit-picky, I'm not going to translate what you say," Stanley threatened.

"Sure you will. And you can eat what you like today," Aleta signed. "You've been active."

"Aleta thinks I lead a sedentary life," Stanley explained. "But that's not true. Nobody could live a sedentary life with Aleta as a wife."

"You're only going to have your diet suspended today because you're going to need your strength," Aleta signed.

His parents chuckled.

"It's not what you think," Stanley protested.

"Oh yes it is," Aleta signed.

"I'm warning you," Stanley quipped as his parents' smiles broadened.

His mother changed the conversation to their expected second child by asking which sex each wanted.

When they had finished eating and were waiting for the check, Stanley received a call from Lyle.

The tables around them were empty, so Aleta signed that Stanley should put the phone on speaker.

"Maybe they found another bomb," his mother said hopefully.

Stanley pressed the speaker button.

"Some good news," Lyle said.

"You're on speaker," Stanley cut in. "Aleta and my parents."

"It's okay. This isn't secret," Lyle said. "We found the farm. Paige figured out the anagram."

"What anagram?" Stanley asked.

"Doyle scratched letters in the metal casings of the voice activation units. We had found M, O, F, R and A and Paige's brain added letters and came up with 'mom' and 'farm' almost instantaneously."

"She deserves a bonus," Stanley declared.

"Hiring her was a smart move," Lyle said. "I dropped the idea that Doyle's mother might be in danger and Peets managed to get Butch to cough up the location of the farm. As it turns out, it wasn't Doyle's mom who was in real danger, but Doyle. Fouts had slugged him and dumped him down a dry well. Dr. Taekman is operating on him now. Prognosis isn't good. His mother was bound and gagged and locked in a closet."

Aleta suddenly began signing.

Without thinking Stanley translated what she was signing, "The plane's not safe."

"What did you say?" Lyle asked, shocked.

"It's Aleta. She's signing at me," Stanley said. "Wait. There's more. The bomb in the plane is not voice-activated."

"What's that mean?"

Aleta signed. "It will explode when you try to take off."

"Lyle, why are you flying my plane?" Stanley charged. "What's going on? And when did you learn to fly?"

"Robert and Hawk were going to fly me. Robert has his license and Hawk can fly."

"Why are you flying here?"

"Fouts took a jet from O'Hare this morning."

"How did he find out where we are?"

"He broke into your office and rifled through Alice's desk."

Lydia spoke up. "He doesn't know I put the hotel reservations in my name.

Aleta began to sign and the first thing she signed was, "Don't repeat anything until we're out of here." '

Stanley nodded.

His parents looked at him puzzled.

He said simply, "Later."

Stanley spoke to Lyle.

"Aleta wants to communicate with you directly. I will point the camera at her. Let me know when you can see her."

Aleta began to sign and quickly spelled out a plan that Stanley had to admit was a clever one.

When she finished, she closed the phone and handed it to Stanley. She got up immediately and the others followed. She headed straight for the Jungle Trek and not until they were half way through did Aleta begin to relax.

"He's gone," she signed. "You can translate for me now."

"Who's gone?" Stanley asked.

"I assume it was Fouts. I should have said the danger is gone because that's all I felt. We're safe now. You can tell Mom and Dad my plan."

Stanley outlined it briefly.

"Lyle, Robert and Hawk are to use Claude's big plane to fly down here. Robert knows where the keys are."

"But can he fly it?" Hubert asked.

"He can call Claude."

"What else?" Lydia prompted.

"We are not going back to the room at all," Stanley said. "We are going to stay elsewhere tonight."

"What about our clothes?" Lydia asked.

"We aren't canceling out reservations. Lyle, Robert and Hawk think he's bringing someone else, so they are going to wait for Fouts in our rooms. We are to leave Lyle the keys and the room numbers in an envelope at the desk."

"If we're going back, why not get our things?" Lydia asked.

"Because we don't know where Fouts is," Stanley said. "To be safe, only one of us is taking the envelope to the desk."

"That would be me," Lydia said.

"Why you?" Stanley asked.

"Because I don't know Fouts and he doesn't know me."

Aleta nodded.

"We will make do with the clothing we have," Aleta signed. "And don't complain about those shorts, Stanley. Mine are shorter, so my legs will get colder."

Stanley grinned as he translated, and then added, "She wouldn't even wear them if I didn't wear mine. I didn't know we... .never mind."

He finished slightly red-faced.

Hubert smiled. "I understand completely. I applaud your choice."

Lydia glared at her husband and Aleta giggled.

"So when do we know the coast if clear?" Hubert asked, trying to ignore his wife's frown.

"Lyle will call," Stanley said.

"Won't Fouts find us at another hotel?" Lydia worried.

"Not likely," Aleta signed. "He won't be surprised if we stay out late, so he'll wait a long time. I'm guessing he's planning to wait in the room."

"So, now what do we do?"

"We go on the Mount Everest ride," Aleta signed. "And we all throw up all over the only clothes we have."

After Stanley translated that, he added, "We go on another trail walk and talk her out of her idea."

Stuart Fouts had spotted the four in the restaurant. The information he'd gotten from Alice's desk told him their exact location and he figured they'd spend the day in a theme park. Considering the number of horses and dogs she had, he surmised that the first day they would visit the Animal Kingdom.

He had been hunting for some sign of them for several hours. When he saw Aleta and Stanley Praetzel in the restaurant with his parents, he realized that his knife wasn't enough.

He had watched one of the waiters hover near their table for an exceptionally long time and realized that their conversation must be noteworthy. He bribed the waiter and got several salient facts from him. Doyle had been found but wasn't conscious. His chances for recovery were slim. There were still undiscovered bombs, so Aleta still wasn't speaking. She was using sign language. The cop was told not to fly. The group knew that he was there.

As he chewed on these facts, he remembered watching the four walk away. Aleta had been in the briefest of shorts. Stanley was in lightweight casual wear as was the older couple. No one had a gun hidden under that type of clothing.

Stanley must have brought his gun, Stuart told himself. He would have been a fool not to and Stanley Praetzel was no fool. He'd left it in his room.

While Stuart Fouts wasn't savvy about bomb making, he was an experienced computer hacker. He returned to his room at the hotel, opened his laptop and hacked into the hotel register. He found no Praetzels listed. Then he remembered the waiter had said something about registration, but he couldn't remember what.

He knew they came in late the night before. He began to look at parties of four in two rooms who had checked in the previous day. There were only two such parties under one name. One was named Castillo and the other, Davis. The latter seemed familiar, but he planned to check both suites of rooms.

He borrowed a master key from a maid after rendering her unconscious with a blow to the head and then locking her and her cart in a room that had obviously been vacated.

He checked the Castillo room first, but the apparel told him that one of the men was quite large and one of the women chunky.

He entered the first of the two rooms registered to a Lydia Davis. He spotted a laptop on the desk. The sight of it upset him. If he wasn't successful, the last thing he wanted Aleta to be able to do was communicate using the laptop. The signing required someone who knew signing. The laptop opened up her line of communication to a much wider range of people.

As he stared at it, his anger developed into rage. That was what had separated him from Doyle in the end. Doyle liked the idea of using scare tactics to extort money from rich people. Lennie and Butch had eagerly climbed on board the original plan. It seemed like an easy way to make money. Plant bombs and then negotiate payment for telling the marks where they were.

Doyle cleverly designed the bombs that could be hidden in unlikely places.

The cops couldn't find them.

Butch had been given the easiest ones to plant. Lennie had been assigned the one in the RV. Stuart, Lukas and Doyle did the trickier ones. But they all knew who planted what. They had argued over which bomb to give up first. Each man hand a proprietary interest in the ones he planted. As a result everyone in the group knew where all the bombs were. That didn't seem to matter. The first exchange of information for fifty thousand dollars netted each man ten thousand dollars. The plan was working well.

Stuart Fouts distributed the money evenly; however, Lennie and Butch got the marked bills and were told not to spend them. Lennie agreed to this which Stuart thought was a dumb move. He had no idea that Lennie planned to rob the Praetzel's on his own.

The second robbery of the Praetzel RV had been as successful as the first until Lennie and Butch went to the same pawnshop to exchange a second necklace for cash. They were caught by Vannella's men and Lennie was worked over. Lennie was in a coma and Butch was in jail.

When Stanley Praetzel offered one hundred grand for the location of the two bombs in the barn, Doyle knew that Lennie and Butch had probably given up more to Vannella. Sergio's men were not under the same restraints as the cops. Fouts original plan to exchange the location of each bomb for a higher amount of money vanished when that request was made. Lukas Kvidahl and Stuart Fouts couldn't pass up the hundred grand. That was too big a payday to let slip by. Only Doyle realized that Stanley Praetzel had set the price. He was a lawyer. A precedent had been set. He wouldn't go higher. Doyle also realized that it was only a matter of time before Butch and Lennie would bargain with the location of the other bombs. The original plan was dead in the water.

That was when Doyle and Stuart Fouts parted company. Doyle shared his conclusions and argued that they should quit after the last large payment Stanley Praetzel offered.

Stuart Fouts and Lukas Kvidahl decided that kidnapping Praetzel was the next move. Doyle went with the two reluctantly, planning to split once he had his share of the hundred thousand. That was too big an amount for him to walk away from.

While he had shot Aleta Praetzel during the kidnapping attempt, and thereby earned himself the right to claim half of the money since Lukas was dead, Doyle had made it clear that he didn't want anything to do with a kidnapping.

Now as Stuart Fouts sat in the hotel room, he looked at his bandaged hand and cursed Aleta Praetzel. No bones had been broken but it still it hurt. He wanted revenge.

With Lukas Kvidahl dead, Stuart Fouts had been forced to put his plan to kidnap Stanley Praetzel on the back burner. He had, however, persuaded Doyle that the original plan was still a good one. They just needed to plant five more bombs and bargain with the location of those. Doyle sensed that Stuart Fouts was still upset with him over his refusal to help kidnap Stanley Praetzel, but he went along with the building of five new bombs and devised radically new locations for each one. When he had been in the house, planting the bomb in the briefcase, he had spotted the brand new laptop on the desk.

Doyle bought an identical one, rigged it and managed to exchange it in the morning when Aleta was riding her horse. That was the one sitting on the hotel desk staring at Stuart Fouts now.

Doyle talked a lot about Aleta Praetzel during their bomb making sessions. He had accumulated a vast amount of knowledge about the prophets and he dispensed it freely. Among other bits of information, Doyle told Fouts that the prophets only prophesied about death. That fact had persuaded Fouts not to kill Doyle outright but to slug him and dump him in a dry well to die days later. He bound and gagged Doyle's mother for the same reason. According to Doyle the prophets only predicted murders that were violent and immediate. His plan had worked. Aleta Praetzel was not the reason that Doyle and his mother were found. Police had gotten the location of the farm from Butch, had raided it and found both Doyle and his mother alive. Doyle, however, was not expected to live.

It soon became apparent that Doyle was right about something else as well. Aleta Praetzel couldn't foresee her own death and so she hadn't been able to tell where the voice-activated bombs were either. The fact that Stanley Praetzel was willing to fork over such large sums of money proved that.

As Stuart sat in the hotel room puzzling over why the police were sent to search the patrol cars in the parking lot, he concluded that when Roger had delivered the gift of the bomb, the police did a search of their cars as a precautionary measure. He noted that they had searched all the cars, not just one. They hadn't found the one in which the bomb was planted and had given up. He hadn't been there when Hawk fetched Topper and the dog located it.

Stuart thought about the one he had with him. It was in pieces so it would pass through airport security. One part was in the pocket of his coat. Another was in his travel case. A third was part of his cell phone. The C-4 was wrapped in a candy wrapper. And now here he was in Aleta Praetzel's hotel room.

And there was Aleta's computer.

He had left a note telling Aleta that there were five more bombs. As far as he knew none of those had been found yet, including the one he was staring at.

It was a powerful one Doyle had said. It would take out a whole room full of people. It would take out not only Aleta, but also Stanley.

And if I am in the room, it will take out me too, Fouts realized.

Suppose she managed to get off a word or two, he thought. I have to do something.

The first idea that came to him was the best.

Deafen the computer temporarily.

First he wrapped the laptop in a bath towel. He still didn't feel safe. He went over the bed, peeled back the spread and the sheet and then lifted the mattress up and shoved the covered laptop between the mattress and the box springs.

He sat down satisfied.

That didn't last long. He was still in the same room with it.

He pulled it out from its hiding place and carried it into the parents' room next door. Aleta would be upset when she found it gone and Stanley and his parents would search for it. Stuart was certain they would find it. And when they did they would consider it safe because he had hidden it. Stanley would reason that if it contained a bomb, that the last thing Fouts would have done with it was hide it.

He carefully remade both beds, and then sat down to wait for Aleta and Stanley to return.

He sat in the room satisfied for over an hour before he remembered that he had the makings of another bomb with him.

He had told Aleta Praetzel there were five more bombs. It occurred to him that if he planted a sixth in a place that would not be considered as a hiding place, and if they found that one, they would stop looking, and she would start speaking again. Doyle had told him that his thinking was too pedestrian.

"You're much too direct," Doyle had said. "The computer is a good idea only because it will take me a lot of time to plant one inside, but stay away from stuff that's too personal."

Stuart had to admit that most of the places Doyle had chosen were unique. Stuart recalled that he had prevailed on two placements. He had chosen to put one in the briefcase and one in her car. They were among the first ones found.

Stuart slouched in his chair and flicked to another channel. The last thing he wanted to watch was a soap without sound. He stopped on a soccer game. He could follow that reasonably well. When the commercial came on he watched the man shaving and an idea hit him.

Put the last bomb in Stanley's shaving kit. They were always traveling. If he was like most men, he had only one traveling kit.

Half an hour later the voice-activated bomb was installed in the traveling kit. It was tucked under the canvas covering on the bottom of the kit with the microphone hidden next to a pocket.

He put it back on the counter where he had found it after he reloaded the shaving gear in the same way it had been when he found it. Stanley would notice if anything were out of place, Stuart surmised. He was a neat freak.

Before plunking himself down in the chair positioned so he could watch the television screen and the door both, he checked the gun, which he had found minutes after entering the room. Satisfied, he settled down to wait.

CHAPTER 8

When Lyle told Robert and Hawk what Aleta had suggested, Paige relaxed visibly.

"That means you can't go, right?" she inquired hopefully.

Hawk hadn't been paying much attention to his wife, but Bertha had. While Bertha was nervous about Robert going, she recognized that Paige was more nervous. While she wouldn't prevent her husband from going to the aid of his daughter, Paige could only see the danger to her beloved husband.

The young wife was trying to stay cool, but she was losing her grip on her emotions.

When Lyle told them about Aleta's plan, Bertha saw Paige panic. They would all be going. Hawk needed to help fly the big plane. They couldn't go without him.

Not wanting to break down in front of the group, Paige rushed into the bathroom.

Bertha hurried after her and managed to push the door open before Paige locked it. She closed herself in with the young girl, took her in her arms and held her close when she burst into tears.

The men heard her crying.

"Bertha's with her," Robert said. "I will go get the keys to Claude's plane."

After Robert left, Bertha emerged.

"You have to come up with a new plan."

"Aleta's in danger," Lyle retorted sharply.

Bertha brushed aside that obvious fact and pursued her own agenda.

"Paige can't be left," she said. "So either Hawk stays here or Paige goes with him."

"Paige can't go," Hawk declared.

But Bertha wouldn't be deterred.

"You're flying the big plane, right?"

"That's why I need two pilots," Lyle stated.

"I don't want Robert participating in the ambush either. That's police work. Why not take trained men, Lyle?"

"I still need Hawk and Robert as pilots."

"So let Paige come along as a passenger. You have room enough."

"Paige shouldn't be pushing her way into police business," Hawk charged. "She hasn't the right!"

Bertha's eyes blazed.

"You have a short memory, Mr. Hawkins Monroe. Your wife has been doing police work all day. Not only has she worked hard, she's done a bang-up job."

Lyle pondered Stanley's last statement. If he could find a way to give Paige a bonus, he should do it.

"You know, Hawk," Lyle said. "The last thing Stanley told me was to figure out a special was to say thank you. If she were on the force, I'd see she got a commendation or time off or a special request granted."

"You mean let her come?" Hawk gasped.

"This is a job for trained men," Lyle went on. "It won't cost me anything to take a trained man with me. Peter French is as good as they come as a police officer. He'll be coming with us."

"But we won't be going anywhere when we get there," Hawk pointed out.

Lyle nodded and said, "That doesn't seem to be the issue here. Go tell your wife that she's coming."

When Hawk entered the bathroom, Paige tried to stop her tears.

"Bertha's been keeping house for two lawyers too long," Hawk said. "You are coming with us."

Paige stared at him, dumfounded.

After a moment, she choked out, "To the shoot-out?"

"No, I've been relieved of shoot-out duty. French is coming for that part. You and I get to sit in the plane and talk to Robert until they catch the bad guy."

Paige sniffled. "Bertha will be glad. She was worried too."

"Lyle said that you earned the right," Hawk said, his tone gentled by her obvious distress.

"Will we stay overnight?"

"Probably not. And we won't be going anywhere. You do understand that."

"I understand. All I want to do is be with you."

"Bring Aleta's Scrabble game," Hawk said.

"We're going right away?" Paige asked, dismayed.

"As soon as Robert gets back with the keys," Hawk said.

"We can't go with our shirts stained with catsup and dog drool."

"We haven't time to go home and change," Hawk protested. "Besides, we will be staying in the plane."

Paige brushed past him.

"Bertha, I need to change. Does Aleta have any casual clothes I could borrow?"

Hawk followed her out of the bathroom.

"We don't need to change. We won't be leaving the plane."

"I won't go smelling of catsup."

"I will fetch some of Aleta's things," Bertha said. "You just step in the shower for a few minutes and I will put them on the counter."

"Paige," Hawk moaned, visibly upset. "We haven't time."

She brushed past him again.

"I can be quick."

Bertha rushed off and Hawk was left standing in the hall staring at Topper who sensed that they were going somewhere.

"What are we going to do with Topper?" he yelled through the door. He heard the water running.

"You're going to leave him here," Bertha said as she entered the bathroom with a stack of clothes. She gathered the ones Paige had draped across the tub and exited.

"Come with me," she said entering the laundry room. She opened a cupboard and rooted around among the clean folded clothes.

"I think I have one of Paul's shirts in here. You're taller, but the neck size should be okay. Roll up the sleeves."

"I can't," Hawk began.

Bertha cut him off.

"Robert will not enjoy living with the smell of catsup for half a day."

Hawk pulled off his shirt and put it in Bertha's waiting hand.

"It was Topper," he explained. "We were sharing our fries and Paige said he wanted catsup on his."

"He told you this?" Bertha smirked.

"Paige seemed to think so."

"King loves catsup," Bertha said, handing him an undershirt.

He pulled off the next layer and then Bertha left him.

Paige was done the same time he was. She smiled at him. He returned the smile. She'd exchanged the jeans for a pair of shorts and a pretty pale yellow top that floated down not quite to her waist. Her shoes matched.

Paige saw Hawk's eyes staring at her feet.

"We're the same size. I am off work, aren't I?"

Lyle cut in. "You've done a good day's work. Sorry the only bonus I have to offer is hours in a plane with your husband."

Paige took Hawk's arm.

"We're going to play Scrabble. We'll have fun."

Hawk sighed, "She always wins. It's that anagram thing."

They had no sooner reached their flying altitude than Peter French undid his seat belt and went up front.

"You interested in flying?" Robert asked.

"I'm taking lessons," Peter said.

Hawk looked at him. "You want to log in an hour in this craft?"

"Would I!" Peter exclaimed.

Hawk joined Paige in back.

"How did you do during the take-off?" he asked.

"I stayed in my seat," she said proudly.

"You've come a long way."

"Is Peter a pilot?" Paige asked.

"He's learning," Hawk said.

"Really?" Lyle questioned. "This I need to know about. Excuse me."

Hawk hugged his wife and then kissed her.

"This is a delayed reward. You look great by the way."

After ten minutes, Lyle returned.

"I've got news for you," he said.

The two gazed at him quizzically.

"Peter has as much flying time as you have, Hawk. He can take your place on the way home."

"You mean as a co-pilot?"

Lyle went on. "That means you and Paige can stay overnight and spend this evening in Orlando and tomorrow as well. Hubert's plane holds six. You can fly home with them."

"Do they know about this?" Hawk asked.

"Stanley asked me to give Paige a bonus," Lyle said. "No one has to baby-sit the plane."

"Aren't you glad you have a clean shirt on?" Paige commented, grinning.

"You aren't going to complain that you have no clothes?" Hawk asked, surprised.

"One does not look a gift horse in the mouth," Paige replied solemnly.

Halfway though the flight, Hawk went forward to relieve French because Lyle wanted to plan strategy.

This turned out to be a wiser decision than Chief West envisioned. When they reached the hotel, both thought that the room would be empty. Just as West was about to insert the key card, French's hand stopped him. He motioned him to enter the next room down.

Lyle followed his suggestion.

Once inside the Senior Praetzel's room, French whispered, "He's there."

"How do you know?" West whispered.

"I can hear the television. He has it on mute, but it makes a high pitched sound I can hear."

"Where do you suppose he is?" West asked.

For the next quarter hour they speculated where Fouts had positioned himself in the room. Then they tried different approaches until they had determined which would be most effective.

"It's time," West whispered, opening the duffle bag carrying the riot gear.

"Do we have to?"

"Do you want a hole in your head or your chest?"

"Aw, Chief, the gear hampers movement. If I'm quick, maybe he won't get a shot off."

"Head and chest gear minimum," West ordered.

French noticed West protected his arms and hands as well. He followed suit, but when West put on leg gear, French opted to do without.

West eyed his second in command reproachfully, and, reluctantly, French donned it all. Armed with stun guns, the two left the room.

West slipped the key card into the slot and French rushed in as soon as the lock clicked open.

Stuart Fouts had heard the card in the slot and had risen, gun in hand, to meet the two as they entered. It was the one scene the two policemen had not envisioned.

Shocked at seeing him in an unexpected position, French managed to shout "Police" because the word was already in his mouth.

Stuart Fouts' finger was already squeezing the trigger, so he was able to get off a shot before two sets of darts hit him. He shot again, reflexively, as he fell.

French took both hits.   The force knocked him backward.

West rushed forward and extracted the gun from the Fouts' grip, turned him onto his stomach and cuffed him. Then he checked on French who was gasping for breath.

People began to gather and stood back as they saw two police in riot gear inside the room. West opened French's shirt and saw where the bullets had hit. They'd been stopped by the vest, but from the way French was gasping, West knew Peter had cracked or broken ribs.

West opened his cell, reported the shooting and asked for a paramedic unit.

He then called Stanley and said he needed both him and Robert. However, it wasn't Stanley who left the group, but his father.

"Aleta needs you here.   You can understand her," Hubert said. "If there's one thing I'm familiar with it's how criminals are handled."

"And I hold a bar card in two states," Robert said. "That fact does carry weight."

"Lyle wouldn't have come down without a warrant," Stanley hastened to tell them. "The minute he had proof Fouts had jumped bail, he would have called Judge Clancy."

"He might have jumped the gun," Hubert cautioned.

Stanley watched them walk away. Aleta tapped him on the arm.

"Go!" she signed. "He's our best friend and he called you. I will be fine."

Stanley ran after the departing figures.

"Hey, Dads. I'm coming too."

"What about Aleta?" Hubert asked when Stanley caught up.

"She will communicate somehow. Right now Lyle may need all of us."

"He didn't kill the guy," Hubert said.

"He stepped on toes," Stanley said. "Cops don't like that. He understands that better than anybody except maybe me. He's been teaching me that lesson for months now, so let's see how well I learned it."

Once at the hotel, Stanley turned to his father and said, "Dad, he asked for Robert and me, so you pay for a room for Hawk and Paige, and a second one for Lyle and Robert and then come up to deliver their key cards."

"Will they be using them?"

"Robert will. He has to fly home tomorrow. He needs to sleep."

The two older men exchanged glances. Stanley had taken charge. That was an unexpected twist.

On the floor, Stanley walked straight through the crowd and past the police guard with a single sentence, "I was called."

Robert, who was following him, was reduced to saying, "I'm with him."

Stanley strode into the room.

"Who are you and what are you doing in my room?"

"Sergeant Darren Cooper. Are you the owner of the gun?"

"Ballistics will establish that unless Chief West can identify it as mine."

"You don't have your own gun?"

"It's police issue. I don't keep track," Stanley said. "Now to whom does Chief West owe an apology?"

"What are you talking about?" Cooper asked.

"He didn't follow proper procedure or you wouldn't be here and neither would I. Whom did he piss off?"

"I guess that would be Captain Arguello."

"Take us to him. Mr. Locke, watch the prisoner."

"I can't leave the guy on the floor," Cooper protested.

"Then please request that Captain Arguello join us here."

"He told me to bring everyone to headquarters."

Hubert showed up with the key cards.

"Mr. Praetzel," Stanley said. "In your opinion, as a long time defense attorney, would it be wise for the police to move the unconscious man on the floor?"

Hubert glanced at Stuart Fouts who was sprawled on the floor and then replied, "Not if they don't want a million dollar law suit."

"And who would be liable?"

"The men who moved him."

"But we didn't stun him," Sergeant Cooper protested.

"I imagine he will sue you both," Hubert said.

"I've asked Sergeant Cooper to call the man in charge," Stanley disclosed.

"That would be wise," Hubert said.

Sergeant Cooper went outside the room and made a brief call. When he returned, Stanley was scolding his chief.

"You know better than to move without going through proper channels. A fine mess you're in now. You didn't come alone, did you?"

"French was shot with your gun. The rounds hit his vest," Lyle responded evenly. "I think he has broken ribs."

Stanley turned.

"Sergeant Cooper, was Officer French taken to a hospital?"

"First thing."

"Will you please check on his condition? We need to know if he can pilot the plane going back to Illinois."

After making his request, Stanley stood quietly and waited.

"You mean now?"

"How long does it take your doctors to X-ray ribs? Or do they put cops on the back burner down here?"

"No, we don't do that," Sergeant Cooper sputtered. "I will check."

"You do know that the chances are good that French won't be able to fly for a week or more," Stanley observed.

"One of your wives is going to be disappointed," Robert said.

"Aleta needs you, Stanley. Let's not lose sight of that," his father said.

Sergeant Cooper returned.

"Your officer has two cracked ribs. He can't be a pilot."

"When will he be released?"

"Soon as someone comes for him."

"Robert," Stanley said. "Get French and take him to the plane."

The steel in Stanley's voice was recognized by Lyle. He hadn't sensed it before.

Who had awakened this quality in Stanley, he pondered.

The murmurs in the hall told Stanley that Captain Ruiz had arrived.

Stanley spun around and spoke first.

"I was profoundly sorry to learn that our town's police chief didn't follow protocol in this matter. I know you have your own methods for handling cases of assassins who are armed and lying in wait. It is your town. You are in charge of all police matters. It was presumptive of him to barge in and take charge. That the serial rapist of four elderly women lies at your feet may help assuage your anger slightly."

"My men could have handled this," Captain Ruiz grumbled.

"Of that I am confident," Stanley submitted. "It was an inexcusable breach of protocol. There is no doubt your men would have taken him alive, so he could tell us where the rest of the bombs are hidden. We have had two crews of police, two forensic experts and three bomb sniffing dogs on the case for several days and we've only found sixteen of the nineteen we know he planted. We are stumped. That Chief West didn't advise you of his presence in your city is indefensible. That being said, may I suggest that you ship this vengeful sociopath back north as soon as possible."

Stanley turned to Lyle.

"Now it's your turn to apologize for not giving the captain his due and then offer to forget this incident where your man was injured and accept your responsibility in the matter, and belatedly hand him the paperwork that should have been in his hands the minute you hit town."

"I have not had a chance to get to a fax," Lyle began, "but..."

"You should have waited!" Stanley charged.

"We were laying a trap. He was already here."

"Some trap," Stanley sneered.

"We didn't get to lay it. French suspected he was already in the room and so we went in."

"You were in full riot gear," Stanley pointed out. "You took time to dress. Why didn't you call Captain Arguello then?"

"Yes, why?" Captain Arguello pressed, still obviously vexed.

Lyle immediately apologized. "I was worried about French. He didn't want to wear the riot gear."

"You order him!" Arguello snapped. "That's what you do."

"I haven't ordered French in a long time," Lyle said. "Another of my weaknesses along with failure to follow procedure."

A glance at Stanley told him it was time. With an honest humility, Lyle apologized.

"I am truly sorry. I planned to sneak in, capture Fouts and sneak back out. Bad plan. An unjustifiable breach of proper police procedure. It won't happen again."

"So what do you want to do?" Arguello asked.

"Take Fouts home to stand trial," West said. "He's already been indicted on two counts of rape. There are multiple warrants out on other charges, the most serious of which are attempted murder and kidnapping charges—fourteen counts as of this morning. We have five more charges pending, one possible murder."

"And you haven't been able to catch him?"

"Not until now," Lyle admitted.

He made no excuse.

Stanley saw Arguello finally relax.

"You can get him out of town right now?" Arguello asked.

"Yes, I can. I have a private plane waiting," Chief West said. "Mr. Hubert Praetzel is a pilot. He will take Lieutenant French's place."

"We will take you to the plane," Captain Arguello said.

"Thank you," Chief West responded.

Arguello ordered his men to take Fouts to his car. Chief West followed Captain Arguello. Hubert fell in behind the two. Stanley watched them go.

As Hubert left the room, he turned briefly and gave his son a thumbs up.

Aleta was overjoyed to see Stanley. She was sure that the signing gift would hers for the whole weekend. However, she was wrong. When Stanley returned, she found she could no longer sign. Her joy turned to despair instantly.

Stanley held her close and told the others to give her a moment to adjust.

"She knew this would happen, " he said. "Fouts is now in custody. There will be no new threats. Once she realizes this, she will be ready to celebrate again."

Still weeping, Aleta nodded. She searched Stanley's pocket for a handkerchief and found one.

"I told Bertha what Hubert said," Stanley told her. "I now have drawer full of clean pressed handkerchiefs. I think she ordered a gross."

Aleta giggled and those surrounding her relaxed.

The remainder of the afternoon was spent together. Everything enthralled Paige. Her enthusiasm soon infected the entire group. As for Lydia, while she missed Hubert, his absence didn't put a permanent pall over her enjoyment over being with this delightful group of young adults.

Hubert's call came as they were finishing supper at the theme park.

"I thought I'd order ice cream from room service," Hubert said.

"We're just about to have dessert," Lydia said. "I'd rather not eat alone."

"Who says you'll eat alone? I expect you to share," Hubert said.

"Share?" Lydia gasped. "Hubert, where are you?"

"In our room, waiting for you."

Lydia turned to those at the table.

"Hubert came back. He's waiting to eat dessert with me in our room."

"Tell him you'll be right there," Stanley said since his mother seemed undecided. "We children can manage to find our way back. Honest."

Lydia smiled as she rose. "I know you can. Can you imagine? He flew back to be with me."

"I can understand him wanting to be with you," Stanley said. "But the fact that he flew back does surprise me."

"I think it's wonderful!" Paige exclaimed. "I'm so glad we didn't ruin your holiday."

Lydia took a moment to say, "Paige, you are the very reason I had a chance to experience another facet of my husband's love. I couldn't be happier than I am right now."

When Lydia entered her room a short time later, she embraced her husband with unabashed fervor.

"I am so glad to see you. I was dreading tonight."

"I've been away overnight before," he mentioned casually.

"Somehow this was different."

Hubert responded softly. "It was for me too."

"I am so glad you came back. It must have been quite a run. Tell me all about everything."

Room service arrived and Lydia stared at the dishes of ice cream.

"How many people were you expecting?"

"Just you, but I haven't eaten all day."

Lydia signed the check and said wryly, "If you die from a heart attack tonight, your son will blame me."

Hubert grinned.

"I believe he might. Under that silver cover is my supper sandwich."

"It better be alfalfa sprouts and tomatoes rolled in spinach leaves."

"Any dressing?"

"Dry," she snapped. "Hubert I don't want to lose you."

"Well, it's not going to happen tonight. Tonight I'm going to tell you what a brilliant job Stanley did."

Lydia joined him at the table.

"He told us Lyle made a nice apology. You mean there was more?"

"Talk about downplaying what happened!" Hubert exclaimed, unwrapping a thick roast beef sandwich.

"But before I begin, let me say that Stanley took charge as I've never seen him do before. He was not only determined that Lyle was going to make it back to Illinois today with Fouts, he was imbued with the drive to make it happen. I'm not sure Captain Arguello realized how cleverly he was prepped for Lyle's apology."

A short time later, Hubert and Lydia found Aleta's computer.

"Who put that here?" Lydia asked.

"Fouts," Hubert responded.

"Why?"

"I'm guessing he was angry because she was using it to communicate," Hubert said. "It's a good thing he didn't see her sign."

"But he did," Lydia recalled. "Remember. Aleta said he was at the restaurant. That was why she told Stanley not to repeat her signing. She was telling Lyle to lay a trap."

"So, he doesn't read signing," Hubert said thoughtfully. "I like the fact that he doesn't."

"He is really clever," Lydia said.

"If it weren't for Stanley, Fouts might not have been spirited back to Illinois," Hubert said. "All they have him for down here is breaking and entering and assault."

"Assault of a police officer is more serious than the rape charges back home," Lydia said.

"So that's why Stanley spelled out how many charges were lodged against him back home," Hubert said. "He didn't stop with the rape charges but added attempted murder and possible murder. I didn't see it at the time, but I just bet Captain Arguello wouldn't have given him up were the offenses in Illinois hadn't been capital offenses."

"We should return Aleta's computer," Lydia mentioned. "Remember how upset she was that she couldn't sign anymore."

"Will she be able to type?" Hubert asked.

"Stanley seemed to think so," Lydia said. "Take it back to them along with the towel. It came from their room."

In a room down the hall, Paige was fretting over not having done enough to earn all that they were receiving.

"Even if there is one in Stanley's plane," she said, "There are still two more out there."

"Don't fret," Hawk said. "We've found most of those left. We also have searched and found nothing. That is valuable too."

"How?" Paige asked. "Aleta still doesn't dare speak, even here where it's safe."

"It's better she not speak at all. It's easier to do that than to pick and choose."

"So us clearing a place isn't worth much."

"It is to them. It relaxes them."

"I guess that's a positive," Paige admitted. "But I feel as if I know enough to find the other two. I just can't put the pieces together."

"Then relax and let your mind sort through its banks of knowledge until it finds what you need."

"Suppose it stops looking."

"It won't."

"How do you know?"

"Because mine doesn't. Believe me, Paige, eventually what you're seeking will surface."

"I had a good day today, Hawk—every bit of it."

"Are you ready for a good night?"

"How many times can we consummate?"

"As many as you want."

"And you won't…"

"Break?" Hawk interjected. "No, I won't break. And considering how turned on I've been all day, I think multiple consummations are definitely on tonight's agenda."

"You are so much fun," Paige said, and Hawk knew it was going to be a good night.

CHAPTER 9

On Wednesday afternoon, his first day back at the office, Stanley received a call from Wendell Kingston the third.

"Trouble, Wendell?"

"It's just me here and I need help."

"I will be right there," Stanley said, rubbing his leg.

He was looking forward to an afternoon in his chair. Elevating his leg had helped with the pain resulting from an active weekend.

He sighed as he left the office. Wendell rushed toward him as he walked up the sidewalk toward the front door.

"They want Grandpa to be here," Wendell said. "I told them you said he couldn't come and he was obeying you."

"Smart move, Wendell," Stanley said. "Let's see if we can calm them down. Did you manage to pick out some things for your grandfather?"

"He told me what he wanted," Wendell said. "They insist that he will want other stuff, so they're all picking out stuff they think he will want, so they won't pay for anything."

"Second guessing their father, are they?" Stanley surmised.

"Yeh. They're not being reasonable. Not even my dad."

Wendell introduced Stanley to his father.

"I charge four hundred dollars an hour," Stanley said. "Whoever forced this boy to call me will pay for my services."

"Aren't you in my father's employ?" Tyler Kingston asked.

"He has retained me to advise him and represent him, if necessary," Stanley said. "I told all of you that if I was called on to adjudicate this matter, you would be billed. Now what's the problem?"

"Wendell doesn't know what Dad wants," Tyler, the second eldest son, said. "We want to take some things for him to look over later."

"And reopen the wells of grief that will envelop and drown him?"

"A lot of these things are connected with good memories," Tyler insisted.

"He misses your mother very much."

"We don't want her forgotten."

"That's why each of you are encouraged to take three items that remind you of her."

"But he doesn't have any."

"He doesn't need mementos to remember her. His love for her is still in his heart. So is his sorrow at her passing. To remind him of the one is to remind him of the other."

"We don't want her to fade from his memory," Valerie, Kingston's eldest daughter, said.

"All we want to do is be ready when he says he wishes that he'd saved something to be able to say that we saved it," Diane said.

"Wendell, what's your take?" Stanley asked the seventeen-year-old.

"Grandpa doesn't need any reminders. Mostly his memories make him sad," Wendell said. "That's why he didn't pick out anything to remind him of Grandma. Everything reminds him of her."

"But a lot of this stuff has only good memories attached," Valerie insisted.

"Then you take it," Wendell said. "You don't know what memories are good for him and neither do I. He told me what he wanted and that's what I got."

"What did you get?" Valerie pried.

"That's private," Wendell said. "It wasn't nothing important."

"I want to know," Valerie insisted.

Stanley interrupted. "Wendell, have you got the log book?"

"Yes."

"Each of you list the three items you want and then the ones you are willing to pay for."

"Who's going to decide what they're worth?" Wendell's father asked.

"Wendell is," Stanley said. "My estimation will be higher."

"I want Mother's china," Valerie said.

"The silver coffee service," Diane put in.

"The painting in the living room," Tyler chose.

"The rare books," Wendell Senior declared.

"Mother's jewelry," Valerie decided.

"The cut glass collection," Diane said.

"The sculpture in the front hall," Tyler stated.

"The framed family photographs," Wendell Senior picked.

"Mother's crocheted afghan," Valerie said.

"Grandmother's crocheted tablecloth," Diane elected.

"The grandfather clock," Tyler selected.

"Mom's rocking chair," Wendell Senior finished.

Stanley checked with Wendell who had been writing as each person spoke.

Next the four children each listed the items they were willing to buy. That's when Wendell took charge.

"My sister Betsy, wants Grandma's quilt with the houses," Wendell said. "One hundred dollars."

"Okay," his father said.

"Sally wants the one with the bears," Wendell said. "Two hundred dollars."

"Why is it more?" Sally's father asked.

"It's Grandma's best one."

"Okay," Tyler said.

"I'm taking the two with the flowers," Wendell said. "I like them best. How much, Stanley?"

"One hundred for both," Stanley said.

"Okay," the seventeen year old said.

One by one everyone named things that they wanted that were made by or loved by their mother. Two hours later, everyone was done.

Wendell's father thanked Stanley and said, "Send the bill to me. I will pay it. I'm glad you're watching out for my father."

"Wendell, does Grandpa want his chair?" his father asked.

"I think he'd like it," Wendell responded positively.

"How about the TV," Tyler asked. "Your father and I will bring it over and set it up once you're settled."

"That he would like," Wendell said.

"Good idea," Stanley said. "Wendell, I will drive you home."

"I've got Grandpa's car," Wendell said.

That night Aleta spent half an hour kneading Stanley's upper leg muscles.

As his leg began to feel better, Stanley said, "You want to know if I talked to Dr. Cook about my leg? You think it's healing much too slowly."

Aleta nodded her affirmation.

"He said he wasn't sure what was going on. He did find a small nodule near the ankle though."

Aleta pointed to his thigh.

"I know," Stanley said. "He doesn't believe there's any connection."

The two heard the dogs messing around in the bathroom.

"What are they getting into?" Stanley wondered aloud. "No, Aleta, don't go look. My leg needs you."

She went back to kneading his leg muscles and he sighed with relief.

"They've never been interested in anything in the bathroom before," Stanley noted.

Just then the two on the bed heard the plastic glass fall on the floor.'

"What's on the counter?" Stanley asked.

Aleta pantomimed his shaving.

"My travel kit?' Stanley guessed. "But there's nothing inside it that would interest a dog."

More scuffling followed. Stanley sat up just as Scooby came into the master bedroom with the leather traveling kit in his mouth. It was open and the contents were dropping on the floor as he walked.

Tank followed Scooby into the bedroom and when Scooby sat, the kit still in his mouth, Tank sat beside him, his tail wagging. Both dogs looked at the two humans expectantly.

"Why do they think they've done something wonderful?" Stanley asked.

Aleta laughed. Then she hugged the two dogs and waved at them to follow her into the kitchen.

"Now I know how Paige felt when Topper dragged her suitcase from the closet and spilled her clothes all over the floor," Stanley grumbled.

He called after his wife, "This is not a trick I want repeated."

She appeared in the doorway with the Scrabble game.

He was immediately distressed.

"You still can't use the computer"

She put the blank tile upon which Lydia had drawn a question mark and put it on the holder.

"You are afraid to try?"

Aleta nodded.

"Don't be," Stanley said. "Go get the computer."

Aleta trotted off to the study and fetched her computer and brought it back.

"Open it up, Aleta," Stanley ordered. "Give God a chance."

Aleta shook her head.

"You'll be too disappointed if you can't. Is that it?"

She nodded.

Her hands fluttered and Stanley read her signing aloud even though there were only two of them in the room.

"It is so hard every time the door is shut in my face again," she signed. "The travel kit must have contained a bomb, but that makes no sense."

"Why?" Stanley asked, more to encourage her than because he wanted an answer.

"Because the dogs have never zeroed in on it before," she signed.

"Before our room was invaded by Stuart Fouts?" Stanley asked.

"Of course!" she signed excitedly. "He put some C-4 in it?"

"To throw our dogs off course?" Stanley questioned.

Aleta shook her head and signed, "To make me think we had found all the bombs."

"Why would he do that?"

"He wants me miserable and confused and upset. He likes my suffering."

"I guess you know what to do then," Stanley smiled.

"Yes," Aleta affirmed. "I stop suffering and I don't talk."

"And how do you do that?" Stanley asked kindly.

"I have no idea," Aleta confessed. "I want to communicate so much."

Abruptly, Aleta's hands stopped their signing. She burst into tears. Stanley gathered her into his arms and let her cry. Once her tears subsided enough so he could speak, he did so.

"You do communicate," he said. "You communicate your love for me with every touch of your hand. You communicate your love to Gerard every time you smile and hug him. You communicate your love to Shadow when you mount him and ride him. You communicate your love to the dogs when you do what you just did."

Aleta shook her head.

"Anybody can give them a treat," Stanley agreed. "You did something much more important. You understood what a great gift they had presented and you showed them that you did."

She pointed at Stanley.

"My slowness would have disheartened them."

Aleta looked at the two happy dogs at her feet and smiled at them. She clapped her hand over her mouth.

"You were going to say something, weren't you?"

She nodded.

"Let me say it for you. Scooby, Tank, you are good dogs," Stanley said. "Keep up the good work. I promise I will pay attention next time."

He let his eyes rest on his wife's sorrowful face and said softly, "We knew at the outset that this was going to be a long-term deprivation. We knew from the beginning that it was going to be the hardest thing you would ever have to do."

Aleta shook her head.

"What would be harder?" Stanley asked, truly surprised.

She pointed upward.

"To be without God?" he guessed.

She nodded, smiling, and then pointed to him.

"And to be without me?"

She laughed and nodded her head vigorously.

"Well, I'm glad I'm near the top of your list." Stanley said. "What you need to do is to learn sign language."

Aleta's eyebrows shot up in surprise.

"And to teach a few rudimentary phrases to Jamara and Bertha. You need to learn to communicate more precisely than you can now."

Aleta moved her hands apart as if pulling taffy and then pointed upward.

"Yes, I think that's what God wants," Stanley said. "We stop worrying about when we will find the bomb and start working on living as if this is going to last a really long time."

"I agree," Aleta signed suddenly.

"Let's start with that sign," Stanley said. "It's one I would like to see often."

Aleta laughed even though her hands were still after that.

Stanley could see the excitement in her eyes.

Silently, he thanked God.

Lauren was called the next day and Aleta began to learn to sign. She was grateful that the ability had been gone when she woke up in the morning. She tried the computer and found that she couldn't type either. Instead of being devastated, she was elated. This was the confirmation she needed. Now she was certain that she was on the right path.

Lauren found Aleta a quick and apt pupil.

"It helps that you can hear," Lauren said.

Aleta raised an eyebrow.

"Because I can tell you what you are saying," Lauren said.

Aleta nodded.

Then Aleta led Lauren to the barn and indicated that she wanted to be able to communicate with Hubbs first.

Lauren explained to Hubbs that Aleta wanted to learn to use sign language so they could communicate about the horses.

"She can hear you," Lauren said. "But sometimes she wants to do more than nod or shake her head. "

Hubbs didn't laugh. Instead he asked Lauren to teach them both certain important phrases.

The first one on his list was "call the vet."

Both women looked surprised and agreed that his idea was a good one. They learned several variations of that phrase, from a question to an order.

They didn't bother with the horse's names. There were other more important words that needed learning. Even though Aleta could hear, both learned all the phrases either one would need to use. It took almost an hour.

Next Lauren and Aleta went to Bertha. Lauren explained that Aleta needed learn to sign and she needed Bertha to be able to read her signing.

"I agree," Bertha said simply.

"What do you think is the most important sign you need to learn?" Lauren asked.

"Call Dr. Cook," Bertha said.

Both women laughed and then they told Bertha what Hubbs wanted to learn first. The lesson started there.

The next sign Bertha wanted to learn was the order, "Call Stanley."

"Tell Jamara" came next followed by simple everyday requests and transfers of information.

Lauren let Aleta teach Bertha and Jamara, knowing that doing so was helping her learn faster. By the morning's end, Hubbs, Bertha and Jamara could communicate in a rudimentary fashion with Aleta using sign language.

Bertha and Jamara noticed that Lauren used sign language when she was speaking to Aleta and to them. They soon picked up an understanding of other words and phrases. At lunch, Lauren dropped speaking and communicated using only sign language. Her companions enjoyed the challenge.

After lunch, Lauren taught them a number of common words and phrases.

"Tomorrow we will tackle the alphabet," she promised.

Meanwhile, Stanley enlisted Lyle's help in learning to sign

That night Stanley brought Aleta her computer and told her to see if she could type.

She put her hands on the keyboard and typed, "I told you I would be devastated if I tried and couldn't type. However, with Stuart Fouts in jail, I can't see why his being angry over my being able to type would make a difference."

Stanley chuckled.

"I think now that you are learning sign language the hard way, God has stopped blocking your use of your computer," he observed.

"Why would He do that?" Aleta typed.

"You are sometimes a hard person to persuade to turn off your chosen path," Stanley ventured.

"I am not!" Aleta typed.

"You wouldn't give up preparing for that Melvin Porter case ad infinitum had I not put the scarf over you eyes every night and insisted that you not work during our evening family time."

"I remember you took the first witnesses in the trial and I could relax because I knew I wasn't going to need to do anything but listen that first day."

"And I kept doing that, didn't I? I kept insisting that you not work during our family time."

"Yes, you did," Aleta typed. "I could never have shed my superstitious belief that I needed to study the case over and over again and get sick the morning of the trial or I wouldn't do a good job."

"You took over eventually."

"You were there and ready to step in," Aleta typed. "That relaxed me."

"You were brilliant," Stanley said. "You won a not guilty verdict in a case where there were a dozen witnesses accusing our client."

"They were all lying."

"You broke them down one by one," Stanley said. "Each in a different way. I loved watching you."

"You wouldn't let me study," Aleta typed. "How did you know that I would succeed."

"You were more familiar with the case than I was and you had a plan of action."

"You didn't let me flounder.'"

"That would have cemented into your head that you failed because you hadn't studied enough."

"And then at the critical time you pointed to the words in the transcript of Mrs. Lee deposition and you gave me the key to win Tommy over."

"He was the hardest one," Stanley said.

"We were a team," Aleta typed. "I liked that."

"I know," Stanley said. "But I had to force you to cooperate. You need to soften your desire to be completely autonomous and recognize that being interdependent is a goal higher than being independent."

"I don't like being dependent."

"We are all dependent at times. No one is totally independent."

"You are," she typed.

"No, I'm not," Stanley countered. "I depend on all sorts of people and I depend on them to be themselves and to be strong when I am weak."

"I've never seen that part of your personality."

"It's there, Aleta, believe me," Stanley stated. "Now it's time for you to believe something else. Look at the computer screen."

He put his finger on her lips as she stared at the screen. She heeded the admonition and typed her shock.

"I can type! I can communicate!"

"You can go back to work on Monday," Stanley said. "But this weekend, Lyle and Lauren are coming over and we are all going to be using only sign language to communicate."

"But I can type!" Aleta protested.

Stanley plucked the computer from her lap.

"I am putting this in the car and you will take it to work on Monday and it will stay there."

Aleta wanted to protest but couldn't.

"I know the first words you are going to have Lauren teach you to sign," Stanley said. "Shall I write them down so she will know where to start?"

Aleta nodded.

Stanley began to recite them. "Don't do that, Stanley."

Aleta nodded.

"Please, don't do that, Stanley."

This time Aleta smiled.

"I don't like it when you do that, Stanley."

Aleta nodded.

Stanley grinned. "Of course, Lyle will have to teach me how to read those words."

Aleta laughed.

The dogs followed Stanley as when took the computer to the car. He opened the trunk and saw the travel kit and remembered that he was going to turn it over to Hawk.

If I put the computer in the trunk, he thought, I'll remember to turn the kit over to Hawk on Monday.

He laid the computer next to the kit. Both dogs sat down and wagged their tails. Stanley reached into the trunk and opened the tin of dog biscuits and gave each dog a biscuit, telling them again that they were good dogs, and then he took them for a walk.

When Stanley picked up Aleta from the office on Monday after her first day back at work, she had a list of questions on a computer printout.

He glanced at the list.

"How about you working for the information? My leg is killing me. I've been sitting in one chair after another all day."

Aleta nodded happily.

When they arrived home, Bertha met them at the door.

"Eat now or it will dry out. Dr. Chesney gave me a late appointment."

"Today's the big day, huh?" Stanley questioned.

"I hope it's a boy," Bertha said wistfully. "I know Robert says he doesn't care, but every man wants a son."

"Everyman wants a baby with the woman he loves," Stanley said.

"I still want it to be a boy," she stated flatly.

The smell of freshly baked pot pies followed Aleta into the nursery. While she was checking on Gerard, Stanley put the food on the table.

He slipped the scarf over her eyes while she was gazing at her sleeping baby. She was surprised. She was certain that wouldn't happen until after dinner and after she had massaged his leg. She could tell he was in pain.

"The pies are too hot to eat," he said simply.

She pointed to his leg and then to the bedroom.

"Good idea," he said taking her hand and leading her into the bedroom.

She was surprised that he didn't undress her. Instead, he dropped his trousers. She could hear him emptying his pockets. She imagined him folding his trousers.

"Hand me your clothes so I can fold them for the laundry," he said.

Quickly she undressed and handed him her clothes. Once naked, she patted the bed, and motioned him to lie down.

She waited for him to finish folding her clothes and climb onto the bed. She felt her way along his body and found that he was still wearing his shirt and tie. Again she was surprised. Something was amiss. She felt for his leg and found that he was undressed from the waist down. She put both her hands on his thigh and began to massage his upper leg.

She could feel the tightness. It was the worse than it had been the night before. She guessed the pain was more intense. Once she could speak again she would tell Dr. Cook how much he was suffering.

She had no idea why this particular wound was so slow to heal completely. She was grateful he didn't limp and he appeared to be able to do anything, except for sitting. Too much sitting made his thigh ache. The ache resulted in the muscles knotting up and more pain.

He started to tell her about his day, but she quickly put her finger on his lips and shook her head. He lay back and let go of the tension that had knotted the muscles in his leg.

He watched her work, the ends of the silk scarf falling like long tresses of each side of her shoulders teasingly blocking his view of her nude body. Ordinarily, he would have been aroused. He knew this, but the pain in his leg dominated his focus. Still he enjoyed the view. She was so lovely.

The day had not gone as planned. He had won a major victory but it had cost them.

Shannon Taylor had been assigned to prosecute Stuart Fouts. She was the fast rising assistant DA who had come into the limelight when she took over for Aleta in the Tina Jenkins trial. With Aleta's suggestions on how to proceed in hand, she had taken the Jenkins trial to a successful conclusion.

Prior to that, the meeting with Lyle and Hawk had gone well. Both were ready to go to trial against Stuart Fouts on the rape and assault charges. The DNA provided solid proof of intercourse and the tearing and other bruising was documented and proved that penetration had been violent and painful. Tonia's black eye had been photographed, as were the bruises on Mr. Brennan's arms.

Stanley had looked at Judge Dennis Clancy's calendar and noticed that a case coming up in a little over a month was one he knew was on the verge of collapsing.

Stanley had talked the DA into asking for that slot for Fouts' rape trial, a colorful case that in an election year offered a strong probability of a win just before the vote in the November general election.   The DA was up for reelection.

Gray Zenon, the public defender, had no intention of so early a trial date. He wanted time.

Stanley had entered Judge Clancy's chambers with Shannon Taylor for the pre-trial conference. Gray Zenon objected to Stanley's presence; however, Assistant District Attorney Shannon Taylor explained that Stanley represented the four victims who wanted an early trial date.   Judge Clancy allowed him to remain.

Shannon suggested the middle of October.

"I can't possibly be ready in so short a time," Gray Zenon insisted. "To force me to trial early will be grounds for a mistrial. I am, of course, ready to proceed on the rape charges of Tonia Morales and Stella Woodbridge since I was assigned that case when Stuart Fouts was indicted on those charges and I had to prepare for the video deposition, but I am not prepared on the other charges.

Stanley smiled inwardly. Gray Zenon was not going to admit that he went into the videotaping unprepared.

Stanley spoke up.

"If we could just add the Brennan assault and rape to the two rape cases for which we have depositions, we have a strong argument for a separate trial for the four victims I represent.   In all four cases, Stuart Fouts acted singularly with neither consult nor help from another person. All the other charges lodged against him involve a group."

"But it's the same man," Gray Zenon argued.   "He should stand trial on all counts in one trial."

"Two of the bombs have not been found," Stanley said.

"We can wait," Gray Zenon declared.

"And let the raped women wait for justice when we are prepared to prosecute Fouts on their charges. Shouldn't they some justice in their lifetime?"

"That's not important," Gray Zenon proclaimed vociferously. "Fouts is in jail. The women know he will be tried."

"They don't know he will be convicted, especially if their main advocate winds up dead. Or is that what you were counting on?" Stanley spat out angrily.

"Mr. Praetzel!" Judge Clancy admonished. "Watch yourself!"

Stanley apologized immediately.

Shannon stepped in.

"There is another reason we need to try Fouts now on the rape charges. We currently have the victims available for the defense to cross-examine. These are frail, elderly people. Too many crimes against the elderly are never punished because the victims lie mute in their graves."

"We don't need to worry about that. I will confirm that during the videotaping the defense was given ample opportunity to cross-examine Fouts' accusers," Gray Zenon confirmed.

"We are off the record here," Shannon said sharply. "I wonder if that will be your stance when you take Mr. Fouts as your client in private practice."

Judge Clancy was quick to pursue this.

"Mr. Fouts can afford a private attorney?" he asked.

"He said he expects to inherit a sizeable sum of money," Zenon replied smoothly. "He doesn't have the money yet."

Stanley, who knew to what money Fouts was referring, remained silent. He could tell Judge Clancy wanted to pursue this on his own.

"You cannot receive extortion money as you fee," he warned. "If you do, I will recover it."

"Of course not," Gray Zenon responded. "I will check the source of the funds."

"So you are planning to take him on as a client if you leave the Public Defender's Office?" Clancy pressed.

"If I leave, if he inherits and if he asks, the answer is yes. However, so far I have not resigned, I do not know that he has inherited any money and I have been assigned to defend him."

"Mr. Zenon is interviewing at three firms in the next ten days which is why he has no time to prepare for this case," Shannon informed the judge. "He will be gone in a month and the case will go to a new man who will insist on starting all over again."

"If I lock him into this trial and his focus is elsewhere, the defendant will have grounds for an appeal," Judge Clancy argued.

"Not if his employment and salary are dependent on how good a defense he puts on in the rape trial," Stanley interjected.

"I haven't the power," the judge said. "And even if I did, I wouldn't use it."

"Nor will I," Stanley said. "But the private sector is well aware of the performances of each of the public defenders. They will be watching this case. Once we announce the trial date and they discover that a candidate for a position in their firm is the defense attorney, they will be interested.

Shannon Taylor added, "Especially if Aleta Praetzel is named Special Prosecutor by you. And there is a positive reason for my request. Mrs. Praetzel has been actively involved with these cases from the start. She is better prepared than anyone to prosecute."

"But she's not able to speak," Gray Zenon pointed out, upset with that possibility.

Shannon brushed that concern aside.

"We will work together. We've done it before."

"She used gadgetry in the courtroom that time," Zenon said disgustedly.

Shannon spoke up quickly. "Special case. Doesn't apply here."

Judge Clancy focused on Stanley.

"No tricks or gadgets or special requests."

"I guess that means you won't let three large dogs search the courtroom on the first day," Stanley responded.

"What?"

"We have trained three bomb-sniffing dogs which is why we've uncovered most of the bombs. Two have eluded us. They are voice-activated by Aleta's voice. If all the bombs haven't been found by the beginning of the trial, we'd like to be sure the courtroom is clean."

"I told you," Zenon proclaimed. "Histrionics!"

"Dogs in my courtroom, sniffing everything and everybody? Is that what you are proposing?"

"One dog," Stanley compromised. "Minimal sniffing."

"Absolutely not!" Judge Clancy declared adamantly.

Suddenly it occurred to Stanley that Aleta wouldn't be able to speak. She could play no active role in the proceedings. He offered a compromise.

"How about a check point at the entrance to the courtroom—a metal detector—and one trained dog? All outside?"

Gray Zenon objected vociferously. "That practically proclaims my client is guilty."

"It does do that," Judge Clancy mused.

"How about as protection against someone shooting Fouts in the head?" Stanley said. "There could be other victims out there ready to avenge themselves."

"I will order a weapons search using a metal detector."

"And one dog?" Stanley posed hopefully.

"Have the dog search your staff at your office. There will be no dog outside my courtroom. Is that clear?"

Stanley began to argue, "Mr. Brennan was sent to our office with a gift for Aleta. It turned out to be a bomb. What's to prevent…"

He stopped abruptly. His demeanor and voice changed drastically.

"On second thought," he said. "I withdraw my suggestion."

Judge Clancy nodded his approval and went on.

"I appoint Aleta Praetzel as Special Prosecutor," Judge Clancy said. "We are going to trial on the charges of the four elderly victims on October 17. Jury selection begins four weeks from today. That should give you enough time to prepare, Mr. Zenon."

"I need to have my client seen by a psychiatrist," Zenon announced.

"We want the same right," Shannon stated.

"Get it done. There will be no delays, no continuances, no fancy footwork," Judge Clancy declared.

He looked hard at Gray Zenon who nodded acquiescence dourly.

Shannon had smiled broadly at Stanley whose face remained an unreadable mask.

And now as he lay in bed he wondered if he could put off talking to her. It would be so nice to simply fall asleep. He closed his eyes as his leg began to feel better and thus shut off any arousal of passion which might have kept him awake.

Aleta could feel the total relaxation of the muscles and she knew her work was done. She looked up at Stanley. His eyes were closed and he was breathing softly and evenly.

He never slept in his shirt. She loosened his tie and removed it. He didn't wake up.

She lay beside him and rested her hand in its usual place and let herself relax, Sleep overtook her quickly.

CHAPTER 10

Tuesday morning, Stanley heard the pans rattling as Bertha began breakfast.

"She's upset," he said, grateful they had awakened during the night and had a very late supper.

Aleta patted her tummy.

"It's a girl?" Stanley asked.

Aleta nodded.

"Should we skip breakfast?"

Aleta shook her head and made a gesture.

They heard the front door open and Jocelyn call.

"I'm sorry, Mom. Please forgive me. Dad says you'll still love me. It's just that Aleta had Grams and Dad, and Jayline had Mother, and when you came along, I was special because, well, you had three sons and I thought Dad wanted a son after three daughters, but I was wrong. I guess he likes me more than I thought. He says he's hoping that she'll be half you and half me. Isn't that neat? I'm so sorry I hurt you. Your love is so… so…"

When she stopped speaking, Aleta and Stanley guessed that Bertha had put her arms around her and hugged her.

"We need to give them a couple of minutes," Stanley decided. "What do you want to do with our spare three minutes?"

Aleta kissed him.

They exited laughing.

"So what's the girl's name?" Stanley asked.

"You heard?" Jocelyn asked embarrassed.

"You were shouting," Stanley said.

"You could have gone and taken a shower."

"In our business suites?" Stanley smirked.

"You take them all the time," Jocelyn declared.

"Not in our business suits."

"You're never dressed this early," Jocelyn contended. "Didn't you look at the clock?"

Aleta giggled.

"What's that mean?" Jocelyn charged.

Stanley lost his smile and switched topics.

"Aleta has an early appointment with Shannon Taylor. Judge Clancy appointed her Special Prosecutor in the Stuart Fouts rape trial."

"Can she talk?" Jocelyn asked Stanley.

"Not yet."

"What will you do if the bombs aren't found?"

"Ask me in three weeks," Stanley said. "I'm banking on them being found."

Robert entered with Paul and Lettie. His first glance told him Bertha and Jocelyn had made up.

"Did you hear the good news?" he asked.

Bertha smiled. "First thing he said when Dr. Chesney said it was a girl was, "Hallelujah!""

"I gather it wasn't the response you were expecting," Stanley said.

"It was the last thing I expected to hear," Bertha said. "You were right, Stanley. He was as anxious to give me a daughter as I was to give him a son."

"They're going to call her Hallelujah," Jocelyn announced peevishly.

"Halle, for short," Bertha said.

"I like it," Stanley said.

"So do I," Paul agreed.

"It's better than Harriet," Lettie commented.

"Don't let your grandmother hear you say that," Paul cautioned.

"I've told her already. She said she didn't choose her name either. She told me that it would grow on me. Hah! Warts grow on people, but that doesn't mean they like them."

"Names aren't warts," Stanley said. "Harriet is a fine name. It has character. And it's unique."

"You're saying that because... why are you saying that?"

"Because that's what I think."

"You're weird."

An hour after Stanley and Aleta arrived at the office, Chief West arrived and asked to speak to both of them. Aleta joined the two men in Stanley's office.

"What brings you here so early," Stanley asked.

"Can I take the guards off the Brennans? And can Toni Morales and Stella Woodbridge return home?"

Aleta shook her head.

"You sense danger?" Stanley asked.

Aleta nodded.

"Today?" Lyle asked.

Aleta shrugged.

"I will check back with you next Monday," Lyle said. "We are actively looking for those other bombs. Hawk wants to know if you'd mind another sweep of the office?"

"He's welcome anytime," Stanley said. "I will have Paige's paycheck waiting at Alice's desk."

"You're still paying her?" Lyle asked.

"Her mind is still engaged with the problem of where they haven't looked," Stanley said. "She has some new ideas, hasn't she?"

"The Tontine offices across the street, the staff cars, and the office when everyone is here," Lyle responded. "Is tomorrow okay?"

"Aleta and I will be at the Brennan depositions," Stanley said. "Zenon insisted they be held simultaneously so there's no chance of collusion. We are each taking one."

"Who is Zenon taking?"

"Ostensibly, the wife," Stanley smiled.

"Why are you going? Where's Shannon going to be?"

"Zenon purposely picked a time when she couldn't make it. He even studied my court calendar. I'm due in court tomorrow," Stanley said. "He's playing hardball."

"And court?"

"Zenon has no idea how much of a team we are here. Mother is taking my place."

The remainder of that day was normal. No new cases were being accepted. Everyone was busy with the ones that had been taken in on the last intake day.

Tuesday evening Stanley again put the scarf over Aleta's eyes and she relaxed into his care. She wanted to tell him how renewed she felt each morning, but Wednesday when he did it anew, she realized that he didn't need to be told.

Stanley was reading her body language and noting her renewed spirit each morning and garnering from those unspoken reactions that this particular therapy was keeping her together enough to spend her days without uttering a word either in protest, argument, joy or surprise.

She did note that he spent more and more time in the chair in his office and at night she still needed to massage his leg; however, during the day, he didn't limp and he appeared to be able to do everything required of him physically.

Her computer allowed her to communicate and to work, but her frustrations, worries, fears and longings stayed buried. She couldn't bring herself to put them up on the computer screen.

Entering the peculiar world that Stanley had created allowed her the freedom to let go. Many minor frustrations accumulated throughout the day faded as she lost her sight, her sense of time, and her ability to do things. The stubbed toe reminded her on Tuesday that moving around without shoes could be painful. The bruised knee on Wednesday told her it would be wise to let Stanly guide her.

She wondered why they had no visitors in the evenings. She correctly guessed that Stanley had arranged it. He'd done it by telling Lauren that Aleta needed quiet evenings to renew her energy for the long days she was deprived of speech.

Lauren had passed the word, and no one disturbed the couple after five.

Paul was allowed to work in the family room only from eight to five. He never even took a breather. He was allowed to work there on weekends as well. The enforced period away from his painting renewed his enthusiasm and Andrea was overjoyed at having him home with her. Frequently, he asked her to pose and he sketched her. This she enjoyed and the sketches made it into this book of sketches for later projects.

Paul persuaded his wife to pose in the nude on the nights Paul Junior went out with friends. It was an exciting delicious experience for Andrea. Her husband's sketches were lovingly done and she carefully hid them all in a huge black portfolio tucked in the back of their closet.

What Andrea didn't know was that Paul had extracted a couple of his favorite sketches of his nude wife and snuck them into the Praetzel's family room where he began to render them in oil. Only the Praetzel's huge Irish Wolfhound, Tank, saw those sketches being transformed. The door was locked each night when Paul left.

On Monday, when Stanley prepped Roger and Emily Brennan for their deposition the following day, Stanley discovered that Roger Brennan had decided to lie. He wanted to claim that he was tied up and couldn't come to his wife's aid. When Stanley pointed out that he had deep bruises on both arms and none on his wrists, Roger decided maybe lying wasn't a good idea.

Stanley prompted him to remember why he had sat silently and done nothing.

He cried when he finally admitted he was too old and too frail to fight Stuart Fouts and he knew it.

"Can I say he threatened me?"

"Did he?"

"Not in words. But he is so strong.'"

"So what were you thinking when you sat there?"

"Mostly that if I tried to stop him, he'd kill me and then he'd kill Emily. He had no heart at all."

"That was sound reasoning," Stanley said. "Wise men weigh the odds and the probable outcome of their actions. That doesn't mean they aren't brave. It means they aren't foolish."

Emily smiled at her husband.

"You didn't keep him from raping her and that was a terrible thing, but you kept him from killing her."

Roger looked at his wife.

"You said afterward that you wished you were dead."

"I felt that way. I still feel that way some of the time."

"Maybe I should have let him kill us both."

Stanley stepped in.

"Don't assume that he would have done it painlessly. This man is into torture."

"How do you know?"

"He rapes frail old ladies. He causes them great pain," Stanley finished. "In the deposition, it is important that you tell only the truth. Suggestions will be made that will repel you. I don't care if you get angry. Just don't lie. I will stop any suggestions that are irrelevant."

Stanley told Aleta about his prep work with Roger. Consequently, the next day at the deposition, Emily checked Aleta's computer screen before answering the young female public defender substituting for Gray Zenon. As a result of the old woman's actions, Aleta was able to block every innuendo that her husband's age made him unable to satisfy her and caused her to encourage Stuart Fouts.

Both Praetzels were surprised that Gray Zenon was taking this tact considering the age of the victims. Then, on Friday, when they talked with Dr. Herve Schwartzman, they discovered that that was indeed Stuart Fouts position. He claimed the women had encouraged him once they discovered that he liked older ladies. Sex had been consensual. He said that's why Tonia Morales hadn't reported him the first time.

As for Stella Woodbridge, according to Dr. Schwartzman, Stuart Fouts claimed she was pulled out of the house because her dog was barking. She did not seek help. And she had to be restrained to keep her from returning. Then her embarrassment forced her to declare that he had raped her.

"Is he believable?" Stanley asked.

Dr. Schwartzman nodded. "Sociopaths frequently are. He's going to want a jury trial

Saturday morning, Aleta discovered a box of large pain patches in the drawer holding Stanley's stash of electric razors that he never used. The prescription label was dated several days earlier. The box originally contained thirty patches. The instructions were that no more than three should be worn at a time. Twelve hours on, twelve hours off. The box was half empty.

She reasoned that he used them when he went riding, but he hadn't gone riding yesterday.

To her surprise, Stanley didn't plan to go riding that morning either. According to her calculations, he was wearing three pain patches that morning.

Stanley had persuaded Robert to take Minx out instead of him, since she was saddled and ready to go.

When Berth brightened at the prospect, Aleta encouraged her father to join them.

"When I come back, Stanley," she murmured to herself, "you are going to answer questions about your leg."

She was wrong.

Stanley had invited Lyle and Lauren, their dogs and their kids over for a barbecue as well as Lyle's parents as well as his own. Andrea had come to spend the day with her husband and daughter since Paul Junior was going to the football game with friends.

Paige called while the riding group was out. Stanley fielded the call. Paige told him that Hawk's grandmother kept calling their dog Tank because he was wearing Tank's collar. Stanley explained that Bertha had probably put one of Tank's collars on Topper when she was taking care of him while they were in Florida, so that if he strayed, whoever found him would call Bertha.

Paige told Stanley that Hawk's grandmother had not been able to understand their explanation, so if she saw the real Tank and she saw the collar slipped on his neck. Maybe that would help.

"Her memory isn't good and she gets confused a lot," Paige explained. "For some reason, she's got it in her head that Topper isn't ours and that we need to return him."

"Come for lunch," Stanley said. "Bring everyone, even Topper. Lyle and Lauren are here with their kids and dogs. Even if Hawk's grandmother doesn't remember people's names, she might enjoy watching the children and dogs. And there's always the horses."

"That would be a lovely outing. Hawk's parents would love to meet his friends," Paige said. "What can I bring?"

"Just yourselves," Stanley said.

"I have a recipe for a great chocolate pudding cake," Paige offered.

"We have a lot of people," Stanley responded. "And if you bring cake everyone will want a piece."

"It serves twelve," Paige said.

"I hate to say it, but we'll be serving nineteen adults counting you five," Stanley revealed.

"I will bring two pans," Paige said. "What time?"

"The riding group will be back at eleven and be ready to eat between eleven thirty and twelve."

"May we come at eleven, so Grandma can watch them come in on their horses?"

"Come a bit earlier if you like. Lyle and Lauren are coming at ten."

"Thanks loads," Paige said. "It will be a nice little excursion for Grandma."

Paige turned away from the phone and told the group about the invitation.

"It's a nice group," she assured her mother-in-law. "Bertha is a practical nurse and she used to work in an elderly care home, and Stanley's mother just recovered from a stroke, so Grandma will fit right in. One of the children is deaf so her parents will be using a lot of sign language. It's going to be a very casual affair. The farm is nice. Grandma can walk lots of places and see things. The house is unique, but mostly, they are our best friends and we'd like you to meet them. Lydia is the judge that made it possible for us to get married. You absolutely must meet her."

As Paige spoke, Hawk watched his mother's face relax. He wasn't certain he would have painted such a compelling picture.

His father's response told Hawk he was glad Paige had taken the lead. She had infected him with her enthusiasm. When Paige asked his mother to help her bake two cakes, he saw his mother's eyes light up. To his mother, bringing a cake meant she wasn't imposing, Hawk knew. How did Paige know?

Hawk had spent last night telling them how Paige and he met and all the particulars about the wedding. His parents had arrived on Friday, half a day early because Grandma thought that was the day they were traveling and she was excited.

When Paige began pulling out ingredients, her mother-in-law asked, "Are we making the cakes from scratch?"

Diplomatically, Paige replied, "That's how I'm used to baking."

"I haven't had the time to do that for so long," Hawk's mother said defensively. "Mother needs constant watching."

"Here's the recipe," Paige said. "Why don't we each bake one?"

"Do you follow the recipe exactly?"

"More or less."

"Tell me when you do either more or less."

Hawk and his father sat on the porch overlooking the lake, talking.

Hawk told him how Paige had the chutzpah to as for more money for her services and his father grew concerned.

"Are you sure this Stanley Praetzel is not going to ask Paige for special favors?" his father asked.

Hawk laughed. "You'd never think that if you met Aleta."

"Isn't she the one who can't speak?"

"Actually, she can," Hawk said and then he filled his father in on the details he'd left out earlier.

"You know both your mother and I were worried about Paige's age earlier, but she seems very mature. You left a lot out of your tale last night. Care to fill me in?"

And so Hawk did, slowly and carefully answering every question.

Finally, his father asked, "Since you were both planning on her finishing her education, why didn't you use protection?"

"Two doctors told us she'd need an operation to get pregnant."

"Abortion was out of the question?" his father probed.

"Absolutely," Hawk returned. "We want this child. Paige made her decision with no illusions about motherhood. That's why she wants you to meet Molly. She raised her from the time she was little. Even after her mother died, Paige didn't slack off on her schoolwork. You should have seen the house, Dad. Neat as a pin. And you've tasted her cooking. The luckiest day of my life was the day she picked me."

His father laughed. "I'd say you had that backwards, but having met Paige, I do believe she did just that."

"She has no parents, Dad," Hawk said. "She wants you and Mom to like her."

"We like her. We just don't think she's old enough to know what she wants," his father commented. "Are you sure she's not just using you?"

"For what?"

"To get a college education, for one thing."

"She has her own trust fund."

"She's a beautiful girl," his father said and stopped, leaving his innuendo draped in the air between them.

Hawk brushed aside the negative implication and simply agreed that Paige was indeed beautiful.

Silence reigned for a number of minutes before Hawk thought of something to say.

"Do you know what she wanted in a husband, Dad?"

The older man shook his head. He had no idea what someone as young as Paige valued.

"She wanted a man who was kind."

His father's eyes widened. "Really?"

"She said that's why I hunch over, so as not to tower over people and make them feel inferior."

"She said that?"

"She also liked my eyes, but she never once asked me to trim my hair."

"I like the cut," his father pointed out, suggesting that she'd managed to get him to do it covertly.

"I let her choose how I would wear my hair. It was my wedding gift to her," Hawk said. "She had the barber cut it just short enough so she could see my eyes and then she told him to trim the rest to balance."

"Who's your barber?"

"She is. She watched every snip he made," Hawk said. "She used to cut her brother's hair. They really didn't have much money when they were growing up."

"Trust fund or no trust fund, you must have seemed like quite a catch," his father remarked.

"Me? With my rattletrap of a car, barely furnished apartment and hodgepodge assortment of clothes? This largess that you see is a boost from some wealthy friends who wanted to give Paige a dowry. She's the catch."

"She used real butter," his father observed. " She has expensive tastes."

"I prefer butter," Hawk said. "And butter makes cookies taste better. I can tell the difference. But she's no spendthrift. If I want cereal, she makes me oatmeal. She says boxed cereals are too expensive and too sugary."

"We had corn flakes this morning."

"I told her you liked corn flakes," Hawk explained. "I've learned to like oatmeal. She sometimes adds cinnamon, sometimes applesauce, sometimes bananas. And I like that she cooks breakfast for me. She packs me a lunch too. I used to just skip lunch."

His father moved on.

"Will we meet any of her school friends while we're here?"

"Jocelyn and Lettie will be at the barbecue. And Jack," Hawk said.

"Good," his father said. "I'd like to meet her best friends."

"You will meet them too," Hawk said.

"People's best friends are their same age."

"Paige never made any at school. She was too busy being a mother. It isolates one. She relates to the women more my age in our circle of friends. She already has a reputation as a baker. And four of those you will meet today are pregnant too."

"All homemakers?"

"Aleta's a partner in a law firm. Bertha is a paid housekeeper. Lauren has five children, so I guess she's a full-time homemaker. Andrea just moved here. That's her house going up over there across the lake."

"What does her husband do?"

"He used to be an architect and then he visited Aleta. Now he paints."

"That was a foolish move. Architects make good money. Artists don't"

"He's amazingly good."

"That just excites critics. It doesn't sell paintings."

"He's already sold quite a few," Hawk said.

"To whom? Friends?"

"Well, yes," Hawk admitted. "I wish I could commission him to do one of Paige, but he's way out of my price range."

"He won't last long overcharging like that."

"Stanley can be blamed for that. When Ed tried to buy one for a couple thousand, Stanley stepped in.

"I'm glad someone brought the artist to his senses."

"Stanley insisted Paul have his work appraised before he sold any. Ed has a good eye when it comes to art. He bought one of Bessie's ruined paintings for a couple thousand. Within a month it was worth a hundred grand."

"So Ed raked in a bundle. Smart man."

"He didn't sell it. He liked it," Hawk said. "That's why Stanley became Paul's agent."

"This Stanley a lawyer or something?"

"He has his own law firm. His father and Aleta's father all work for him."

"A powerhouse, huh?"

"Sometimes he works as a volunteer deputy for Chief West. We worked a couple of cases together. He's got a terrific brain."

"His law firm struggling?"

"West doesn't pay him. He wins their bets."

"Bets? He's a gambler."

Hawk chuckled. "He bets on competitions where he's pitted against Lyle. Lyle wins most of the time. Then Stanley owes him deputy time."

"Chief West uses untrained men as officers?"

"Stanley knows the law. And he's a crack shot. On top of that he has great instincts," Hawk said. "You know, Dad, I just realized how much of a pessimist you are."

"It's a hard world, Son. You need to be cautious. Things aren't as good as they seem."

"Nor are they as bad as you envision," Hawk said. "Excuse me. I need a dose of Paige."

Abruptly he left, sought out his wife and said, "I need you."

She followed him upstairs to their bedroom. Topper trotted along at their heels.

"Your parents?" Paige asked instinctively.

"My father…" Hawk began. "Oh, Paige, you buoy me up so. I just needed to hold you."

"Hawk, I love you. I am not too young to know you are the kind of man I want to be married to for the rest of my life. I know they think I'm too young to know what I want because I don't know what career I'm interested in. But that's secondary. Primarily I want to be a wife and mother. And more importantly, I want to be your wife and the mother of your child whom, by the way, may not be the son you want."

Hawk burst into laughter.

"Paige, you are so good for me!"

"What does that mean?"

"I don't care whether you have a girl like you or a boy like you."

Paige giggled.

"If he looks like me, he won't be a boy. You obviously need a lesson in anatomy."

"Are you going to give me one?"

"Not today."

Hawk turned serious.

"Paige, I'm so sorry. I had things backwards."

"Backwards?"

"I wanted them to like you," Hawk explained. "What I really want is for you to like them. Dad is sure there's a cloud somewhere ready to block out the sun."

"Yes, I know," Paige said softly. "Is your father's only objection to me my age?"

"Pretty much."

"He also thinks I'm too pretty?"

"Pretty much."

"And he doesn't think you're handsome enough to hold on to me?'

"Pretty much."

"Anything else?"

"He thinks Stanley is trying to buy your favor."

Paige laughed.

"Stanley doesn't even see me. He is too wrapped up in Aleta."

"But you are prettier."

"Only to you," Paige returned. "Is your father wearing you down?"

"Yes. I forgot why I moved so far away until now."

"You can't change him," Paige said.

"I know. But he puts doubts in my head and I hate it."

"Where did you get your confidence from?"

"I don't have a lot."

"You gave me mine."

"And you increased the little I had."

"So we're good together," Paige said.

"That's a truth I believe.'

"Me too," Paige said. "Help me change."

"Change?"

"We're going to the Praetzels. I'm not wearing slacks while Aleta is wearing shorts."

"How do you know she'll be wearing shorts?"

"Because Stanley likes her to."

"My parents?" Hawk asked.

"They already think I'm a kid, so I will act my age. Let's live in the truth, Hawk. I love you. You love me. I'm young and you're ancient."

"I'm not ancient."

"You won't wear shorts."

"It's a man thing. It has nothing to do with age."

"Wear what will please your parents or wear what will please me," Paige challenged.

"I better not be the only one in shorts."

"So what if you are?" Paige charged. "You won't be dressed inappropriately. We'll look like a pair."

Hawk nodded and began to change, uttering his usual complaint, "My legs are too long."

"You're a tall man," Paige said. "Tall men have long legs. Did I ever tell you I really like tall men?"

"No," Hawk murmured.

Paige laughed. "You're the perfect height. Now kiss me and tell me we will survive this weekend."

Hawk gathered Paige in his arms and Topper nosed in between them. They kissed but each put a hand on Topper's head and ruffled his ears.

"We are a family," Hawk said.

"Mother told me parents have a hard time with that concept when it comes to their children. I think we're experiencing that phenomenon now."

"Which is why Dad is questioning everything?"

"So let's give him something to be a bit unnerved by."

"Our shorts?"

"You've got it."

Hawk chuckled.

"You are a clever one, Paige. It will keep him off balance all afternoon."

"Just remember, wearing them is another way of consummating our marriage—a public way."

"Where do you come up with this stuff?"

"I pick your brain."

"You do not.

She threw her arms around him and kissed him again.

"I love you so," she whispered.

Hand in hand they left the bedroom with Topper trailing along behind.

"The cakes are ready to come out," Hawk's mother announced. "Oh, I see you've changed."

"It's a casual affair," Paige said. "If you and Dad want to change, we still have time."

"Er... Hawk, wouldn't you be more comfortable in jeans?" his mother asked.

Hawk squeezed Paige's hand.

"These are cooler."

"Your legs are too long for shorts," his mother criticized.

Paige laughed and said. "He'd look weird if they were short. He's a tall man."

"You'll be out of place," his mother commented.

"Everyone there knows I like Hawk to wear shorts," Paige said.

"But proper is proper," his mother sniffed.

"Different groups have different ideas what's proper." Paige said.

"Are you being smart?" the older woman carped.

"Just quoting my mother," Paige said politely.

Hawk put his arm around his wife waist and said, "Her mother was a sociologist. Paige has a lot of knowledge of sociology tucked in that brain of hers."

"I will get Grandma," his mother announced brusquely.

"Oooh, shorts," the old woman said when she saw Paige. "Are we going on a picnic?"

"Yes," Hawk said.

"We need to return the dog," the old woman insisted.

"That's where we're going," Hawk said. "To return the collar and have a picnic."

"I will follow in my car," his father said. "And we will take the cakes."

CHAPTER 11

Approaching the Praetzel farm, Phillip Monroe came up over a rise, spotted Hawk's turn indicator blinking and announced that they had arrived. He surveyed the jumping ring in the pasture to the right of the house. On the other side of the drive was an orchard. At the end of the drive was a modest one story remodeled farmhouse.

Phillip Monroe commented to his wife, "Certainly isn't rich, is he?"

"I wonder who uses the horse ring," Elba questioned. "Those jumps are pretty fancy."

"Such a long driveway," Phillip commented. "Looks like he put all his money into concrete only to run out by the time he came to the house. He should have used asphalt. Cheaper."

As Phillip Monroe pulled in behind his son, Lauren and Stanley came out to greet them. Bessie Dobbins, dressed in paint-splattered jeans, appeared beside them.

Hawk's parents watched Paige approach the old woman and greet her.

"Did you miss going out with the group?" Paige asked as she held the car door open for Topper.

"Hubbs and I exercise the horses on the weekends. I didn't know Stanley was having a party."

"Neither does Aleta," Stanley said, introducing everyone.

"We brought Topper," Paige said. "He's wearing Tank's collar."

"Tank's wearing Topper's," Stanley said. "I thought a total exchange would be easier for your grandmother to understand."

Bessie interrupted the exchange when Hawk walked around the car, carrying one of the cakes.

"You're in shorts!" she exclaimed.

Hawk reddened.

"I asked him to wear them," Paige said.

"And well you should have, my dear. He has great legs!"

"They're too long for shorts," Hawks mother put in.

"Don't be ridiculous!" Bessie snapped. "A tall man needs long legs. But yours are beautiful, Hawk. Paul will want to sketch them."

"Sketch my legs?" Hawk gasped, reddening even more.

Lyle, who had come out of the house carrying his youngest son, shouted back inside. "Bessie needs a sketch pad, Paul. She's going to paint Hawk's legs."

Paul rushed out.

Phillip and Elba Monroe were surprised at the tall, masculine-appearing man with the handsome features. He wasn't what either pictured when they heard he was an artist-in-residence.

Paul had two sketch pads in his hand as he stopped and stared at Hawk who was standing stock still holding Paige's cake.

"He need to be holding something else," Paul said.

"I do animals and landscapes," Bessie commented.

"Someone take the cake," Paul said. "Where do we want to put the legs?'

"You leave them on his body," Paige quipped.

"She's the one with the nice legs," Hawk said.

Both artists studied Paige up and down.

"Nude," they agreed adamantly.

"Nude?" Hawk said. "She's not posing nude!"

"We're just saying that every part of her body is lovely," Bessie said. "But right now, we want to sketch your legs."

"This is ridiculous!" Hawk blustered.

"Lauren, can we borrow Locke?" Paul asked.

"He won't sit still," Lauren said.

"Over by one of the apple trees, I think," Paul said, ignoring her warning.

"Maybe with a horse?" Bessie suggested.

"He is not sitting next to a horse," Lauren proclaimed adamantly.

Bessie whispered to Paul.

He nodded eagerly and asked, "Which horse?"

"Lyle," Lauren called. "Tell them that Locke is not sitting at a horse's feet."

Lyle chuckled. "I think you just did."

"Come on, Lyle," Paul said. "Bring the baby. Paige, bring Hawk."

"He's absolutely not sitting at a horse's feet," Lauren repeated as her children gathered to find out what was going on. She signed to Camay and her two younger brothers watched.

Bessie told Hubbs what they were doing and he put a bridle on Sterling and moved him out of the barn and in front of the orchard.

Lyle's parents drove up and Camay signed to them and told them what was going on. Stanley's parents came in just as she finished.

Kurtz West chuckled as he told them that Bessie Dobbins had come over to visit Hubbs and saw Hawk's legs and now she and Paul were going to paint them.

"Hawk's legs?" Hubert asked, his surprise coloring his tone.

"He does have nice legs," Lydia commented.

"You looked?" her husband asked.

"I'm not dead. Of course, I looked."

Her comment shocked Hawk's parents who'd hung back bewildered at the happenings. Stanley quickly introduced the new arrivals to Hawk's parents.

"The two wanted to paint Paige in the nude," Elba Monroe reported. "But Hawk said no."

"It was an indecent proposal," Phillip Monroe declared.

"Not from an artist," Stanley said. "Perhaps it would help if I showed you Paul's first oil"

"Oh, Stanley! Is it done?" his mother exclaimed.

"Hanging over the fireplace."

"What about Bessie's painting?"

"The far wall."

The seven went into the house and stood and stared at the painting over the fireplace.

"I heard you had to pay more," Stanley's father said.

"Someone else saw it and offered Paul more and I matched his offer."

"But he had agreed to sell it to you for two hundred and fifty."

"I wanted to pay what it was worth. It's his signature piece. What he gets for it will determine how much the others are worth."

"So how much?"

"Double."

"Five hundred?" Hubert questioned, amazed. "That's a lot."

"That doesn't seem like too much," Phillip Monroe said. "I've seen worse ones going for a couple thousand."

"Five hundred thousand," Hubert said quietly.

"Half a million!" Phillip Monroe gasped. "Why did you pay? He promised to sell it to you for half that. You should have held him to the deal. You could have resold it and made a handsome profit."

"I did tell Paul that if anyone offered him more, I wouldn't match it," Stanley said. "And to seal the deal, I paid him on the spot."

"He's still putting it in his show, isn't he?" Hubert asked.

"Yes."

"This is a nice painting," Elba Monroe commented pointing at Bessie's landscape—one of the rare ones that had been ravaged by the heat of the fire and the water damage from the firemen's hoses, the combination of which had given the painting an ethereal quality.

"That's Bessie's painting," Stanley said. "It was one of the dozen or so that made it through the fire."

Elba Monroe looked around.

"Where's Grandma?"

Stanley pointed through the window facing the pathway to the barn.

"She went to join the others."

"Come on, Phil. Let's go after her."

After the two left, Lydia said. "Paige doesn't have a mother, and that woman won't be one."

"They're Hawk's parents," Hubert said.

"You can be so dense sometimes," Lydia shot back. "Young women need their mothers. Aleta has Bertha."

"And you, Mother," Stanley put in.

"Paige has no one," Lydia said. "I think she was hoping Hawk's parents would be the parents she is missing."

"Then be her mother, Lydia," Hubert said softly. "You've been on her side from the beginning. Let her know you still care."

"But…" Lydia began.

Stanley chimed in, "Mother, she needs an older friend. She had a wonderful mother. She just may need someone to go toe to toe with Elba Monroe."

"She's Hawk's mother."

"And we're Paige's family," Stanley said. "So, let's go watch our resident artist immortalize Hawk's legs."

A few moments later, Lydia came up beside Paige who was standing alone. Lydia noticed that neither of Hawk's parents had joined her.

Lydia put her hand around Paige's waist and whispered, "I thought he had great legs the day you first made him wear shorts."

Paige responded, "He's so embarrassed. I'm not sure what to do."

"These are two serious artists," Lydia said. "And they picked him as a model. I love the pose."

Paige smiled.

"Lauren said it was okay for him to set Locke on the horse. He was so gentle that Locke never even cried. Not once."

"In-laws are difficult for most couples, Paige. Sometimes they turn out to be the kind you can be friends with. Sometimes they don't."

"They think I'm too young. They think I don't know what I really want. I know I haven't decided on a career, but mother always said a woman's first job was to be educated."

"That's wise advice, Lydia said.

"You would have liked my mother," Paige said.

"We probably would have been best friends. I know she would have approved of your choice of husband. I certainly do."

"Hawk wore the shorts even though he knew his mother world be upset. He did that to please me."

"And to declare his independence," Lydia stated.

"And now they will ridicule him," Paige predicted. "They haven't said a really positive thing to him since they got here. I don't understand it."

"It's their way," Lydia said. "They were like when they saw Paul's painting. They are the first ones not to be moved by it."

"The one of Aleta nursing Gerard?"

"Yes," Lydia replied. "Stanley and Hubert played around with it's worth, but they still didn't get it. Not really."

"I'm not getting through either, although I'm really trying."

"Paige, I'm only interested in you right now. You need some buffers between you and them. In-laws are one of the leading causes of marital break-ups."

"Mother taught me that," Paige said. "That's why I want them to like me."

"Hawk has already chosen you," Lydia said. "Now let me give you a little sociology lesson. It isn't what they think of you that counts. It's what hold they have on Hawk that matters. He's trying to break free. Do you understand what I am saying?"

"Just before we came over here, he took me aside and said we were a family—him, Topper and me."

Lydia chuckled. "I'm so glad Topper was included."

"That's why I didn't invite Ed and Beatrice over. Hawk's parents don't think Topper was a good wedding present."

"I have an idea," Lydia said. "You need a little neighborhood brunch to welcome Hawk's parents. It would make them feel special. Have they met Molly yet?"

"No."

"They should meet her with her father. They are the kind that are impressed by doctors," Lydia continued.

"Evelyn would come," Paige said.

"I don't want you to invite them. I want Hawk's parents to be invited by Evelyn or Beatrice or even Bertha. I will arrange it. Don't you worry. We're your family. We've adopted you."

Paige's mouth fell open.

"We love you, Paige. We want your marriage to succeed."

Lauren approached Paige.

"I think Lyle has nice legs too," she said.

Flustered, Paige stammered an apology.

"Don't apologize," Lauren said. "Hawk's legs are nice and he's tall. I don't think the painting would have looked as good with a shorter man."

"It's mostly his legs," Paige remarked. "He has his back to us."

"Did you see Paul's rendering?" Lauren asked. "He put Hubbs in as well."

"I've been watching Bessie," Paige said.

"Come look at Paul's," Lauren said.

Paige followed her a few paces to the left.

"It is different," Paige said.

As she lifted her eyes and looked around, she saw Hawk's mother pulling out her camera. Somehow Paige knew this was wrong. She walked up to her mother-in-law and whispered, "Mom, we need to help."

As she said that, she put her hand in front of the camera. Stanley's mother saw and heard Paige. Lydia quickly approached Hawk's mother and said," Elba, let me take some pictures for you while you and Paige help Andrea."

"I want one of Hawk," Elba said.

"In his shorts?" Lydia asked, mildly surprised.

"Maybe if he saw what he looked like…"

"I understand. I'm quite good with a camera. I will get some nice shots for you."

"Of Hawk?"

"Of course."

Elba gave her the camera reluctantly and followed Paige to where Andrea was working.

"We're here to help," Paige said.

"You are a dear," Andrea said. "I could use some extra hands."

After Paige left with Elba, Hubert moved near his wife.

"What was that about?" he whispered.

"Paige didn't want her mother-in-law to take pictures of Hawk posing."

"Why not?" Hubert said. "We're all watching."

"There are pictures and then there are pictures," Lydia said. "I intend to take some positive ones."

The riders returned. The artists stopped sketching.

Hawk sought out Paige. He recognized the scared look that he remembered from their first days together.

"Are you okay?" he asked.

"We can't talk here," Paige said.

"The bedroom in the house," Hawk said, taking her hand and hurrying away with her.

When he closed the bedroom door, he asked, "What happened?"

"Your mother was going to take a snapshot of you posing," Paige blurted out. "I stopped her."

Relief flooded Hawk's face. "Thank you!"

"Judge Davis took your mother's camera," Paige went on. "She promised some nice pictures."

"Not…" Hawk began.

He stopped when Paige shook her head.

The door was flung open and Hawk's mother entered. She was fuming.

"You were a laughing stock," she declared.

"No, he wasn't," Paige countered fiercely. "No one was laughing. Paul is a talented man who's going to be great someday and Bessie is a well-known artist. Everyone was watching them work. It was a special magical moment."

"You put your hand in front of my camera," Elba declared. "I saw you."

"I don't think that was right of me," Paige said. "I'm sorry."

"Then you dragged me off so I couldn't get another shot and had that, that person take pictures for me. She should have been helping not me. I don't like being treated like a servant."

"I'm sorry," Paige said. "I thought you liked helping."

"No woman likes helping."

"I do," Paige said.

"Well, you're low class. You don't know any better. And to these people you're a toy.

They'll discard you as soon as they're tired of you."

"They're my family," Paige stammered.

"Ah, there you are," came a strong firm voice from the living room. "I came to return your camera. I got some nice shots of your mother and husband besides some of your son. I went around and got his face. You must be so proud of him."

"Proud?" Elba tossed out the word like a dead rat. "Ashamed would be a better word."

"That would be a foolish word," Lydia said. "We are all so glad Hawk decided to settle here. He is tops in his field."

"He could have been a doctor," Elba said,

"I'm glad he's not. We don't need another doctor. Him we need. I wish you could see him in court. He is very impressive. And I've been told Paige has made sure he is as impressive in appearance as he is in handling the forensic evidence."

"Putting shorts on him impressed no one in a proper manner."

"No one put shorts on me," Hawk inserted. "Paige let me choose. I chose to please her."

"Shorts are proper attire for the occasion," Lydia said. "Lyle never dresses inappropriately. He comes from one of our finest families."

"The one with all the children?" Elba queried with disdain.

"He can well afford them," Lydia remarked. "He's a multi-millionaire. No one, however, is as rich as my son. Even Hubert and I aren't. And he would be in shorts were it not for his injured leg."

"Is it bad?" Paige burst in. "He didn't get shot again, did he?"

"No dear. He didn't get shot. He says it's nothing. He's making a big deal out of it to keep Aleta's mind off herself,"

"Don't believe him," Paige declared.

Elba interjected, "Foolish words from a child."

Lydia brushed aside Elba's comment. "Why not?"

"He would never tease Aleta like that," Paige said. "He's trying to keep both of you from worrying."

"You know, I believe you're right. He and Aleta tease each other so much I never gave a thought to the fact that they never play tricks on each other."

"Let me know if I can help," Paige said.

" A hollow sentiment," Elba quipped.

"Not with Paige, Mother," Hawk inserted. "She's a capable woman."

"Paige, come with me," Lydia said. "Hawk needs to talk with his mother."

Hawk nodded and Paige let Lydia lead her away.

"I don't understand," Paige confided. "He's not like either of his parents."

"Someone shaped him differently from either of them."

"You mean like an aunt or a grandfather?"

"Yes, someone he's had a long term relationship with," Lydia said. "The influence of a teacher or coach would be too fleeting for him to be so radically different. Someone loved him deeply."

"Oh, I'm so glad you see it too," Paige said enthusiastically. "I was beginning to doubt everything my mother taught me."

"Don't," Lydia said. "And be careful. All families have secrets."

"I shouldn't pry?"

"I would suggest you study them," Lydia suggested. "They were and are a big factor in his life. Help him settle into the man he has become."

"He said his father raised doubts about me and he hated that," Paige confided.

"He doesn't share their value system," Lydia mused. "And they really don't care. That's what I don't understand. They really don't like him."

"You saw that too?" Paige asked.

"Paige, I'm sorry. I've been analyzing Hawk's family," Lydia said. "That's not my place. One thing I want you to remember."

"What's that?"

"I married you two. I want your marriage to succeed. His parents are bad news. Distance yourself from them."

"It seems wrong somehow," Paige confided. "They are his parents."

"Whom he chose to move away from."

"Honor his choice?" Paige asked.

"Yes, Paige," Judge Davis said. "That's what marriage is—choosing. He chose you. He did it publicly today. It was a brave act."

"Not defiant?"

"He disobeyed no one. He simply chose your reasonable request over his mother's unreasonable attitude. Two artists confirmed his choice."

"I wish I could buy one of those pieces," Paige said.

"Which one?"

"I like them both," Paige said. "That reminds me. Lauren invited me to do something with her, but I said no. Now I'm not sure I should have."

"What was it?"

"Posing for Paul's new painting."

"The pregnancy piece," Lydia said knowingly. "Sorry, Paige, you're legally underage. Lauren forgot that. She was seeing you as an adult."

"She said it isn't a sex thing with Paul."

"I know it isn't. If you're interested, I could talk to Paul. You can pose, but not nude."

"What about Hawk?" Paige questioned.

"If you're not nude, would he object?"

"No, I guess not."

"I will take care of it," Lydia said. "But let me tell you what I will insist upon. No sexually suggestive poses. Never nude. A bikini I will allow. Some reliable adult woman in the room with you at all times. Any of the women scheduled to pose will be acceptable."

"Can I tell Lauren?" Paige asked excitedly.

Lydia smiled and nodded.

Paige is still part child, Lydia concluded. That Elba woman has got to keep her hands off.

Paige ran out and cornered Lauren.

"Lydia is going to fix it so I can pose with you."

"Lydia?"

"I'm underage," Paige said.

"Oh my God! I forgot!" Lauren exclaimed.

"She said you did. I feel complimented," Paige said.

"How is she going to fix it?"

Paige told her and then added, "It's my tummy he wants."

Lauren laughed. "I guess that's right. With five of us, Paul can probably work something out."

"It won't bother everyone if I'm not nude too?"

"No, Paige," Lauren responded smiling. "It won't. None of us wants Paul to get into trouble. And you belong in the group. Lydia is right to protect you,"

"Thanks for including me."

Lauren chuckled. "Remember I'm using you to squeeze in myself."

Paige giggled. "We are a naughty pair, aren't we?"

"We are all that, but only because we are all basically proper women."

"And our daughters won't know about this until we're ninety."

Lauren laughed. "You've got it."

Aleta joined them dressed in shorts. They threw their arms around her simultaneously and both began to talk at once. She laughed as the story unfolded.

She nodded when Lauren said, "There should be five in that painting."

Aleta pointed at the house and the three went in to tell Paul. Lydia was just coming out.

Paul frowned.

"Don't throw parties on my work days."

"You've been working," Lauren accused. "Don't blame us if a fellow artist distracted you. Let Aleta see the sketch of my baby."

"And my husband's legs," Paige added.

Paul pulled out the sketch.

Aleta pointed at herself.

"Yes," Paul admitted. "I caught you and Hubbs behind your horse. I'm so glad I could please all three of you. Call me for lunch. Otherwise I'm busy."

"You know, Paul," Paige said. "You don't have to finish them all by the show."

"You can't put on a show with unfinished pieces," he protested.

"Sure you can," Paige said. "Walking in here is fascinating with sketches all over the place and half-finished pieces. How come you work on more than one at a time?"

"I guess it's because I get in different moods."

"You're an artist," Paige said. "You can't be boxed into a time table. You had enough for a show with that one of Aleta, Stanley and Gerard. It alone is worth a visit to the gallery."

"She's right," Lauren said. "These partially finished pieces are stirring."

Paul stood back.

"I will finish them," he declared. "But I like to go with my moods. I do my best work then."

"If the buyers have a deadline, tell them you aren't a photo shop. No twenty-four hour service is offered," Paige advised.

"But will they wait?"

Aleta laughed. She pulled Paige in front of her and motioned Lauren to get behind her.

"They'll line up?" Paul asked. "Aleta are you sure?"

All three nodded.

Lauren blurted out. "Paige and I want to be in the Pregnancy Project."

"Pregnancy Project? Is that what it's being called by everyone?"

"Can we?" Lauren pressed.

"Only if Aleta will let Gerard be in it."

"I thought you wanted Locke," Lauren said.

"I do. Five women. Two babies."

Aleta nodded.

"Okay, Ladies. All of you need to expand right after my show."

The three giggled.

"We will," Lauren promised.

"Now shoo. I've got at least ten minutes more work before... Hell, Andrea, why are you so prompt?"

"Paul's going to do five in that pregnancy project of his," Lauren announced excitedly. "Paige and I are included as well as Gerard."

"I will explain later, Andrea," Paul said. "But it's going to be better than I first imagined."

"You sound excited," Andrea noted.

"I am."

Andrea turned to Lauren and Paige. "He does his best work when he's excited. Time to eat. Stanley and Robert say the hamburgers are done."

"I better hurry. Lyle doesn't like to have to feed all five."

"Aren't his parents here?" Paige asked.

Lauren chuckled.

"They are. I forgot. Let's not hurry."

Andrea and Paul rushed out, but the Paige slowed. Aleta and Lauren, sensing that something was troubling her, hesitated.

"Lydia said I should build a new family, not look to Hawk's parents. I could use a couple of older sisters."

The two stopped dead. Aleta reached out and closed the front door.

"What's wrong?" Lauren asked.

"My in-laws don't like me," Paige stated bluntly. "But that's not the worst of it."

"What could be worse?" Lauren asked.

"They don't like Hawk either," Paige said and then began to cry.

Aleta and Lauren gathered the young woman in their arms.

"And that you don't know how to deal with," Lauren murmured.

Paige nodded.

"Any idea why?" Lauren asked.

Paige nodded and then rattled off her observations.

"He's too tall. They don't think he's handsome. And he's not a doctor. I know Hawk was hoping they'd be impressed with out new house, but they weren't. He was so hurt by some of the things his father said. He said he was weak. He's not."

"We don't think that," Lauren said. "No man who's weak would wear shorts in the face of such obvious parental disapproval. That was a brave act, not a weak one."

Paige nodded her acceptance of Lauren's vies.

"You can't do anything about their feelings," Lauren went on. "But to go back to what you asked us to do. We'd love to adopt you as our sister. Aleta can't speak or she's apt to blow us all up, so let's just shake hands. I'm not into doing the blood brother thing."

The three held hands and Lauren announced they were sisters forever. Aleta bowed her head and Lauren whispered.

"Don't you dare say 'Amen'. I just got into Paul's project."

Paige giggled.

The door opened and Stanley entered.

"Ladies, you're missed. Lyle needs help. Hawk needs help. I need help."

"It's our day off," Lauren quipped.

"That doesn't work," Stanley said. "Paul's out there talking about Paige's brilliant suggestion about his show. And he's going to talk about his big project next."

"He wouldn't!" Lauren gasped.

"He said he had an announcement," Stanley said, grinning.

"Not in front of Hawk's parents!" Paige wailed.

"Or Lyle's," Lauren cried. "I haven't told Lyle yet."

"Hawk doesn't know either," Paige worried.

Stanley laughed. "They both know. How do you think I found out?"

Aleta clapped her hand across her mouth.

"Lydia!" Lauren guessed. "Well, if the secret's out, the secret's out."

The three marched out resolutely, red-faced.

Paige headed straight for Hawk, threw her arms around him and buried her head in his chest. He embraced her and whispered, "It's okay, Paige. You asked Lydia. You did a wise thing. I'm proud of you. I'd love to have you in a painting of Paul's."

She squeezed him and he knew she felt better.

"Come," he said. "Let's fill your plate."

Lauren headed straight to the table where Lyle had a plate waiting for her.

"Lydia told me," Lyle signed. "It's okay."

"I was just poking the ball," Lauren signed. "And it rolled down the hill and I couldn't stop it."

"I don't understand, Mommy," Camay signed.

"It's a metaphor," Lauren signed, spelling out the new word. "The word ball stands for another word."

"Like sex?" Camay asked.

"Not sex," Lauren said as she signed, reddening even more. "I may not be able to keep this a secret until I'm ninety."

"What secret?" Camay signed.

"If I told you, it wouldn't be a secret," Lauren returned.

Lyle was grinning during this exchange. His parents were puzzled, but they gathered it was not something to be discussed around children, so they said nothing.

Aleta sat down and Stanley filled her plate and presented it to her. She looked at him.

"I made the hamburger," he said.

She smiled.

Her father explained the exchange to the people sitting at the table.

"That translates into you'd better eat every bit of the hamburger."

Aleta nodded.

"Okay, Paul," his brother said. "Your announcement."

Paul stood up.

"I have this big project in mind. It involves seven nude models, so it will take a long, long, long time."

When the laughter subsided, Paul went on.

"It has been underwritten by a patron of the arts."

"Mother?" Robert asked.

"Someone else," Paul said. "Don't ask. The person wishes to remain anonymous. But my studio is off limits the day after my show in October."

Paul sat down amid a buzz of excitement.

That night as they were dressing for bed, Hawk said, "That was a brilliant idea, Paige, sending Mom and Dad to a dinner and a movie."

"It was Bertha's idea," Paige said.

"Evelyn's going to have a brunch for the neighbors tomorrow, so they can all meet my parents," Hawk said. "But then we have the afternoon to deal with."

"We're Grandma sitting," Paige announced. "I suggested to Elba that she and Phillip might want to do a bit of shopping."

"Dad doesn't shop."

"Aleta suggested it. She told me she wanted to talk to me and she didn't know enough sign language yet. Lauren translated that much. Then Stanley let her take her computer out of their car trunk, but we had to take it into the bedroom to use it. He said she could do that because that was her work computer and I was a client. He told her she was to leave the computer in the bedroom when we were done."

"Stanley is determined that Aleta learn enough sign language to function," Hawk said. "It's his way of giving Aleta some control over her ability to communicate. And he knows how hard it is to learn sign language. That's why he restricted the computer to work only. Aleta's a social creature. He knew she would strive to be able to communicate with her friends."

"We don't all sign," Paige said.

"He wanted to counter the feeling of despair that came over her when Fouts planted a second set of bombs. It didn't help any that we only found four of the five. And now it seems that he threw in another one when he invaded their hotel room in Orlando."

Paige spoke up. "I know. Stanley is still paying me. He asked me to focus on the one from the first group that was never found."

"I guess Stanley will make exceptions," Hawk said.

"Only for clients," Paige said.

"Are we paying for Aleta's advice?" Hawk asked.

"Stanley takes payment in chocolate cakes," Paige said. "I guess I owe him another chocolate cake."

"So what did Aleta tell you that is worth a chocolate cake?"

"She told me that there was nothing I could do about your parent's negative feelings toward us, so she suggested I look for ways to make their visit fun for them."

"That was definitely worth a chocolate cake, maybe even two."

"And then Lauren said she thought that Hawk's mother would enjoy shopping on Main Street in Willow Glen. Aleta said she loved the street even though she didn't like to shop. She told me they had a lovely little jewelry shop with all sorts of special jewelry, and Lauren said there is no woman who wouldn't like piece of jewelry that was unique. So I suggested to Dad that he take your mother to that jeweler and buy her a pin or a bracelet, and he liked the idea."

"Those are the only kind of jewelry she wears," Hawk said.

"Bertha joined us. She said caretakers never get enough time off. It makes even the nicest people contentious."

"Mother was like that before Grandma came to live with them," Hawk said. "Aleta's right. She can't be changed."

"As long as we don't let her control our actions, we'll be fine."

"Speaking of actions," Hawk said casually. "The door's locked."

"But Topper is inside the room with us," Paige noted.

"He's sound asleep," Hawk said.

"If we move, we'll wake him," Paige said ruefully.

"We've had a rough day."

Paige threw her arms around her husband's neck and kissed him.

"Are we going to do this standing up?" Hawk asked jokingly.

"Can we? I mean, is it possible?" Paige bubbled.

"Oh, my dear Paige, not only is it possible, I'm not even sure I could make it to the bed if I wanted to. You have no idea what you do to me."

"What if we wake Topper?"

"We'll swear him to secrecy," Hawk said.

CHAPTER 12

Sunday morning, Aleta woke with a start. Fortunately, she woke Stanley when she jumped.

She looked at him and he saw a query in her eyes that weren't yet fully alert. She opened he mouth and he kissed her before the words were spoken. As they kissed, she began to realize what she had almost done.

She reached for the laptop that she had set on the nightstand after her talk with Paige.

"Don't every let me fall asleep without the blindfold again," she typed.

"It reminds you not to speak?" he asked.

She nodded.

"You had a question?"

"Do florists deliver on Sunday?" she typed.

Before Stanley could answer, she typed, "Call Lyle."

Stanley picked up the phone. Lyle answered on the third ring.

"Aleta is typing as fast as she can," Stanley said. "Get Peets on another line. We have only one phone."

"What's going on?" Lyle asked.

"Three bombs are set to go off at the same time," Stanley responded. "Do you have Peets on the line?"

Stanley nodded at Aleta and she typed, "Tell Peets to tell Kurt to take the vase of flowers just delivered by the florist and put it in the hollow of the old oak tree across from the garage. While he's doing that, Dixon is to take the three women out to the barn. Tell him not to forget the dog. Stella will go back for it."

Suddenly Aleta banged her hands on the wall and began typing furiously.

"Kurt is not obeying. He thinks he knows better than I do!" Aleta typed. "Kurt is to put the vase in the hollow of the rotted tree, not behind the one farthest from the barn! Make him do it right or someone will die."

Stanley's voice matched Aleta's in anger.

Then he reported back, "He's arguing with Peets."

"He's wasting time. I need to warn the others!" Aleta typed.

As she typed this, she cried out in agony. She saw the death of Bessie Dobbins and screeched, "Not Bessie!"

All those in the house froze in terror.

Lyle allowed Peets to hear this. Then he heard Peets roar over his phone.

After a few seconds, Aleta began typing again, tears of anguish gushing down her cheeks.

"Lyle, tell Brad to obey me exactly and he will save three lives," Aleta typed, her fingers finding the keys her eyes couldn't see.

"He is to run as fast as he can and grab the little girl that just got off her tricycle. He is to take the flowers from her hand and deposit them on the porch. One of the flowers is a bomb."

Stanley could hear Lyle barking the orders to Brad.

"Then he is to run like a quarterback going for a touchdown," Aleta typed. "The child will scream. Her father will try to tackle him. Brad is to keep going. He is not to stop. He is to encourage both parents to chase him."

Aleta's family had rushed to the door of the bedroom. Stanley's voice had carried into the kitchen and family room. He didn't realize he was shouting her orders.

Quietly, Bertha opened the door and the group watched open-mouthed as Aleta, tears streaming down her face, cries of anguish coming from her mouth, continued to type.

Lettie started to speak but Jocelyn hushed her. "Aleta is having visions of people dying."

"But she's…" Lettie started.

Jocelyn clapped her hand over her cousin's mouth.

Stanley read the words as Aleta typed them.

"Lyle, call the fire department. Send them to Stella Woodbridge's house and Bessie Dobbins place. Now!"

"Peets man is chasing the floral truck," Lyle reported back.

Aleta began typing rapidly again. Stanley was still relaying what he was reading.

"Have Lance stop his chase. Now!" Stanley shouted.

Aleta continued to type. Her torment had been reduced to loud moans.

"Tell him to back up as fast as he can," Stanley shouted. "Peets, the truck is going to explode."

"The driver?" Peets asked Lyle who asked Stanley who saw the answer being typed by Aleta before the question reached her ears.

"Tell Lance to back up and he will save the driver's life."

Peets roared at Lance to back up and save two lives.

He added, "If you don't, you'll not only be dead, you'll be fired."

The action of the cop giving chase told the driver of the truck what was about to happen. He slammed on his brakes and leaped from the truck and began to run toward the police car. He was halfway there when three explosions rent the quiet of that Sunday morning.

"One more," Aleta typed.

Stanley repeated the words.

"Go ahead," Lyle said as sirens could be heard rushing to the three locations of the bomb blasts.

"Voice-activated," Aleta typed.   "Call Reid on his radio then repeat every word of my instructions."

"I have him," Lyle reported back.

Aleta's typed words were read by Stanley as they appeared on the screen.

"Don't finish. Don't tuck yourself in. Pull out your Taser. Run to the back door. Shoot Mrs. Morales as soon as she opens the door and sees the kitten."

Stanley read the words rapidly, and then added his own.

"Now!" he cried. "Shoot! Or you will both die!"

"He shot," Lyle reported a second later.

"Call the bomb squad," Aleta typed. "Stuart Fouts has learned to make bombs. The three in the floral truck were Doyle's work. The one laid at Tonia Morales back step was Stuart's work. His mother has been watching the house is my guess."

Suddenly, Aleta's fingers stopped.

"She's done," Stanley reported.

Aleta could feel herself trembling as she grew cold. Her stomach churned and she knew it wouldn't take much for it to try to vomit up what she had seen even though that wasn't possible. Her throat tightened and she found she couldn't swallow. Too much had been ingested too fast, all of it horrendous.

The trembling increased. She couldn't stop it. She felt Stanley's arms around her and she couldn't understand why she was feeling so sick.

She could scarcely hear the words being said around her. Someone said something about shock.

She didn't know if she nodded or not. Whoever said that was right. Shock was the word for what she felt.

The scenes that had been viewed by her swam back and forth in her mind like waves on a seashore, none the same and yet all alike. One half of her mind was trying to cast them back in to the nether regions where the terrors of the world dwelled while the other half was trying to categorize and file them as if by so doing they would be reduced to forgotten memories.

Her reason couldn't cope with the vividness of the images. It was difficult to put them into the vague category she called visions which portrayed what might have happened, but, because she obeyed, didn't.

Her mind saw them as reality. Her prophecies would not have carried the emotion necessary to command attention and adherence to her directions had she seen them as fantasy.

"God, I can't do this anymore," she prayed silently. "I thought I could, but I was wrong. I am not strong enough. I don't want to fail You, but I can't handle this."

Aleta felt herself being lifted by arms that were not Stanley's. She couldn't figure out to whom Stanley would give her. She heard Bertha's voice, but she couldn't hear what she was saying.

She couldn't see. Where was Stanley? Why wasn't he with her?

Suddenly a silk scarf was tied across her eyes and she realized Stanley was there after all.

They will know, she worried. Our secret will be out.

She heard him talking with her father and Bertha.

"It relaxes her," she heard him say. "It tells her she is going to be taken care of. It reminds her not to speak without her having to strain to remember that."

"I can see that," Bertha said softly.

The next words she understood were Stanley saying he couldn't kneel.

Then she heard nothing more until she heard Dr. Cook's voice asking, "How long has she been like this?"

"An hour before we called you. We thought she'd just fainted," Stanley said. "We knew she was exhausted."

Aleta realized that the scarf was gone. When had it been removed?

Stanley's words told her he knew she was awake.

"You still can't speak," Stanley said gently. "Please squeeze my hand if you understand."

Aleta wasn't sure if she squeezed it or not.

"I felt that, Aleta," said the soft, deep voice she loved. "You saved them all, Aleta, even the driver of the florist truck. No one died today."

She squeezed his hand. It was a faint pressure but it was a response.

"She's terribly weak, Wayne," Stanley said.

Aleta could hear the worry in his voice.

"Just keep talking to her," Dr. Cook ordered. "Let me tell the rest of the family she's awake."

Stanley began speaking. "The front of Stella Woodbridge's house was demolished by the explosion. What was left, the fire would have taken care of had the fire department not been given that head start you gave them. As for Bessie's house, it's safe. The tree practically exploded. Its trunk flew straight up and pierced the garage roof and then fell away from the house and caught fire.

"Bessie told Peets she was thinking of building a new studio. She mentioned that his men had missed moving four paintings, but she hadn't said anything. The paintings each had a sign on them that read 'do not touch'. The signs were meant for Hawk not to experiment with them. Peets men obeyed the signs. Bessie is hoping for another miracle.

"The garage is smashed and charred. It's probable that none of her good paintings survived. But Bessie is happy. She says the bomb dug a hold big enough to plant a new tree to replace the one her grandfather planted a hundred years ago. And she's looking forward to finding a miracle in the charred wreckage despite all evidence to the contrary."

Dr. Cook returned, picked up Aleta's wrist, glanced at his watch for a few seconds, and then said, "Better. Are there any more prophecies in your future?"

Aleta smiled wanly.

"This means no sitting in the hospital waiting room, Stanley. Find something else for her to do. It is a minor operation, after all."

Aleta sat up, clapped her hands across her mouth and stared at the doctor.

Dr. Cook turned to Stanley, "You didn't tell her?"

"She magnifies everything. I only told her about the test part."

"Mistake. Big mistake," Dr. Cook snapped.

"Well, yes, with you coming in here and blabbing about the rest," Stanley shot back, irked.

"You didn't think she'd notice you were in the prep room where we put the patients before surgery?"

"I was going to have her wait in the waiting room."

"In the surgical wing?"

"I was going to ask your grandmother to sit with her. But then she started prophesying."""

"You were going to leave a fearful, upset wife with my grandmother?" Dr. Cook asked, perturbed.

"It sounds terrible when you put it like that," Stanley acquiesced.

"How do you want me to put it?" Dr. Cook charged.

"I was going to leave one prophet in the hands of another prophet."

"Wow! You lawyers are really good!"

"You doctors are the same," Stanley spat back, losing his cool. "You're the one who is proclaiming this is a minor operation when, in fact, it is a biopsy and I could lose my leg."

Aleta gasped.

"Worst case scenario," Dr. Cook said hastily. Then he answered Aleta's unspoken questions. "There's a tiny tumor pressing on the nerve in his ankle. It's an odd place for a tumor and we need to look at it."

He turned to Stanley.

"You scared her," Dr. Cook accused.

"It's what she thought the minute she heard about the operation. I haven't been able to hide the pain from her."

Aleta nodded.

Dr. Cook relaxed. "He reads you well, doesn't he?"

"She nodded again.

"I still don't want you hanging around the hospital."

Aleta shrugged.

"I don't know what you can do. There must be a million things."

"She can watch my mother in court," Stanley decided.

Aleta shook her head and gestured to say she was going to be with him.

"And mess up my mother's concentration?" Stanley questioned.

Aleta hung her head.

"She'll be in court," Stanley told the doctor.

Aleta nodded. It was an order.

CHAPTER 13

Monday morning Aleta dressed for work. Stanley did as well. He planned to check in at the office before going to the hospital.

Aleta wondered fleetingly if he would be back.

Stanley had asked his father to escort Aleta to court to watch the city dog park trial. He said he might be detained at the hospital. If he could, he would try to make some of the trial. If he were detained too long, he would go straight to the office and work on the School Board presentation. The Board had shoved its meeting forward a week to avoid too big a crowd over what they suspected was going to be a controversial issue.

Aleta was glad that today would consist mostly of being a spectator.

His secretary reminded Stanley that Brittany and Sophia had a one o'clock appointment.

"I won't forget," Stanley answered her a bit forcefully.

Despite his tenseness, his mother relaxed. She knew Stanley hated medical procedures, even minor ones. That he didn't ask anyone to cover these appointments caused her to glance at Aleta and give her an assuring wink.

Today was the biopsy, Aleta told herself. There would be time for discussion after the results were known.

She returned her mother-in-law's wink with a smile.

The scarf had only been partly to remind her not to speak when she woke in the morning. It had another purpose. She now realized he had not wanted her to ask questions. He hated discussing options before the facts were known.

The Willow Glen police officer assigned to Aleta drove her off to court as soon as Hubert mentioned that they needed to leave early in order to be assured of getting a seat. The associates had already left.

When Stanley left the office a short time later, he found that he too had a police escort-- none other than Chief Lyle West.

"The hospital is my bailiwick," Lyle commented, smiling.

"You have men," Stanley quipped.

"They're busy," Lyle said, opening the passenger side door.

"I'm in no danger," Stanley protested.

"Stop trying to be brave. I'm here mostly as a friend."

As he sank into the seat, Stanley's bravado collapsed.

"We spend entirely too much time with Taekman and Cook."

"And Chesney," Lyle added, climbing in behind the wheel.

"Until Aleta came, I'd never even seen the inside of the Tri-City Hospital, and now I feel as if I know every square inch.

"When you are able to ride in a wheelchair, I will show you a couple places you haven't seen," Lyle said as he pulled onto Second Street.

"I will be back in the office at noon," Stanley declared.

"You're going to be in the hospital a bit longer than that," Lyle countered. "A room has been reserved for you."

"I have a one o'clock appointment," Stanley said. "And I meet with the School board tonight."

Lyle's voice was gentle, but firm.

"Not tonight. Maybe next week."

"Stanley was quiet for several minutes before he spoke.

"My grandfather died of bone cancer. It ended in his leg."

"I know," Lyle said. "But this is a tumor."

"Cook told you?"

"My parents told me," Lyle said. "Our families have both been here a long time. I'm surprised Aleta didn't come."

"I ordered her not to."

"I thought you did that only for her own good."

"Lyle, she was so exhausted yesterday we had to call Dr. Cook."

"So you sent her to watch Lydia."

"My mother is always exciting to watch. Whatever will happen will happen. Aleta worrying won't change anything, but it could hurt her."

"Our silent prophet did a fantastic job," Lyle declared. "The truck driver will testify against Mrs. Fouts. We got a search warrant and found a number of bombs in Stuart's room. The sheriff's men are searching the Conan farm this morning. I sent Hawk to help because Peets said they had looked in every room and they didn't find the bomb paraphernalia."

"So are Hawk's parents gone?" Stanley asked, willing to discuss matters other than his upcoming procedure.

"They left last night," Lyle reported, happy to switch to a neutral subject. "Hawk said Paige turned the visit around after talking with several of the women at the barbecue—your mother and Bertha, as well as Lauren and Aleta."

"So how did that help?" Stanley asked.

"Bertha gave her a direction. She told her caretakers are under tremendous stress and it brings out the worst in some people."

"Well, I guess an explanation might help some."

"Paige did more than listen. She acted." Lyle explained.

He then told Stanley about the activities Paige had set up for Hawk's parents sans Grandma.

"Were they happy when they left?"

"Hawk's mother complained that she had hardly spent any time alone with Hawk," Lyle said.

"How did he handle that guilt trip?"

"He was smiling when he told me he promised her that he and Paige would watch Grandma any weekend they visited. He said he could see her eyes light up."

"Paige is a sharp young woman," Stanley said.

"Her mother taught her well," Lyle agreed. "Did you know your mother offered to be her friend?"

"My mother?"

"You've seen her as a judge too long."

"Aleta found her soft side. I didn't know she had one."

"Does Aleta know?" Lyle asked, referring to the upcoming procedure."

"No. I implied it wasn't serious," Stanley responded.

"Half-truths are whole lies," Lyle said. "That's a Yiddish proverb."

"Is it your job to make me feel bad?" Stanley asked.

"When you deserve it, it most definitely is. You shut everyone out. I know you're basically a private man, but women don't like that."

"Dr. Cook gave Aleta all the facts," Stanley said defensively.

"But you scrambled them, didn't you?"

Neither spoke again until Lyle pulled in front of the Emergency entrance.

"I'm not an emergency."

"Which is why we're going in this way," West said stiffly. "I'm still in charge of your safety."

"You're not going to watch them operate, are you?"

"You're not leaving my sight."

"You just don't want to stand watch in a bare hallway for an hour."

"Watching them cut off your leg will be much more exciting."

"Lyle!" Stanley gasped. "Where's your sensitivity?"

"Buried with you ability to face reality."

"I don't want to face reality."

"And I don't want to be sensitive."

"I'm not inviting you to my bedside when I'm dying," Stanley proclaimed as they walked through the door.

"I will invite myself," Lyle declared.

"You would, wouldn't you?"

"That's a promise."

"Thanks," Stanley said. "Now let's get on with this leg chopping session."

Dr. Cook heard the exchange.

"What's this about chopping? I didn't take off the whole morning," he said leading the way to the elevator.

"Don't make promises you might not be able to keep," Stanley cautioned. "And, by the way, Lyle plans to be in the operating room. He's going to guard me from anyone from the outside killing me. You guys get first crack."

Dr. Taekman entered the elevator with the group.

"We aren't going to kill you," he said.

"You do know which leg you're operating on, don't you?"

"The one with the scar," Dr. Taekman said.

"They both have scars," Stanley retorted. "Get me a pen and I will mark it."

"You will not!" Michael said. "I know which leg it is. It's your right leg."

"Left!" Stanley declared.

"Which is on my right, right?"

"I will get a marking pen," Lyle said. "You do know which leg it is, Stanley, don't you?'

"It's the one that hurts."

When the nurse took Stanley into pre-op, Lyle turned to the two doctors.

"We are kidding, aren't we? He's not losing his leg."

"It's a strange place for a tumor," Dr. Taekman remarked.

"He's not ready," Lyle said.

"He signed the release," Dr. Cook said.

Lyle looked surprised. "He did?"

"Most tumors are benign," Dr. Taekman said. "But with his family history, the odds aren't favorable."

"And you told him this?"

"Of course," Dr. Cook said. "He's not an ostrich. He faces danger."

"He ordered Aleta to court, you know," Lyle said.

"I helped with that," Dr. Cook said.

"She wouldn't have been able to handle being here?" Lyle questioned, a tinge of surprise coloring his tone.

"Aleta is a very strong woman when it comes to handling the truth," Dr. Cook commented.

"He made appointments," Lyle remarked.

"He didn't want to worry anyone," Dr. Cook responded.

"He's smarter than I thought. He's actually handling Aleta's cases right now. He knows she'll take care of them," Lyle mused aloud. "So he figures the tumor is cancerous and you're going to remove it before it infects the bone."

"The cancer is in the bone in the ankle," Dr. Taekman corrected. "Osteosarcoma."

"The pain is in his thigh," Lyle argued.

"Referred pain is our guess," Dr. Taekman offered.

"That's because it was recently wounded by a bullet," Dr. Cook added.

"My God!" Lyle exclaimed. "How long has he known?"

"We did the biopsy last week," Dr. Cook said.

"You're going to cut off his leg!" Lyle gasped.

"Half a leg," Dr. Taekman said.

"Are you supposed to be telling me this?"

"You're the only one we're allowed to tell," Dr. Cook said. "He knew you'd be here. You're going to break the news to Aleta and his mother."

"Me?"

"Sure," Dr.Cook said. "He says you owe him."

"I owe him? That would mean that he will owe me."

Dr. Cook grinned. ""That's what he said you'd say. He said to tell you he will give you one day for each member of his family you tell."

"That's not near enough!" Lyle blurted out.

"You've got about twenty minutes," Dr. Cook said. "Better go mark that leg."

"You guys won't mess up, will you?"

"Keep him relaxed," Dr. Cook said.

"I don't relax him," Lyle protested.

"Sure you do," Dr. Cook said.

"I'm doing a doctor's work," Lyle grumbled. "Where do I find a thick black marking pen?"

"Don't look at me," Dr. Taekman said. "I only use purple pens."

"For Pete's sake, give me your purple pen," Lyle demanded. "Why do I get all the nasty jobs? I'm not paid enough for this."

Dr. Taekman offered him a pen. Lyle grabbed it and stormed away.

"Won't he upset him?" Dr. Taekman asked.

"Not a chance. He'll yell at him and Stanley will yell back, and that will relax him."

"It wouldn't relax me," Dr. Taekman commented.

"I will remember that if ever I need to chop your leg off."

"Let's scrub up," Dr. Taekman said. "You aren't too close to this one, are you?"

"Closer than most, but then so are you. That's why Stanley chose us."

Lyle stormed into the hospital room where Stanley was sitting up in the hospital bed and shouted, "You toyed with me!"

"I didn't. I just didn't tell you everything all at once. Nothing you said was undeserved."

"For God's sake, Stanley..." Lyle started.

"I did talk with Him, you know. I planned to talk with Aleta on Sunday. And you know what kind of a weekend we had. It didn't seem important right then."

"She should be here crying over you, not me."

"It would be too much for her. She and I will grieve together after."

"You're too calm."

"Are you going to mark my leg or not?"

"I got Taekman's purple marker," Lyle said.

"I guess that will do."

Lyle pulled back the covers.

"What do you want me to write?"

"On the right leg write 'malpractice is in your future. Wrong leg.' Put the last in caps. Doctors don't like to read too many words."

Lyle painstakingly printed the words.

"I may run out of ink."

"Don't. And stop tickling."

"I didn't know you were ticklish."

"I'm not."

"It's done," Lyle announced after another couple minutes. "What do you want to say on your other leg? Should I print 'right leg'?"

"And have Taekman think that's my right leg. He knows to take off the left one."

"We could say 'left leg'."

"He might think we're sending him to the other leg," Stanley said. "You know you have to keep everyone in the dark until Mother has finished her argument."

"Concentrate on what we're going to put on your leg, the one with the cancer," Lyle ordered.

"That's it!" Stanley said. "Put 'leg with cancer'."

As Lyle was writing, Stanley said, "Aleta will have to take the School board meeting tonight. She can't know before then."

"How am I supposed to do that?" Lyle asked.

"Put me in the room with the bulletproof glass. It has two beds. Tell her she can spend the night because it will be easier to guard both of us here."

"That's a stretch."

"You know she won't leave. She never does," Stanley said.

"She'll want to be here when you wake up," Lyle said.

The orderly arrived. "Time to go."

"You'll think of something," Stanley said as he was moved onto the gurney.

"Lie?"

"You can't lie to Aleta," Stanley murmured.

Lyle walked beside him. "You don't believe in making things easy, do you?"

"The course of several lives will depend on Aleta being at the School board meeting tonight."

As the doors to the operating room opened, Lyle said, "I will handle it."

Shortly afterward, the operation began.

Every so often one of the doctors would ask Lyle West how he was holding up. West would choke out, " Fine".

Fine was the furthest thing from the truth, but Lyle knew they'd invite him to leave if he said anything else. He was glad Lauren had insisted he carry handkerchiefs. When he saw the nurses wipe the doctors' brows, he took one out and used it to blot his eyes, which were tearing up despite his efforts to remain stoic.

What happened to the first stage of grief—denial, he wondered.

He'd plunged straight into whatever stage created tears. He had joked with Stanley about wanting to watch the doctors chop off his leg. He never dreamed it would happen.

The thing he knew is that Stanley would expect him to do it. Even if Stanley didn't, he expected himself to do it.

He knew from the outset he wasn't prepared for this. He'd seen severed limbs and carried on. He'd even watched doctors operate on prisoners and held it together.

I can do this, he told himself repeatedly. The first part where the skin was excised and folded back to make the end flap for the leg was almost bearable.

As the operation progressed, he couldn't help but want to stop it, to protest the severing of a limb, to shout out that there must be another way. He guessed he was in the denial stage. He was denying that this procedure was necessary.

The tears stopped when the anger took over.

I'm not doing this right, Lyle berated himself inwardly. I'm not handling it right.

I have to think, Lyle told himself. I have a job to do and only until noon to figure out how. When court breaks, Aleta will head straight here to check on Stanley. She will expect him to be ready to go back to the office.

As he began to think of how to carry out Stanley's wishes, his mind stopped focusing on the operation and he managed to survive the placing of the severed leg on a tray. It was draped and removed from the operating theater.

Lyle watched them hang another pint of blood and wondered if Stanley had asked his parents to donate. For some reason that small, ordinary question brought to Lyle's mind the realization that this was a major operation. With that thought came the awareness of the tremendous loss Stanley was undergoing. Tears sprang unbidden into his eyes. He dabbed them surreptitiously.

Then he forced himself back to the task Stanley had given him. As he did so, a plan emerged.

CHAPTER 14

Chief Tom Milani met the Praetzel family outside the courtroom. He led them to a quiet room.

"I'm doubling the guard on you, Aleta. I want you in one of two places right now—your office or the courtroom."

Aleta looked distressed.

Tom continued, "Chief West said to tell you that Stanley is in Recovery right now. The operation went well. Aleta, Stanley asked that you take his one o'clock appointment with Brittany and Sophia. He also wants you to take his place at the School board meeting tonight."

Aleta's distress was more pronounced.

Tom hurried on, "Chief West is asking that none of you visit now. He's afraid Mrs. Fouts may have a tail on you and West doesn't want you to lead that tail to Stanley. Aleta, I will sneak you in tonight after the School board meeting. Chief West has arranged for you to spend the night.

Aleta's face brightened.

"Can we talk with him?" his mother asked.

"Not yet," Tom answered.

"Can we talk to the doctor?" Lydia persisted. "I need information."

"Please, for Stanley's sake, don't call the hospital. He's under an assumed name," Tom reported. "Don't blow his cover."

"Do you think Mrs. Fouts is that clever?" Lydia asked.

"She almost blew up three women over the weekend," Tom replied. "If Aleta hadn't prophesied, they would be dead. West's men turned away the floral delivery to the Brennans, but the one to Bessie Dobbins got through. So did the delivery to Stella Woodbridge's house. A child accepted the delivery of the vase of flowers, which we assume was addressed to Stella Woodbridge. Tonia Morales was tempted by a kitten with a voice-activated bomb that was placed at her back door."

"How come the police at Bessie Dobbins didn't stop the delivery?" Hubert asked.

"Clear vase, just stems in the water," Chief Milani responded. "On top of that it was addressed to Bessie Dobbins, not Stella Woodbridge. It was delivered by the Oakwood Flowers truck and the driver was wearing the uniform they all recognized."

"Very clever," Hubert said. "Especially, the kitten one."

"At this point, I'm following Chief West's lead," Tom said. "He says no visitors, no phone calls, no calls to the doctors."

"This is too weird," Lydia protested. "I don't like it."

"Stanley agreed to letting Chief West be in charge, West is being overcautious, but we almost lost several good men this past weekend because we underestimated how clever Mrs. Fouts was and what lengths she would go to protect her son from going to prison."

"Come on, Lydia," Hubert said. "You'll have to agree those attacks were terribly clever. I don't like the fact that she switched tactics with Tonia Morales."

"I guess." Lydia temporized. "I agree that right now Stanley is pretty vulnerable, but we need to know how he is."

"That's the good news," Tom interjected. "West has arranged for you to meet with both doctors at eight tonight."

"At the hospital?" Lydia asked hopefully.

"At Stanley's house," Tom replied. "We don't want the family anywhere near the hospital. As for you, Aleta, Lyle says that Stanley is ordering you to go to the school board meeting."

Aleta nodded.

"So you're going to do it?" Lydia asked.

Aleta nodded again.

"Chief West will pick you up there when it is over."

As the group left for the office where lunch was waiting, Lydia whispered to her husband, "This smells fishy."

Hubert nodded and hissed, "Don't upset Aleta."

"I guess I can wait until tonight," Lydia said loudly enough so that Aleta heard her. "I do have to focus on my case. Leave it to Stanley to keep our noses to the grindstone."

Aleta smiled. The firm was very important to her husband. She, personally, was certain that something had gone wrong during the operation. Tom had said he was okay, so it's not that serious, that is, it's not life threatening.

"And it's just like Stanley not to want us thinking about him when we have important cases in the final stages," Lydia concluded.

Once back in the office, Aleta sought out Tim Jordan and told him that he was going to speak for her at the School board meeting that evening. She handed him her prepared arguments and told him to practice them after he sat in on the appointment with Brittany and Sophia. At two she told him she planned to go back to court to listen to Lydia cross-examine the plaintiff. Hubert heard her and promised to save her a seat.

"After the jury has the case," she typed on the computer while Tim stood watching, "you and I will practice your speaking as I'm typing. We need to be as smooth as possible. Then we need to go over your introduction."

"Mine?" he asked.

She nodded as she typed, "You're good at that. And tell Alice to order supper for us and to tell Bertha I won't be home for supper."

"I'm just wondering," Tim said, "why you are so intent on going to watch the dog park case."

"Because the plaintiff is Charlene Brockbank who is Carlton Brockbank's mother. She will be at the School board meeting tonight and I want to be prepared."

The last half of the operation hadn't interfered with Chief Lyle West fine-tuning the plan in his mind. He hadn't dared focus on what he was witnessing. He had surmised that if he became engrossed in what was happening on the operating table, he would become so caught up in the drama of the moment that he would fail his best friend.

When Stanley was rolled into the recovery room, Lyle followed him. He pulled a chair up to the side of his bed and he made one brief call.

"Tom, he's in Recovery and he's doing fine," Lyle reported almost an hour after the court had adjourned for lunch.

"That's it?" Stanley had muttered.

Lyle looked at his friend and asked him if that was the truth.

"I'm feeling rotten," Stanley replied.

"I didn't say you were feeling fine," Lyle stated. "I said you were doing fine. You're in a hospital recovery room, for Pete's sake. You're supposed to be feeling rotten."

"I don't want to feel rotten," Stanley snapped.

"He's complaining, Tom. Everything is normal," Lyle reiterated.

"So he wasn't on his way to Recovery when you called before?" Tom asked.

"Things were going well," Lyle said. "It took over four hours, Tom. If he wasn't in Recovery, there would have been no stopping that family."

"So is he really okay?"

"He's alive and the doctors are pleased. They told me the operation went very well. They don't anticipate any complications."

"You've never lied to me before," Tom said, his tone transmitting his displeasure.

"Tom, I honestly thought we were minutes away from being done," Lyle admitted. "They both said something about being glad that was over and I thought it was only going to be minutes before he'd be rolled out of there and I knew court was going to recess for lunch. I thought I was only jumping five minutes ahead. I'm sorry Tom. I guess the bottom line is I was rattled."

"I can live with that. It must have been hard watching that operation."

"Yes," Lyle admitted. "It was the hardest thing I've ever done."

"At least you didn't ask me to lie," Tom said. "I think I'm actually grateful you miscalculated."

"Thanks for understanding, Tom."

When he finished talking to Tom Milani, Chief Lyle West looked at Stanley.

"I'm not a complainer," Stanley said referring to a crack made in the middle of the conversation with Milani.

"You are when you're feeling rotten."

"Did you do what I asked?"

"When have I had time?"

"Lyle, it was important."

"I took care of half of the list."

"Which half?"

"Well, Aleta's not here, is she?"

"Did you tell her?"

"Not yet."

"Did you tell anyone?"

"I told Tom," Lyle said. "I did that an hour ago, so he could tell them you were in Recovery and everything had gone well."

"How far along was the operation when you told Tom it was over?"

"The leg was resting in the morgue."

"What's it doing there?"

"That's where they keep bodies they are going to autopsy."

"It's a leg, Lyle."

"It's dead," Lyle retorted.

"I know that," Stanley shot back.

"Do you want me to arrange for you to witness the autopsy of your leg?"

"That's the most macabre suggestion I believe you've ever made," Stanley said. "Is that why it's there?"

"I don't even know it's there actually. It was rolled out of here on a gurney and I made an assumption."

"How's our patient?" Dr. Taekman asked entering the room.

"Drifting in and out of consciousness," Lyle said. "Is morphine supposed to make one irritable?"

"I'm not irritable," Stanley said. "I asked Lyle to do a few simple chores for me and instead he's been guarding me."

"That's my job," Lyle said.

"I'm in no danger," Stanley said. "You have Stuart Fouts under lock and key."

"Not exactly."

"What's that mean? You arrested him in Florida. I was there. I remember."

"Judge Gutterude was handling arraignments when Stuart Fouts was arraigned on the new charges—you know, the ones involving Doyle and his mother. Since he had jumped bail, no one thought Judge Gutterude would release him on bail again. That little jaunt to Florida cost him twenty five thousand. But then Gray Zenon persuaded the judge that Stuart needed time to make arrangements for his mother's care, so Judge Gutterude doubled his bail to fifty thousand and released him."

"She was arrested!" Stanley exclaimed. "She tried to kill every witness against her son."

"He'd already released Stuart when he found out we had arrested the mother on the bombing charges," Lyle said. "Zenon handled that arraignment on a temporary basis.

He told Judge Gutterude that he believes that she will plead insanity. He said he wasn't handling her case and didn't know about her arrest when he was in court earlier. He apologized nicely it seems. Then he persuaded Judge Gutterude to lock her up in a mental institution so she could be evaluated. Fouts had persuaded Zenon to get her placed in a facility with two psychiatrists on staff."

"Is Zenon still acting for the public defender's office?"

"Yes," Lyle said. "Judge Clancy locked him into that case, but the mother has one of the top criminal firms in Chicago representing her. Zenon is working with them. I think he's hoping that will result in them offering him a position."

"So I'm really not safe, am I?" Stanley said. "You really have been guarding me."

"Fouts is wearing a bracelet. He's being monitored," Lyle said.

"He's probably already slipped out of that and paid someone else to wear it."

"We have eyes on him as well. He's not stepping a toe out of line."

"How many banks has he visited?"

"A couple."

"Two? Three? Five?"

"Four." Lyle said. "His mother has accounts in two. He has access to her money, but he is being careful about only using it for her expenses. He has a small account in another bank. In the fourth one he has a safety deposit box."

"The money isn't stashed in it," Stanley stated. "It's a red herring."

"We searched his mother's house with a warrant when we were looking for bomb making materials," Lyle said. "No one uncovered any large amounts of cash."

"No one was looking for that."

"We looked everywhere."

"Where did you find the bomb paraphernalia?"

"In the basement."

"Did anyone look in Stuart's room?"

"Yes."

"And his mother's room?"

"Yes," Lyle said. "We suspected he might have squirreled some away just in case the house was searched."

"So you took Hawk?"

"No, but Tom's men did a thorough job," Lyle said. "Mrs. Fouts isn't Stuart. She didn't hide the stuff very well."

"That's where the money is," Stanley said. "And Stuart hid it."

"None of the listed money has shown up."

"We gave them the list," Stanley said. "They knew they weren't to spend that money locally. My guess is that Stuart took it to make sure no one would slip up. I can't see him trusting Lennie or Butch to follow orders not to spend the bills on the list."

"I think that's exactly what he did," Lyle said. "Think about it, Stanley. What better place to hide it?"

"I don't follow," Stanley said.

Dr, Cook entered.

"We're moving you up to 406," he said.

"I'm keeping you under police protection, Mr. Stanley," Lyle said as the orderlies entered the room. "You're far too vulnerable, even on the fourth floor."

While the orderlies transferred Stanley to the gurney, his attention was focused on the last suggestion Lyle had regarding the ransom money. As he was being wheeled out of the intensive care ward, he asked the men to wait a minute.

They hesitated in the doorway and Stanley said, "I think you're right, Lyle. He's too smart to hold on to the bills I put on the list even though I gave the list to him with the money. All I had to do was memorize the numbers on a couple of the bills."

"And did you?"

"Aleta did. She has this head for figures."

"Are you working on a case?" Dr. Cook asked.

"Yes," Lyle admitted.

"I want him to rest," Dr. Cook said.

"I will leave. I have to go arrest Peets."

"What did he do?" Dr. Cook asked.

"Butch is lonely," West said. "How is Lennie doing by the way?"

"He's going to make it."

"I have an idea about how you can get Butch to open up," Stanley said.

"Dr. Cook says you need to rest, so I'm leaving," Lyle said. "Remember, don't eat anything. I will bring you a cup of soup tonight."

"I will bring Mr. Stanley his soup," Dr. Cook said. "I don't want him working. I want him resting."

"Not chicken soup," Stanley called as he was wheeled down the hallway toward the elevator. I hate chicken soup."

After the elevator doors closed, Lyle looked at Dr. Cook and asked, "Is he going to be all right?"

"Would you be if you were him?"

"I hate to leave him," Lyle said.

"What errands did he give you?"

"I'm to tell his family what happened after the court day is done, except for Aleta. I'm to tell her after the School board meeting."

"Won't they descend on the hospital at noon when he doesn't return to the office?"

"Tom is taking care of that," Lyle said. "By the way, you're meeting with the family tonight at eight at Stanley's house."

"Why?"

"Because I won't be able to answer all their questions."

"Are you setting me up to tell them?"

"No, I will manage to do that before your meeting."

"I'm bringing Michael."

"That's what I told Tom to tell them," Lyle said. "You're sure Stanley will be all right?"

"He needs to rest," Dr. Cook remarked. "His body has under gone a serious trauma."

"I could sit quietly. I don't need to engage him in conversation," Lyle said.

"Take care of the tasks he gave you. He's not able to handle the emotional outbursts that will result from his family learning about the decision he made without consulting any of them. And right now he needs to live with it for a while himself."

"You're the doctor," Lyle acquiesced. "My job is to protect him."

Stanley dozed during the ride up the elevator. He didn't know he had done so until he found himself in a new bed and heard the orderlies talking as they were leaving the room.

"Should we tell the doctor?"

"We forgot the chart," the other orderly said. "We'll tell the nurse he didn't wake up when you took his vitals. Hand her the slip you wrote them on and she can put it on the chart. We're due for a break."

"Poor bastard," the first orderly said. "One of my friends lost his leg in Iraq and when he got back, his wife divorced him."

"Most wives wouldn't."

"She said that his stump was a big turn-off."

Stanley lay back and thought about the conversation he had just heard.

He knew Aleta would be upset because he didn't tell her, but he never even considered the possibility that she would divorce him.

I've been sent a reality check, he concluded. What was I thinking?

He lifted the sheet and stared at his bandaged leg lying under the protective hood. There was no foot at the end of it. It was almost surreal the way it just ended mid-calf.

Stanley let the sheet drop and closed his eyes.

Lyle had said I would owe him deputy time if he told everyone about the amputation of my leg, but I know full well that Lyle will never collect. I can't function as a police officer with only one leg.

Lyle needs a man beside him with two legs. Even as a sharpshooter for the force, I would be limited. Lyle had climbed on top of a roof once. I can't do that. More than once I have been called upon to shoot from uneven terrain. That takes balance--balance I no longer have.

His mind continued to ruminate upon the changes that the loss of his leg would visit upon his everyday life. Try as he would, the concept of balance clung to his mind the same way a cat's claws cling to a sweater. You can't shake some things loose.

So, think about balance, he told himself. What do I do that takes balance?

Dancing with Aleta was one. They had been doing that almost every night. They both enjoyed it and together they had become more and more proficient. He had taken a few private lessons and had pleasantly surprised her with new moves. He had planned to keep doing that. He was half way through learning the rumba and had found it exciting. He knew Aleta would love it.

He had been told that he had to learn to walk again with a prosthesis. He had been told he'd be awkward at first. No one thought he'd ever be able to dance again. One therapist warned him that if he did dance, he'd be limited to the simplest of moves.

And he was just learning how to ride a horse. That took balance. He wondered if he could ever jump a horse. It was not something he had as a goal, but he didn't want to lose the option of being able to choose to do it just once. Aleta said there was nothing as thrilling as sailing through the air on a horse.

What about their other hobby—dog showing?

He couldn't show Tank any more. There's no way he could do the twisting and turning and the minute adjustments necessary without a good sense of balance. He'd stumble and possibly fall. Or he'd trip his dog. That would be worse.

He wouldn't have to get up with the baby at night. That was not necessarily a plus. He liked doing that once he'd shaken off the last vestiges of sleep. He could foresee the necessity for a nurse at night after Michael was born. He liked the fact that Aleta and he were alone at night. He savored privacy.

How many other things am I going to have to give up, he wondered.

His mind jumped from one thought to the next in no particular order.

Unless he wore a prosthesis, he couldn't pilot a plane or drive a car.

A man in a wheelchair would be at a decided disadvantage in a courtroom. He would have to raise his hand instead of stand to command attention.

Why am I thinking that I am going to be in a wheelchair, he wondered. They fit artificial limbs before one even leaves the hospital. I will walk out of here.

Will Aleta ever look at me the same, he thought. How could she?

She will pity me, he surmised. She won't leave me. She will take pity on me. That's not what I want.

What do I want?

Not to have lost a leg, he realized. That's what I want. I want to be whole again. I want to rethink this all again. I want to find another solution. I don't want to live with the solution I chose.

The bottom line is that I don't think I got rid of the cancer. I didn't defeat it. I chopped off half my leg, but the oncologist that I hate was right. I temporized. I needed to lose the whole leg.

The cancer is still there. I know it. Dr. Taekman and Dr. Cook both felt that I should amputate above the knee. The cancer had already invaded the bone at the ankle, which meant that it was probably in the lower leg bone as well.

"How was losing only half a leg any better than losing the whole leg? I didn't save any ability to do anything."

Why was saving my knee so important?

Why when I drew my line in the sand, did it fall below the knee? Why couldn't lose my knee? Was it because the knee has the unique ability to twist the leg as well as bend it? Doing without the foot and ankle was nearly incomprehensible. I know I considered it. I honestly did consider it. What did I think—that it would be easier if I chopped off my leg in stages? I think that's exactly what I did think. I thought it would be easier to lose half a leg than to lose the whole leg. I was wrong. This is an unbearable loss. Saving my knee doesn't mitigate my loss one bit. But for some inexplicable reason I couldn't give up my knee. I was clinging to the remote possibility that there was still a chance I could beat this cancer and save that precious piece of my leg. But deep down I know that the cancer is still there. It had invaded the bone marrow. The blood took it from the ankle to the leg and it didn't stop mid-calf.

There is nothing I am certain about except that I have taken the first step. I have rid myself of the part of my leg infected with cancer. I have taken a radical step. I feel as if all God was asking me to do was to take this first step. He didn't ask me to do more. This was all He asked.

Then why am I so miserable? If I did what God was asked, why am I not at peace?

Why am I not happy? Not only am I not happy, I am unhappier than I can ever remember being.

I want my leg back.

He looked around the empty room and despair overtook him.

All my life I've struggled with being ugly and just when an accident allows me to fix my face so it's a bit more pleasing, I am suddenly plunged into the role of cripple.

"God, I want my leg back!" Stanley cried aloud.

In the silence that surrounded him, he never felt more alone.

CHAPTER 15

In the Intensive Care Unit at the lowest level of the hospital, the ICU nurse discovered that the orderlies had taken the patient and left his chart attached to the bed. Muttering, she called administration and asked what room had been reserved for Mr. Stanley. She realized as she was doing so that the orderlies had been caught up in the discussion between the patient and the police chief. Mitch wouldn't have made such a mistake otherwise. Charlie on the other hand was a flake. She didn't want to get Mitch in trouble, so she was circumspect when she solicited the information.

When Mitch came down with the scrap of paper on which Charlie had written the patient's vitals, she was tempted to doubt their veracity, but she thrust the chart at Charlie and told him to copy his reading onto the chart. He was in a hurry but she insisted he come back to sign the chart.

"Put down that he was sleeping," Mitch prodded.

Charlie did that and handed the nurse the chart.

"Did you put down the room he was moved to?" Mitch asked.

"No need," the nurse said. "I called Administration and they told me."

"But…" Mitch started.

"She knows," Charlie cut in impatiently. "Let's go."

Mitch smiled at the nurse. "Thanks for covering for us."

The nurse sent the chart up to Room 232 with a volunteer nurse's aid. The young woman, not seeing the head nurse anywhere, went to Room 232 and fastened the chart on the end of the bed.

She was surprised that the bed was empty, but not alarmed. It was not uncommon for a patient to be moved somewhere else for a test temporarily. He would be returned when the test was done. She said nothing to the ICU nurse about the patient not being in the bed.

The nurse on the second floor told the head nurse at shift change that Mr. Stanley had not arrived from intensive care.

"Why is his chart here?"

"Someone put the chart in the room when I was elsewhere. I called Administration and they said that this room that was reserved for him. Something must have happened during transport. Sooner or later someone will find a patient without a chart and call administration and it will be straightened out," the floor nurse said. "All I know is that he's not on this floor."

Meanwhile, on the fourth floor the new head nurse found two guards on the door to Room 406. She entered the room and looked for the chart. Not finding one, she went to her station and fastened a blank form to a clipboard and carried it back to the room with her.

She found the patient asleep and took his vitals. She went into the hall and asked the guards the name of the patient.

"Mr. Stanley..." the one guard began.

His partner cut him off abruptly.

"That's it. Mr. Stanley. We weren't told his first name."

The nurse wrote that name on the chart. She checked the IV bags and noted what he was being given. The meds were standard ones. She didn't worry. She'd check with ICU and see if there were any special orders.

A short time later, Hawkins Monroe entered Room 232 and saw that the food on the tray had been uneaten.

"Good," he murmured. "Someone warned Stanley."

He glanced at the chart and saw that his vitals had been taken within the last two hours and he relaxed. Things were looking good for Stanley. He wondered briefly where he was, but he wasn't worried. Stanley hadn't eaten the food. That had been his biggest worry. His job was to test for poison. Since Stanley hadn't eaten any of the food, he wouldn't need to rush the tests.

He emptied each of the plates of food into separate bags and put them in his kit. He headed straight for his lab.

A short time later, the nurse, seeing that the food tray was empty, put it in the hall to be picked up. She noted on the patient's chart that he had eaten his entire meal. She hadn't seen him rolled into his room or out, but she had had a busy afternoon and realized that there were long periods when she was involved with one patient or another. She couldn't believe that he had been transported without her knowledge, but the food on his tray was gone which meant that he had been there long enough to eat supper. She decided to check the floor one more time. She then checked with the entire staff. No one had seen Mr. Stanley. She called Administration and asked if Mr. Stanley had been assigned a new room. She was told that he hadn't. She was about to call ICU when she saw two lights on her board. She vowed to check with ICU after she took care of those two patients.

Down in Emergency, Dr. Cook had been handling one emergency after another all day. He finally got a chance to check into his clinic and one of his interns asked him if he'd eaten. That's when he remembered his promise to Stanley. He headed straight for the hospital kitchen and asked Donno, one of the kitchen help, for a bowl of soup for one of his patients.

"We just finished serving supper and we just cleaned the soup pan," Donno said. "What's the name of the patient?"

"Mr. Stanley."

"I picked up that tray myself," Donno said. "He ate everything on his tray."

"Are you sure?"

"I was a bit surprised because those trays rarely come back that clean," Donno commented. "He even ate the crackers."

"What was on the tray?" Dr. Cook asked, unsatisfied.

"Chicken noodle soup, jello, tea, and crackers," Donno replied.

"He doesn't like chicken soup," Dr. Cook said.

"He must have really been hungry then."

"I guess he was," Dr. Cook said. "Well, as long as he ate, I guess I will head back to the clinic."

Shortly after five, when he was talking to Robert and Bertha," Chief West excused himself and fielded a call from Hawkins Monroe.

"You were right to have me check Stanley's food," Hawk said. "It was poisoned."

I lifted some prints from the tray and ran them against the hospital staff and got a match."

"That doesn't mean she poisoned the food."

"She put the food on the tray and she put the tray on the cart," Hawk said. "I'd start there. Her name's Shawna Smith. She's a new hire."

"Thanks, Hawk."

"I didn't see Stanley in his room," Hawk said. "It was empty."

"Which room?"

"232."

"We moved him."

"A supper tray was delivered to 232."

"That was his original room. Only Dr. Cook and I know which room he's actually in."

"His chart was still there."

"I will check on that," Lyle said.

"What about Shawna Smith?" Hawk worried. "She might disappear after her shift."

"I take care of that first. Dr. Cook did say he was going to personally bring Stanley his supper," Lyle said.

Chief West called French and told him to pick up Shawna Smith and bring her in for questioning. He told him Hawk had analyzed Stanley's supper and found poison.

"Hers were the only fingerprints found on the tray," Lyle added. "See how much information you can get from her without telling her we suspect her."

He turned to Bertha and Robert.

"They delivered the food to the room that was originally reserved for Stanley," Lyle said.

"We figured that out from your conversation with Hawk," Robert said.

"Does the kitchen know to send up meals to his new room?" Bertha asked.

"I'm not allowing hospital food or any other kind of food, except what I deliver," Lyle said. "I volunteered you for breakfast with fresh rolls at seven. I invited both Wayne and Michael."

"So, breakfast for six?" Bertha said, her smile telling her husband she was not only pleased at being given something to do, but she was also pleased that the task needed to be done before her workday began. That meant that making breakfast for Stanley and his visitors was something that she would do as Aleta's mother. Only Robert realized that Bertha treasured being able to do extra things. Those done during her work hours didn't count in her thinking.

"Aleta will be staying for at least a day," Lyle said. "If Dr. Schwartzman is there, he'll expect to eat. Better plan for eight. Chesney always manages to wrangle an invitation. I swear he lives at the hospital."

"He is an obstetrician," Bertha said. "Most women deliver at night. We're too busy during the day."

Both men laughed.

"Andrea just drove in," Bertha said. "You can tell her and Paul while I fix Stanley some soup.'

"Dr. Cook said he'd bring Stanley soup," Lyle said.

"Stanley doesn't like chicken soup."

"He told Dr. Cook that."

"And what do you suppose Dr. Cook did when the kitchen told him that's all they had?" Bertha quipped.

"Did you tell Stanley's parents?" Robert asked.

"I told them first," Lyle said. "They'll be coming over here at eight to meet with Dr. Cook and Dr. Taekman. Please don't tell Aleta. She has that School board meeting tonight."

"I left her at the office with Tim. They were practicing his reading as she typed," Robert said. "How come Stanley told you about his operation?"

"He didn't," Lyle said. "I decided I would be the best one to guard him at the hospital. He will let me accompany him anywhere. Well, that's not true. I have to pull rank on him."

A few minutes later, Bertha handed Lyle a thermos of soup for Stanley.

"I had some homemade beef and vegetable soup in the freezer," Bertha said. " I put it in the microwave. It's too hot now. It should be perfect by the time you get it to the hospital."

"I will just make it there and back in time for the School board meeting." Lyle commented.

"Here's a second thermos for you," Bertha said. "Take time with Stanley. Let French guard Aleta. School board meetings can be pretty dull."

"I just might do that. Reward him for his timely capture of Shawna Smith with guard duty."

"I'm not as worried about Aleta as I am about Stanley," Bertha went on. "If she senses danger she can do something. Stanley can't."

"You have a point," Lyle said. "I will take your suggestion. Stanley is currently completely helpless."

As Chief Lyle West was driving to the hospital, he called French.

"Have you got her?"

"Yes.

"You can't put her in our jail," West said. "We need no distractions for Peets to do his best work."

"I've got her in interrogation. I can keep her there for hours."

"You're taking my place guarding Aleta at the School board meeting tonight. I need to keep an eye on Stanley. There are some lose ends at the hospital I need to clean up. And I'm bringing him soup for supper."

"What do you suggest I do with Shawna Smith?"

"Give her to Gary Donaldson in Willow Glen," Chief West said. "She is involved in an attempt to poison a Willow Glen citizen. We need to concentrate on protecting the two main targets tonight."

"Chief Milani guards their house," French pointed out.

"And we guard the hospital and the high school and that's where the Praetzels are going to be tonight," Chief West said. "Tom needs an important piece of the Stuart Fouts case to sink his teeth into."

"But I'm asking Gary Donaldson to house my prisoner."

"He's on your level," West said. "Tell him you will help him investigate, but tonight you're on guard duty. If he gets anything out of Shawna Smith, he has my permission to follow up any leads at the hospital or elsewhere."

"Should I tell him Peets is using our jail?"

"Of course."

"Peets' method won't work on Butch, you know," Peter French said. "Butch won't do anything without Lennie telling him to."

"There's one exception," Chief West said.

"Peets tell you this?"

"I told him and he agreed."

"What's the exception?"

"You've got all the pieces. You put them together," Chief West said. "You can tell me what you deduced when you deliver Aleta to the hospital. Personally escort her to me. Tell her I have a surprise that she's to take to Stanley."

"Suppose she insists on seeing him immediately."

"Handcuff her and call me," Chief West said sternly. "She's in protective custody. We call the shots."

"Isn't that pretty drastic?"

"I will explain the situation if you need to use the cuffs, but not before. You have your orders."

"Yes, Chief," French said. "I will tell her you ordered me to cuff her if she didn't follow the plan."

"Smart move," West said. "You can tell her that only I can rescind my order."

"She'll be pissed."

"Yes, she will. But she'll be pissed at me, not you."

"There is that," French agreed.

When Peets was escorted into in the cell next to Butch, he was in full uniform. Butch didn't even look up.

"You still here?" Peets asked.

Butch responded to the voice and the question.

"Yeh, I don't know what to do. They won't let me see Lennie."

"He's the guy in the hospital, right?"

"Yeh."

"What you need is a lawyer."

"They give me one only he says he can't do nothing," Butch complained. "He says the cops got a good case."

"You're the guys that pissed off Vannella. Right?"

"We didn't know."

"You held out on him," Peets said. "He's still pissed."

"They beat up Lennie bad."

"He almost died," Peets said.

"I need to see Lennie."

"You need to protect him is what you need to do," Peets stated flatly.

"There was two of them and they had guns."

"I'm talking about in the future."

"My lawyer said I need to plead guilty, but I ain't doing that until Lennie tells me to."

"You need a better lawyer."

"How do I do that?"

"First, you fire the one you've got."

"I told him to go to hell!"

"I guess that'll do," Peets said, smiling.

Butch looked up. Shock mingled with recognition made Butch stutter, "What the hell!"

He scooted backwards on the bench.

"You got a chief's uniform on," he stammered.

Before Peets could explain, Butch rushed on, "If you want to play a cop, you can't pretend to be a chief. Everybody knows who the chiefs are."

"You don't," Peets retorted.

"Sure I do." Butch proclaimed.

"Who's the Police Chief in Willow Glen?"

"Some fat Italian guy, only he ain't connected with the mob. He's a straight cop."

"How about Arborville?"

"Some short, white dude named West. Lennie says he smarter than anybody."

"And Oakwood?"

"A big black guy that don't mess around. If he latches on to you, you'll wind up confessing to everything you done. Lennie always made sure we didn't do no crimes in Oakwood. He says that wasn't a dude he wanted to come up against."

"That was a smart move on Lennie's part," Peets said, smiling.

"Yeh, Lennie's smart."

"So, how come he didn't know the Praetzels were protected?"

"We wasn't robbing nobody around here. We was robbing a rich guy in an RV."

"You did it twice."

"He was rich and we needed the money."

"You got a cut of the money Praetzel paid for the location of a couple of the bombs."

"Yeh, only Lennie says we can't spend it because it has numbers on it that will give us away."

"Why did Lennie take that money and not the unmarked money??

"Because we was given twice what everyone else got."

"Didn't everyone get ten thousand?"

"Yeh, but we got twenty."

"That's because there are two of you."

"I don't scare Stuart none. And Lucas was a whole lot bigger than me."

Rather than try to puzzle out what Butch was thinking, Peets moved back to his agenda. "Was Stuart pissed that you gave Vannella the location of the bombs?"

"We didn't tell him. We didn't tell nobody. Lennie wound up in the hospital and I wound up here in jail before we saw them guys again. Hey, how come you know?"

"I'm a cop. I'm supposed to know," Peets said.

Butch chewed on that statement for a minute and then said, "Yeh, I guess that's right."

"Vannella isn't happy that you held out on him."

"I told him most of what I knew. I can't remember where all the bombs were put. There were too many. Only Stuart and Doyle know that because they planned the whole thing. I just put a couple where I was told. I learned about some of the others when they were arguing over which ones to tell Mr. Praetzel about."

"Do you think that you and Lennie can take that money you got and run and hide?"

"Yeh," Butch said. "That's what Lennie said we was going to do."

"He's going straight from the hospital to jail." Peets said. "And if you don't make things right with Vannella, Lennie's going to get beat up again in prison. Vannella's got guys on the inside."

"So, what do I do?"

"You make a deal that'll let you go over to the hospital to see Lennie."

"Lennie don't like me doing that."

"Just a little deal," Peets said.

"Like what?"

"The location of one more bomb."

"Lennie won't like that."

"Lennie will still have the others to bargain with."

"I guess Lennie would think that was okay."

"You need a good lawyer," Peets said.

"Do you know a good lawyer?"

"I know lots of good lawyers. The best criminal lawyer in Chicago is Kurtz West."

"Is he expensive?"

"He's Vannella's lawyer."

"So, he's gotta be good, huh?"

"You better believe it."

"How much he cost. I ain't got a lot of money."

"The first appointment is free," Peets said. "And he lives in Willow Glen."

"Do you know him?"

"He's a friend of mine."

"All I need is one appointment for Lennie and me together," Butch decided.

"I will arrange it." Peets said.

Then Chief Peets got up and opened his cell door.

"Hey, they didn't lock you in," Butch said.

"I wasn't impersonating the Oakwood Chief of Police," Peets said. "I am the Oakwood Chief of Police."

"I didn't tell you nothing."

"On the contrary, you told me everything I needed to know."

"You already knew everything. You told me."

"I did know a lot. Now I know more."

"Lennie will kill me."

"Not when you bring him a really good lawyer," Chief Peets said. "But don't worry. Kurtz West will be able to make sure I can't use anything you told me in court."

Butch brightened when Chief Peets said that. One thing no one knew about Butch was that he could tell when he was being lied to. Lennie did it all the time, but Butch knew that Lennie just didn't think he'd understand, and he never lied to him about being his friend. This big black chief wasn't a liar at all. When he said that Kurtz West would make sure that nothing he said would be used against him, Butch believed him.

Two hours later, Butch was ushered into Lennie's hospital room.

With Butch were two men. One was wearing the uniform of the Oakwood Chief of Police. The other was a much smaller man, dressed in a very expensive suit.

"Lennie, I got us a really good lawyer," Butch announced. "His name's Kurtz West and the Oakwood Chief is an honest cop. He don't lie at all."

"Did you confess?" Lennie asked.

"That's what the crappy lawyer I had at first wanted me to do, but I didn't. And then Chief Peets told me that if I'd tell him where one more bomb was, he'd see I got to see you and he'd get us a good lawyer. And well, there are lots of bombs left, so I give him one more. Turns out they already found that one, only my giving it counted Chief Peets said. So here I am."

"I will be outside," Chief Peets said. "I will make sure no one interrupts you."

Half an hour later, Kurtz West emerged.

"I need to see Stanley Praetzel," he said. "What room is he in?"

"Are you done?"

"Not yet," Kurtz West said. "I'm guessing my son is with Stanley. I need to see him as well."

"I will watch the prisoner," Chief Peets said.

He turned and entered the room. He had no idea how propitious a decision that would turn out to be.

Kurtz West went up to the fourth floor and walked up to the guards.

"Is my son in there?"

Chief West came to the door.

"Dad, what brings you here?"

"I need to see Stanley."

"Come on in."

"How are you doing, Stanley?' Kurtz West asked the man elevated only slightly in the bed.

"Your son says I'm doing fine," Stanley quipped. "I feel rotten."

"How's your brain?"

"They took off my leg, not my head," Stanley snapped.

"He's not happy because I didn't tell Aleta, even though he told me I couldn't tell her until after the School board meeting and it's not over yet," Lyle explained.

"So he's crabby," Kurtz said. "Is that a good sign or a bad sign?'

"Why are you asking him? He's not a doctor?" Stanley charged.

"He's worried that Aleta won't love him anymore," Lyle stated flatly.

"I didn't tell you that," Stanley protested.

"Well, what else would put you in such a foul mood?"

"Losing half my left leg."

"He's coming to grips with reality," Lyle explained. "Why did you need to see him?"

"Peets volunteered me for a pro bono case. I'm not even sure I should take it, considering the two idiots pissed off Sergio Vannella."

"Lennie and Butch," Stanley guessed quickly, grateful for a change of focus. "Kurtz, they need you. Butch is retarded and Lennie is not only the only friend Butch has, he takes care of him."

"Lennie's a thief," Kurt West pointed out.

"A short, little thief that needs a bodyguard."

"I don't do short, little thieves," Kurtz declared, then paused and said, "That came out wrong."

"Time for you to expand," Stanley said. "Butch is big. He's also retarded."

"You mentioned that."

"That's the point," Stanley said.

"I can get him a reduced sentence."

"You're missing the point. Butch can't function without Lennie."

"You want them both to get reduced sentences?"

"Lennie's too small to make it in prison without Butch."

"They broke the law," Kurtz West said. "Why am I arguing your side?"

"Because Lennie is taking care of Butch. That's a pretty big thing."

"Butch protects him in return," Kurtz West noted.

"And that makes Butch feel good about himself."

"There's no way Lennie will go straight," Kurtz West said. "I speak from years of experience with criminals like Lennie."

"Finding them a job isn't the answer," Stanley said. "Lennie's whole mind-set is geared to the fast snatch. Lots of money. No work. But my guess if that Lennie wants a few other things as well."

"Like what?"

"He doesn't want to go to prison. He doesn't want Vannella mad at him. He doesn't want to give up his dream of making a really big score. He's like a fisherman who enjoys every catch and dreams of the big one at the same time."

"Stanley, I'm a lawyer, not a therapist. I can't straighten out Lennie's mind-set."

"We build on what's positive," Stanley said. "We impress upon Butch that Lennie needs not to anger Sergio Vannella again and he needs not to upset Stanley Praetzel either."

Lyle broke out laughing.

After a minute, Kurtz West joined him.

"The trouble with you two is that neither of you is married to Aleta," Stanley barked.

"I'm not touching that one with a ten foot pole," Lyle said. "What's your point?"

Stanley took a deep breath and plunged in.

"They plead guilty and they get a suspended sentence for the two robberies at the dog shows. Vannella won't be happy if they don't get the maximum, so when they plead they request the maximum. Then, at the request of Stanley Praetzel their sentence for that crime is suspended. In return for my requesting that their sentence be suspended, they have to do one job for me. That's part one of my plan.

"In part two, they return the marked bills extorted from me and agree to testify against Stuart Fouts in exchange for having the charges on accessory to the attempted murder and extortion dropped. We need those bills to get a search warrant for Mrs. Fouts house. I want Fouts to be unable to use my money to fund his defense. That's what I want. And I am willing to give these two an out-of-jail free card to get that."

"That's it?" Kurtz West asked.

"No, there's the job."

"Testifying against Stuart Fouts isn't it?"

"I'm soft on that part. I insist on the money though," Stanley said.

"So, what's the job?" Kurtz West asked.

"Lennie must find out what Butch would like to do for a living—be a plumber's helper, plaster walls, plant trees, guard warehouses at night, drive a garbage truck--and then see that he is trained for that job. Butch's job is to see that Lennie doesn't break the law while they are serving their suspended sentences, because if they do, they will both go back to jail, but not together. That's the kicker. They get to stay together if they obey my rules."

"That just might work," Kurtz said. "The one thing they both value is their friendship. I think you've just handed me the key. Friendship is a good foundation to build a new life on."

"Can you sell it?" Stanley asked.

"Stanley, are you insulting my father?" Lyle interjected.

"No, I'm asking my friend, Kurtz West, who just happened to have produced you, if he can foresee any problems with getting Lennie and Butch to swallow the whole deal," Stanley responded. "I think the biggest hurdle is going to be that Lennie likes being boss."

"And how would you get around that?"

"By telling him that even the smartest boss listens to someone who's an expert."

"Butch is no expert," Kurtz West said.

"Butch knows what will make Vannella mad. Ask them both," Stanley said. "By the way, they get a finder's fee of ten percent of all the money I recover."

"I will start there," Kurtz West decided. "Thanks, Stanley. And about the other, from what I've heard, your leg isn't the appendage Aleta is the fondest of."

"Lyle!" Stanley roared.

"Cut it out, Stanley," Lyle said evenly. "He talks to Claude a lot."

"Claude doesn't know."

"Claude is a politician who's at the top of that game. He knows," Lyle stated. "Just be glad he knows."

"Why should I be glad?"

"Because then he won't dig up any really big secrets."

"That is my big secret."

"Then you have nothing to worry about."

"I'm the one with the morphine drip in my arm and you're the one making no sense."

"You can go do your thing, Dad. Just get us some reason to ask for that warrant to search Stuart Fouts' mother's house for the money," Lyle said.

"Take Hawk this time," Stanley insisted. "I want Stuart Fouts broke."

As he was saying that, two stories below them, Chief Alan Peets had pushed the chair back into the dark corner and sat smiling as he recalled Butch's words about the reputation he had on the street. It was a unique one and he rather liked it. He still didn't think Butch had put him together with the Oakwood Police Chief that Lennie had warned him about, but Butch would never forget that he kept his promise to him.

He didn't pay any attention to the nurse that entered to change the IV bag until he watched her dump it in the wastebasket.

One thing no one but Chief Lyle West knew about Alan Peets was that, once alerted, Peets' brain reacted with lightning speed. It was that very speed that had saved West's young life when they were paired on a case involving a crooked cop from Peets' home state. The two of them were escorting the New Jersey cop to his seat on the plane that was taking him back home to face extortion charges. As the cop was moving up the aisle in the empty plane, both Peets and West alerted to a strange movement on the part of the supposedly unarmed cop. Peets' bullet hit the cop just as he was squeezing the trigger on a gun he had drawn from deep inside the front of his pants. West and Peets had been fast friends ever since.

He acted just as quickly this time.

Before the nurse had finished adjusting the flow of the fluid from the new IV bag, Peets had lifted it from the stanchion and thrown it on the floor with his right hand. His large left hand had imprisoned one of the nurse's wrists while the other one reached for his cuffs. She screamed when she saw the large black hand grab her wrist. Shock stilled her voice a second later when the first cuff was locked onto that wrist.

She recovered quickly, however, and shouted at him to let go.

"I will report you," she yelled. "You can't manhandle a white woman in Chief West's city whether that uniform is real or not."

"Chief West and I go way back," Peets said, wondering why he blurted that out. "And you're mine."

"He'll take your badge," she threatened.

"Lennie, tell her who I am," Chief Peets said.

"Lady, he's the one you don't never want to get on the wrong side of. I don't know what he does, but he does it better than even West."

"What do you know?" she spat back.

"I know enough to stay clear of him," Lennie said. "He's the goddamn Oakwood Police Chief and even Vannella's lawyer does what he says."

Peets opened his radio.

"Williams, I've got a collar for you to practice on," Peets said. "I'm on the third floor of the hospital. She should be easy. She's dumb, she's white and she thinks West will interfere."

There was a pause and Peets said, "I don't care what your plans were. You wanted in. This is your ticket."

After another pause, Peets voice turned harsh, "I did my stint for this week. You better do it right. That's the last word on the subject."

"I want my lawyer!" The woman declared.

"After you're booked," Peets said. "Let's go outside and wait in the hall.   Williams needs bread crumbs to follow."

He pushed her out of the room and radioed Hawk.

"I'm outside Lennie Archer's room holding onto the perp. I've got Williams coming," Peets said. "Yes, I hear you. I just don't know if I can do it to her."

That particular exclamation frightened the young woman.

"Please don't hurt me. I will tell you anything you want to know," the woman said.

"Tell me your name."

"Rosie Reed."

"I know for a fact that it's not," Chief Peets said.

By the time Williams arrived the woman was thoroughly frightened. How did Chief Peets know she lied?

"One of her aliases is Rosie Reed," Chief Peets told the only other black officer on the Oakwood force. "That's what she wants to be called right now. No questioning. She isn't under arrest. She hasn't been Mirandized. She doesn't have a lawyer."

"Why do I have to go with you?" Rosie Reed asked.

"Because we're the police and we are asking you to do that, and because you don't want to be arrested."

"So I can just walk away?"

"No, you can't."

"What am I supposed to do with her?" Williams asked.

"Put her in a cell and guard her," Peets said. "The two she's working for clean up loose ends by killing them."

"Yeh, like Lennie here," Williams said, picking up the initial idea Peets wanted planted in the woman's brain. "Poor guy. He hasn't said a peep and still they send her after him."

"Keep the cuffs on. We need to get a woman to search her."

"Who you got in mind?"

"Emma."

"I guess that would work if he hasn't locked her up for the night."

The prisoner's eyes widened in fear.

"Is there no other choice?"

"One. But she has other concerns."

"Ask Lyle."

And that's what Chief Peets did.

Sergeant Williams drove into the parking lot behind the offices of Praetzel, Locke and Praetzel and took the prisoner upstairs. Aleta met him at the elevator door and escorted the woman into the bathroom.

When the door was closed, Sergeant Williams called through the door that Rosie was to strip and hand her clothes to Mrs. Stanley. Aleta took the clothes and handed them out to Sergeant Williams. They were stuffed in a plastic garbage sack and Sergeant Williams gave Aleta hospital scrubs to give the woman after the cavity search.

Aleta found a small plastic packet of some unknown drug in one of the cavities she searched. Hawk would tell them what it was. It was put in and envelope and placed in the plastic bag. Sergeant Williams drove to the forensic lab first and then to the Oakwood Police Station.

He put his Rosie Reed in a cell in the basement and settled in a chair outside the cell.

"Now what?" she asked.

"Nothing," Sergeant Williams said.

"What's that mean?"

"It means you say nothing and I say nothing and I shoot anyone who tries to kill you."

"Okay by me," Rosie said with forced cheerfulness.

She was not rewarded with a smile. The scowl remained in place.

The first two hours, Sergeant Williams told himself that he could do this. The problem was that he didn't know why he was doing this. Chief Peets even told him Rosie

Reed probably didn't know anything. Peets didn't need her to confess as he had caught her red-handed. The cases against the Stuart Fouts and his mother were solid.

Sergeant Williams was handed the phone once during the third hour of his watch. Peets told him that Lennie Archer and Butch Lennert had agreed to hand over the ransom money. Lennie had put in a blue suitcase which was in the trunk of his impounded car. A warrant had been issued on the basis of it. Hawk was going to search the Fouts' house for the rest of the ransom money. The IV bag from the hospital and Rosie Reed's clothing had been put on the back burner at the lab.

"Sorry, Williams. You won't have any forensic evidence to spit out at the right time," Chief Peets said.

"Shit!" Williams grumped.

"I suggest you hold it." Peets said sternly.

As he sat in the basement watching a criminal of no consequence, Sergeant Williams became increasingly angry. What a monumental waste of time this was. While he said nothing, his scowl became more pronounced. Rosie decided to ignore him completely and catch some sleep. She turned her back on the sergeant and tried to sleep. But sleep wouldn't come. She was still too afraid to relax.

She turned around an hour later and found that Sergeant Williams' eyes were still staring at her. The frown was just as threatening. Her fear mounted. Lennie's words rushed back into her mind.

What was it that Chief Peets did? And what was it that this Sergeant wanted to learn to do so badly that he would sit in this cold basement as darkness fell and wait for the chance to try it? And why was he so angry?

That's when it occurred to her to try talking to him. Men liked women to listen to them.

"Why are you so mad at me?" she began, trying to keep her tone pleasant.

"Because you're a goddamn waste of time."

"So leave. There's nothing stopping you," she shot back angrily.

"I was ordered."

"I'm in a jail cell in a basement. No one's going to break into jail to kill me. I don't know anything."

"Yeh. I know that. Chief Peets told me that. The forensics on your stuff won't be done for at least twelve hours."

"Why are you telling me this?" Rosie asked, confused. Cops didn't tell you they had no reason to hold you. They always made you believe they knew more than they did.

"That's why I'm pissed off," Williams snapped, obviously irked. "You asked a question and I answered it, but that's the last question I will answer."

"The time will go faster if we talk," Rosie suggested.

"No it won't," Williams growled. "So just be quiet."

"I want you to stop frowning at me," Rosie demanded.

"Then stop talking until you have something important to say.'"

"But I don't know anything."

"Everybody knows something," Williams snarled. "You're on somebody's hit list. If you didn't know anything, you wouldn't be. And that's why I want you to shut up. I don't want to be on anybody's hit list."

"But…"

"You're talking."

"But…"

"If you don't shut up, I'll call Chief Peets and give you to him."

Fear grabbed hold of Rosie and her voice shook when she said, "Please don't. I'll be quiet."

An hour later, Rosie asked, "What's he want?"

"He wants me to practice on you."

"Practice?"

"Yeh," Williams said. "Stop talking."

Another hour passed before Rosie asked, "Practice what?"

"Getting you to make a choice."

"What choice?"

"You know," Williams said. "What the hell! I'm going to fail the damn test and I don't care."

"What test?"

"Shut up!" Williams growled. "I told you. No talking."

"Go grab yourself a cup of coffee," Rosie suggested.

"You're talking."

"There's no law against that."

"I'm not ready to do this. I just can't do it." Williams grumbled and then was silent.

Rosie waited for him to go on.

Another hour passed.

"He said I'd be easy," Rosie said. "What did he mean?"

Fifteen minutes passed before Williams replied to her question.

"That you were smart enough to figure out what choice you should make."

"But I don't know nothing."

"Yeh. Too bad."

"What's that mean?"

"Just shut up so I can think about how to do this right."

"Do what?"

Williams decided that he'd talked too much already. He'd probably blown it. Maybe if he didn't say another word, Peets would relieve him come morning.

He frowned as he thought about that. The one thing Peets wouldn't do is relieve him. Peets never asked to be relieved. But then he scared the bejabbers out of the perps. And they always had something to bargain with. Here he was stuck with someone who had nothing to give him.

He sat muttering to himself, and even though Rosie tried, she couldn't make out a single word he was saying. Then suddenly he was silent and Rosie wished he'd go back to muttering.

CHAPTER 16

Lieutenant Peter French was at the School board meeting in full uniform when two Willow Glen officers entered with Aleta Praetzel. Tim Jordan trailed in her wake.

Aleta didn't see French because she focused on moving as quickly as possible to the seat at a table in facing the tables at which the School board members sat.

As they were in the high school cafeteria, there was a plethora of tables to use for such purposes. Most had been folded up and stored and chairs brought in to replace them. The cafeteria was packed with people.

Aleta had told Sophia and Brittany to bring all their adult relatives and friends. She had warned Sophia not to panic in the middle of the process.

"It's a three-fold process," she had typed while Tim read her words aloud during their meeting at the office. "If I win Brittany's case, I can win yours. It may seem as if I am arguing that Brittany is a special case. That's the first step."

"What if you lose?" Sophia had asked.

"Then I fight for both of you with the same arguments I have reserved for your case. If they turn down your petition, I have a third presentation that will persuade the Board to reverse its decision, so don't despair until I'm finished."

"I won't," Sophia had promised.

"And don't rejoice until I'm done," Aleta had typed. "I need to present my third argument because if I don't, Carlton Brockbank will continue on his course until he graduates."

The girls had both nodded solemnly.

Now, in the crowded high school cafeteria, Tim Jordan stood up and introduced himself and Aleta Praetzel, partner in the law firm of Praetzel, Locke and Praetzel. His voice was strong and clear as he continued.

"We have three matters to bring before the Board this evening. Since each is unique, we will present each separately. We only ask that you consider each on it's own merits. From now on I will be speaking only the words Mrs. Praetzel types or those given me in advance. No words will be mine. As you all know, Mrs. Praetzel has chosen to remain silent until the last voice-activated bomb that has been planted is found. What you may not know is that these bombs have been cleverly hidden inside such items as a dog's collar, a horse's bridle, the steering wheel of her car and behind her bedroom wall. So bear with us."

Tim then took the first folder and passed around copies of Aleta's argument regarding Brittany's petition to remain in her regular classes until graduation. As the members read the arguments, Tim spoke the words that were written. Blessed with an uncanny memory, which stood a law clerk in good stead, Tim delivered the argument as if it were his own.

The questions began as soon as he finished.

The first to speak was Jane Ratner, a forty-five year old woman with brown bangs streaked with gray.

"It was consensual sex, was it not?" she charged.

"Yes, it was," Tim read, his eyes on the computer screen. "However, a minor cannot legally consent to sexual intercourse; therefore, it would be considered statutory rape were not the young man, Carlton…"

"No names," cut in the chairwoman Maureen Watson.

"We are using the name of the girl," Aleta typed. "However, we will agree to refer to the young man by his first name only."

Chairman Watson nodded.   The name had already been spoken.

Tim went on. "The young man is himself underage. However, in this case, there may be mitigating circumstances that will motivate the District Attorney to make an exception."

"When that happens, we will consider the case again," the brown-haired woman with bangs declared.

Aleta remembered that ploy from a previous encounter.

"And at that time, Mrs. Ratner, will you grant her petition?"

"Yes," Jane Ratner said. "Because it will have been proven that it wasn't her fault."

Murmurs of approval were heard.

Aleta continued unperturbed.

"This pregnancy was visited upon Brittany, a naïve young woman with no sexual experience by a devious young man who deliberately impregnated her.   This was done without her knowledge or consent. Here you have a young woman who has a bright future ahead of her and you are going to punish her for an act perpetrated by someone else. Isn't that what rape is? A sexual act forced upon someone without his or her consent. How is this so different?"

"It really isn't," the moustached Board member, Derek Knott, remarked.

Aleta remembered him from her previous appearance on behalf of Paige.

Several heads nodded.

Derek Knott had a following on the Board. He was considered a man of reason.

"We can't send the wrong message to our children," Jane Ratner declared stiffly.

Tim read Aleta's response.

"Let me tell you what you are telling the young women in your school. You are telling them that you support abortion."

"No! We are not! Absolutely not!" Jane Ratner protested. "We are telling them to abstain."

"You are sending another message as well," Aleta argued. "If Brittany gets an abortion, she can continue to take her regular classes, correct?"

"She's got you there, Jane," Derek Knott chuckled, stroking his moustache and tipping his chair back.

"Worse than that," Aleta continued. "You are teaching the young people in your school that lying is preferable to telling the truth."

"I don't see that at all," Jane Ratner said, pursing her lips.

"She will be able to stay in her regular classes if she hides her pregnancy, has her baby secretly and abandons it," Aleta stated.

"She's got you again," Derek Knott said, tipping his chair forward.

He continued to speak.

"I suggest we not add to this young woman's problems by denying her a chance at a college scholarship. She's worked four years toward that goal. She is the type of student of whom we are proud. So, she made a mistake. She trusted the wrong person. That is no reason to take away her future. She is behaving as an honorable, responsible adult. I move we allow her to continue in her regular classes."

The motion carried with only Jane Ratner voting nay.

The audience clapped.

Brittany and Sophia stood up and shushed them.

Sophia Antonopolous's case was next.

Jane Ratner was again the strident voice of opposition. "She's not naïve. She's not a scholar. The same arguments won't hold true this time."

"If you will listen," Tim said reading as Aleta typed the words onto her computer screen, "you will realize that I am not using the same arguments. Sophia and Brittany share only one thing. What Carlton did to Brittany, he did to

Sophia as well. She did not consent to be impregnated. In her case, her religion forbids her to have an abortion."

"It also forbids her to have pre-marital sex," Jane Ratner declared sanctimoniously.

"There is that," the gray-haired woman on the Board agreed.

"So is this Board going on record as saying that if one errs, there is no redemption?" Aleta asked.

"We aren't saying that," Jane Ratner huffed. "There's always..."

"Don't get on that horse again," Bob Davenport quipped. "We are not arguing religion here."

"She is," Jane Ratner argued.

Derek Knott turned to Aleta, "Are you?"

Aleta shook her head. "Let me try to use words that don't wave flags. Is the Board saying that if a teenager is caught stealing a candy bar that he should go ahead and steal a car?"

"You are making no sense," Jane Ratner spat out.

"She's making perfect sense," Derek Knott argued. "We are telling a girl that committed a sin in the eyes of her church that if she commits a bigger sin, we will forgive her for that one."

"She should be held accountable for the first sin!" Jane Ratner charged.

"By us?" Derek Knott asked politely.

"Yes, by us," Jane Ratner declared vociferously.

"Are we going to go after every young woman in our school that has sex or just those who get pregnant and don't have an abortion?" he asked.

"We can't go after every one. That's why we must punish those we can," Jane Ratner proclaimed.

"The ones who don't have abortions? I thought you were pro-life."

"I am. But I'm not for allowing sex in schools."

"It's already happening," Derek Knott argued. "We haven't been able to stop it. I say we stop acting like fools."

"Fools!" Jane Ratner exploded. "Upholding morality is not foolish."

"We are promoting dishonesty, deception and murder of the unborn. What's moral about that? Here we are about to punish a young girl for holding onto her religious beliefs," Knott contended. "I move we allow Sophia Antonopolous to complete her schooling in the regular classes."

The gray-haired woman seconded the motion despite a scowl from Jane Ratner. It passed as well.

"Our third and final petition," Tim read, "has to do with the Board's decision regarding Carlton Brockbank, the young man who not only impregnated Brittany and Sophia against their wills, but also attempted to impregnate Elise Steinman. I am passing out copies of signed affidavits from all three. We are petitioning the Board to assign him to the continuation school until he graduates."

"No! You can't! It would ruin his chance of going to a top-ranked college," shouted a well-dressed woman of forty-three who rose from her chair in the middle of the room.

"Sit down, Mrs. Brockbank," the chairwoman said. "We will hear from you later."

"This is a vindictive act, Mrs. Praetzel," Jan Ratner snapped. "It has no place here."

"It has every place here," Tim said, barely able to fathom how fast Aleta could type.

"You, Mrs. Ratner, were adamant that these two pregnant students be sent to the continuation school as an example to the student body. Why are you arguing against sending the male participant?"

"It would ruin his life."

"And his life is more important than that of any of these young women?"

"In society's eyes, yes," Jane Ratner stated boldly. "He is the future bread winner."

"And they are not?"

"They'll get married. Girls like that always do."

"You're married." Aleta typed and then stopped.

"So are you," Jane Ratner sneered.

"But I am a lawyer. I have a career. I want the same not only for these young women but also for all the young men and women in our high school. I do not personally believe that pre-marital sex is wise or even moral, but I am not ready to cast the first stone."

Jane Ratner shouted in rebuttal, "I move that Carlton Brockbank not be sent to the continuation school."

"What's good for the goose is good for the gander," Bob Davenport said. "I do believe Carlton Brockbank needs to be held responsible for his actions."

"We aren't a court of law," Jane Ratner argued.

"We are not asking you to be one," Tim spoke up as Aleta typed the words. "The court will rule on his obligation as father of these two children. He will have more than eighteen years of child support payments to make. He will have other obligations."

"Like what?" Derek Knott asked. "We need to know."

"As Brittany is keeping her child," Aleta typed. "She will need Carlton to share in caring for it on alternative weekends and several nights a week. If her social life is curtailed, his will be as well. I will be representing Brittany and Sophia in court."

"They can't afford you!" Jane Ratner barked.

"My fee for this night's appearance has been fully paid," Aleta typed. "Now let's return to the matter before us this evening. If this Board does not want to ruin Carlton Brockbank's life by sending him to Continuation school after not only one but three sexual acts, then the Board is guilty of discrimination. The female students in the school are not being treated the same as the male students who are guilty of the same behavior. The last time I was before this Board, I was told that you couldn't punish the boys involved in pre-marital sex because you didn't know who they were. Now you have one. So what are you going to do?"

Mrs. Brockbank insisted she be heard and the chairwoman granted her permission to address the Board.

She ranted for twenty minutes before the chairwoman asked her to conclude so the Board could ask questions. She did so immediately.

There were no questions.

Derek Knott addressed Aleta Praetzel.

"You said that you insist on equal treatment for both sexes, Mrs. Praetzel. Please answer me honestly. Are you prepared to go to court?'

"Yes, Sir, I am. You will lose. What you are doing is unconstitutional. And Sir, if I go to court, you will pay for my services plus punitive damages."

"This Board will not be threatened!" Jane Ratner spat out.

Derek Knott spoke up immediately.

"She didn't threaten. I asked her what her plans were and she tacked on her evaluation of our chances. She did this as a courtesy, so we wouldn't be blindsided."

"She won't do it. Her children will be going here," Jane Ratner crowed.

Bob Davenport laughed. "Stanley Praetzel's children will attend the prep school he attended."

"She has a sister in this school who I know carries a condom in her purse," Jane Ratner revealed with a smug expression.

"Well, good for her!" Derek Knott exclaimed. "Tell me, has she ever used it?"

"She belongs to the so-called 'condom club'. The boys won't go near them."

The audience snickered.

Derek Knott chuckled. "We need to hire the person responsible for that. She seems to know the secret. But, putting that aside for the moment, it is the duty of this board to provide quality education to all its students. If our continuation school is little more than a baby sitting service, which Mrs. Brockbank claims it is, we need to look into that; however, if we are going to continue to send our pregnant girls there, then we must send their partners. I move Carlton

Brockbank be sent to the continuation school to serve as an example to the other male students."

The audience roared its approval.

Bob Davenport seconded the motion and when Jane Ratner voted nay, the entire board took her to task. The vote became a unanimous one.

After the meeting was adjourned, Derek Knott approached Aleta while she was still at her computer.

"I hear your husband's father joined your firm. Will the name be changed to Praetzel, Locke, Praetzel and Praetzel?"

Aleta laughed and typed, "He's semi-retired. He wants to just try cases other than criminal ones."

"I'd heard that."

"It's true," Aleta typed. "Stanley's mother is going back on the bench."

"Good!" Derek Knott said. "Nice presentation, by the way. You both did an outstanding job."

"Thank you, "Tim said before Aleta typed the words.

She nodded.

"Here comes Lieutenant French. Are you really in danger?"

Aleta nodded.

"Ready to go?" Lieutenant French asked. "The chief has a surprise for you. And no, I don't know what it is."

CHAPTER 17

When Lieutenant Peter French drove up to the Emergency entrance of the hospital, Chief West was there to greet him. French was glad he'd called him. Aleta, flush with her success at the School board meeting was acting like a woman who would not be stopped by a mere lieutenant. She meant to see her husband and find out first-hand what was going on.

Lyle escorted Aleta to an empty room two stories below the one Stanley was in. It held the usual bed and nightstand. In addition there was a wheelchair.

"You're going to strip," Lyle said. "Put all your jewelry in your purse and then put your purse and everything else in the yellow bag.

Aleta held up her computer.

"That too. Absolutely everything," Lyle said. "When you're done, put on the gown and slippers and get in the chair. French is going to take everything to Bertha. She'll send fresh clothes over in the morning."

Aleta nodded. She really didn't need to speak. Stanley would ask questions if he wanted to know anything. And she had had Lauren teach her a few new signs that Lyle told her that he had taught Stanley. They were odd signs which would make Stanley laugh.

As she began to strip, she began to realize that something had gone wrong in the operation that had changed Stanley's appearance. Something that would generate a shocked verbal response. All she could think of was that when the anesthesiologist put the mask on Stanley's face, he did something to Stanley's freshly operated on nose.

Certain that she would utter some word of exclamation, Lyle was taking no chances. Neither would she. She slipped off her wedding ring and put it in her purse, stuck her feet into the slippers and sat in the chair, completely naked except for the gown.

Lyle handed the bag to French and sent him off.

"Are you ready to see Stanley?" Lyle asked, his tone solicitous, thus confirming her suspicions.

Stanley's nose had been injured somehow.

Aleta nodded vigorously in response to Lyle's question. He wheeled her to the elevator and then when they were on the fourth floor, he stopped at the nurse's desk and looked out the window. When he saw French drive away, he came back.

"I've removed everything from your person and everything from Stanley's as well," Lyle announced. "So you can talk. That's my surprise."

Aleta shook her head.

He rolled her into Stanley's room and bluntly announced, "I couldn't tell her. I was afraid she'd say something."

"Is that the reason for the gown?" Stanley asked.

"I couldn't take a chance. She's wearing nothing but a hospital gown and slippers."

"You checked?"

"No, I didn't check," Lyle exclaimed. "I told her to strip. She's been in jail. She knows what the word means."

Aleta held up her left hand and pointed to the finger that usually held her wedding band to show him that she had indeed stripped--jail-style.

"I still want you to tell her," Stanley said.

Aleta kept looking from one face to the other, trying to make sense of what was happening. Stanley's nose was fine.

She noticed the housing that kept the sheet off his leg. It would effectively protect the area around the ankle where the nodule had been. Her attention was drawn to the IV bottles and she wondered why there were two.

Suddenly, she knew what had happened.

She hopped out of the wheelchair, rushed toward the bed, yanked aside the sheet and grabbed the protective housing covering his leg and stared at the bandaged stump.

The silence was profound.

"Your leg!" she cried. "They cut off your leg!"

"Bone cancer," Stanley said calmly. "They had to."

"You didn't consult me!" she charged.

"I did," Stanley said. "I conjured up every argument you would have used."

Lyle's mouth dropped open at the exchange.

"Did they do a good job?"

"I got two of the best surgeons in the area to do it."

"Taekman and Cook?"

"Yes."

"Can they put it back?"

"No."

"Why not?"

Lyle began to move toward the bed.

"Aleta, what are you saying?" Stanley asked gently.

"I want you go have your leg back," she cried.

Then the tears began to flow. Stanley held out his arms. Aleta sat on the edge of the bed and cried into his shoulder.

"You lost," Lyle said. "Double six is twelve."

"How did my parents take it?"

"Your mother shrieked and your father had to do what you're doing now. Bertha broke into tears and Robert had to do what you're doing now. Andrea almost fainted and Paul had to do what you're doing now."

"I was so sure about Aleta. She's seen some horrible visions," Stanley said.

"Your mother was incensed that I was paid in deputy days."

"You told her that was my idea, not yours?"

"I had to promise that you wouldn't walk a beat," Lyle said. "However, none of my men walks a beat anymore."

"So that means I'm…"

"Going to be used whenever and wherever I need you," Lyle said. "You will recall, I put you and Scooby on guard duty when you were on crutches."

"I remember. I shot up a car."

"And scared the entire neighborhood," Lyle remarked.

"That's what cops are supposed to do."

"We're called peace officers," Lyle declared.

"That's a misnomer," Stanley insisted.

"Lyle looked down at his belt and said, "I've got a call. Be right back."

Stanley hugged his wife.

"I'm so sorry," he murmured.

She cried harder. He held her tight and let her cry. Seconds became minutes and the minutes became parts of an hour.

"I did pray," Stanley said softly once her sobbing had lessened.

Aleta pulled her head away and looked at the half leg. She put her hand on his thigh gently.

"Tell me everything," she said, leaning back against his arms which folded around her.

She rested her one hand lightly on her slightly bulging stomach and the other on the thigh of his half leg.

He told her about the tests they'd done. There had been three. He'd had a hard time accepting that there was anything wrong with his ankle and lower leg bone as all of the pain was at the site of the bullet wound.

"I kept thinking they were wrong," Stanley went on. "Then I thought about what to do."

"Did you ask God?"

"Yes," came the simple reply.

"Then it's okay," Aleta said.

He continued on for several more minutes and then stopped. Aleta turned and looked at him.

"Put your hand back," he said.

"My hand?"

"On my thigh. It's making my leg feel good."

Aleta replaced her hand and Stanley sighed happily, "Thank you."

"But I'm not doing anything," Aleta protested.

"Just leave your hand there," Stanley said. "I want to try something."

He reached up and closed the clamp on the line from the IV bag.

"Stanley, what are you doing?" Aleta gasped.

"Getting rid of the morphine drip."

"Should you do that?"

"It's a pain killer. But it doesn't work as well as your hand," Stanley explained as he removed the needle in his wrist.

"Heck!"

"Heck?" Aleta questioned.

"I took out the wrong needle," he said as he extracted the other one and then peeled off the tape.

"There. Now I feel better."

"Didn't one of those have antibiotics to prevent infection?" Aleta asked.

"Probably."

"Stanley, I don't want you to die!" Aleta wailed.

"I will tell Dr. Cook when I see him and he can give me a shot if I need it, okay?"

"You're not thinking straight," Aleta said. "It's the morphine."

"Blame my actions on the morphine then," Stanley said. "I'm glad to be rid of it. It was messing with my head.

By the way, I'd like my sheet back. You've left me hanging on the line."

"You are not hanging on the line. You're right where you're supposed to be."

"I don't think it was damaged."

"Do you know how far your penis is from your knee cap?" Aleta charged. "There's no way they should have even touched it."

Stanley looked up as Dr. Cook walked in.

"Well, did you mess with anything but my leg?" Stanley asked.

Wayne Cook laughed. "Come on in, Michael. I told you that would be the first question he'd ask."

"What happened to your IV's?" Dr. Taekman asked.

"I removed them," Stanley said. "The morphine was messing with my head and I pulled the other one out by mistake."

"We have a competent nursing staff," Dr. Taekman scolded.

"You're going to scold a patient the same day you chopped off his leg?

"We didn't chop it off," Dr. Taekman said. "We did a good job. Ask Lyle."

"Lyle was there?" Aleta questioned. "In the operating room?"

"You're talking," the doctors chorused.

"Lyle stripped me of everything. I match Stanley now in just a hospital gown."

"I thought you weren't taking any chances," Dr. Cook said.

Aleta thought for a long moment.

"Strangely enough, I'm not. It's safe here. I exploded when I saw Stanley's leg. I couldn't help myself. And since I didn't blow up…"

"That makes sense to me," Dr. Cook said. "Enjoy your stay."

He turned his attention to Stanley.

"I must admit, Stanley,' you are looking good for having sustained a major trauma to the body," Dr. Cook remarked.

Dr. Taekman picked up the chart and wrote, "IV discontinued at patient's request."

"Did Aleta tell you that we're having a boy?" Stanley asked.

"Bernard told me he hadn't done the ultra sound yet," Dr. Cook said.

"That's because he hasn't," Stanley said. "Aleta knows. I'm ecstatic. I didn't think I cared, but I really wanted Gerard to have a brother."

"I won't tell Martha yet," Dr. Taekman said.

Aleta laughed.

"She'll be just as happy as Stanley. Tell her we're naming him Michael Taekman Praetzel."

Dr. Taekman grinned.

"I guess your prediction can't be any worse than Bernard's," he said. "You remember how Bernard kept telling me I didn't know a boy from a girl when I delivered Lauren's baby. That I learned when I was six."

"Speaking of which, I want my sheet," Stanley crabbed. "They gave me an ultra sort gown this time."

Aleta pulled up the sheet part way with one hand, complaining, "Honestly, Stanley, these two men stared at you for several hours."

"I was draped."

"I asked you once before if you looked like everyone else and you said yes, so why this modesty? It's not as it we're in Grand Central Station."

Lyle entered with a large insulated bag.

"Who's going to New York?" he asked. "Are we having a party? Because if we are, I brought the ice cream. And why is Stanley uncovered. Is anything wrong?"

"I've only got one hand," Aleta said.

"I don't know where the hood is," Michael said.

"I don't need the hood," Stanley claimed. "Just the sheet."

"It will hurt," Michael said.

"No, it won't."

Aleta and Dr. Taekman each took one end and brought the sheet up to Stanley's waist.

"Why did you bring ice cream?" Aleta asked.

"Bertha said you celebrate by having ice cream," Lyle said. "We found another bomb. That's why I was gone so long. It seems when French brought home your clothes, the dogs got agitated. I called Hawk. He brought over Topper who reacted as Scooby and Tank had, so we separated out your stuff. And the culprit was…"

"My computer?" Aleta guessed.

When Lyle confirmed her guess with a smile and a nod, she gasped, "Suppose I had insisted on bringing it up here?'

"But you didn't" Lyle said.

"So we have only one to go," Stanley said.

"I'm sure it's not in your house," Lyle said. "Paige gook Topper through the entire house in case your dogs had been ignored when they pointed it out. She says you're still paying her."

"She'd our best shot at finding that last bomb," Stanley said. "I like the fact that she searched the house again."

"By the way," Lyle said. "Harriet's back. Stoney won the Chesapeake National. She got two Best in Shows on Auggie. She's done, she says. Hunting season is almost here."

"Spoon up the ice cream," Stanley said. "I need something decadent right now. Tomorrow Aleta will cut my caloric by an eighth because I'm missing half a leg."

Lyle opened the insulated bag and took out a stack of plastic bowls and plastic spoons. He dipped into the tub of fudge swirl and began scooping.

"Put Aleta's scoop on top of mine. Her hand is busy making my leg feel good."

"Are you sure it's your leg?" Wayne Cook asked.

"Does it matter?" Stanley returned. "I'm a happy patient right now. And considering the changes I've undergone, be glad."

"She can stay as long as she likes," Dr. Taekman decided.

"Bertha is sending over breakfast," Lyle announced.

"Hospital's serve food," Dr. Taekman observed.

"I've mentioned that on previous occasions, Michael," Wayne Cook said. "What time are we having rolls?"

"Seven," Lyle replied. "Unlike doctors, police chiefs need to go to the office."

Aleta looked at her husband. "I don't have to go in."

"Then don't. I need you."

That was the first time in their marriage that Stanley had said those words in quite that way. He had said them when he wanted her to know that she was essential to his happiness, but this was different.

This time he said them as a man who was suffering. She knew it wasn't physical because he had rid himself of his pain medication. He was suffering in another way. He'd lost a part of himself. She had no idea what that felt like, but it had to be devastating. People lost limbs in accidents but this had the added burden of his deciding to sever a big part of himself.

In one morning, he had gone from an able-bodied man to a cripple with limitations. He would have to work hard to regain what he had once had as a natural part of being a whole man.

How could she possibly help him?

After the beds had been moved next to each other and fastened together and the nurses had been told not to check on the patient during the night and the men guarding the door had been instructed to phone anyone either of the pair asked them to call, everyone left Stanley and Aleta to cope with their grief.

Aleta pulled back the sheet and kissed his bare thigh and then the top of his bandage.

Her tears flowed unhindered and Stanley felt a warmth in the love she was pouring out.

He put his hand on her head and she lifted it to look at him.

"I don't know how to help you," she said softly, her voice breaking. "I know you chose wisely. I know it was your love that made you shield me, but, Stanley…"

She paused and her voice grew stronger. "If ever you decide to discard another limb, you will tell me beforehand so I can stop you somehow."

"I like that you don't have any guilt in this."

Aleta smiled weakly. "You did succeed in that endeavor, but don't gloat too long. As soon as the shock wears off, I am certain I will be able to come up with a reason to feel guilty."

"I'm counting on it."

"Why?"

"Because then you'll do what I ask."

"I do that now."

"A man can't hold too may trumps."

"Anything you want, you've got," Aleta promised.

"What if I ask you to give up the Fouts trial and just stay home and hold my leg?"

"The answer is yes."

She scooted around in the bed and laid her cheek against his bare thigh. "My hand may forget its duty half way through the night. My head won't."

"It was a what if," Stanley murmured as his leg began to feel pleasantly warm and he let his thought fade as he closed his eyes and fell into a dreamless sleep.

Aleta's hand found its usual place and she too dropped into a pleasant sleep.

Just before dawn, Stanley spoke. "They wanted to take the leg off above the knee, but I said no. I couldn't give up my knee. I just couldn't."

Aleta's hand went down to the bandaged knee and patted it as gently as one pats a kitten.

"I'm glad," she murmured.

Her hand stayed on his kneecap. Stanley dared not move because the sensations he was feeling were pleasant.

Did she have the gift of healing, he wondered.

A second later another more disturbing thought followed. Could she have rid his leg of cancer?

He'd never even asked that.

"Did I make a mistake?" he murmured aloud.

Soft as his query was, Aleta heard it.

"God didn't tell me what was happening. He could have," she whispered.

"He wanted me to lose my leg?" Stanley asked, this time his voice loud enough to be heard even by a person half asleep.

Aleta didn't move. When she spoke her voice was soft and gentle.

"God doesn't give people cancer. People get it—good people and bad people. It rains on the just and the unjust. This time a good person got wet."

"Go back to sleep, Aleta. You are healing my soul."

Aleta lifted her head and protested, "I don't heal souls. I don't heal bodies. I don't do miracles."

"Lay back down. Let's sleep until morning," Stanley said softly.

To his delight, her head sank down where it had been and her hand stayed on his knee where it had been. The other hand tightened its grip on his penis just a little.

I am going to be embarrassed when the nurse comes to wake me in the mourning, he thought.

But as he lay there basking in the glow of an anticipatory sexual state, as well as feeling a pleasant warmth in his knee, he decided he didn't care. He no longer felt alone or undesirable. Aleta's love for him was still intact.

I am truly blessed, he thought as he again fell asleep.

CHAPTER 18

A nurse did indeed come in before it was light and she did find them in their usual juxtaposition. She backed out of the room and called Dr. Cook.

"Don't disturb them," Dr. Cook ordered firmly. "Don't bathe them or take their temperatures or feed them breakfast. Don't open their drapes or change their bedding. I want them to sleep as long as possible. I will be there with Dr. Taekman at seven. Tell the guards that no staff is to go into that room until after we get there."

The nurse wrote a notation on the chart at the nurse's station. Thus when Dr. Taekman and Dr. Cook walked in at eight, the two Praetzels were still sleeping in the same position in which the nurse had found them earlier.

"Obviously the weight of her hand is bearable," Dr. Taekman commented, picking up the chart.

"I'm surprised he can handle the weight of her head against his thigh," Dr. Cook commented. "Note that too."

"Do we note where the other hand is?" Dr. Taekman asked.

"Just say 'usual position' higher up on the body'."

"Come on, Wayne," Michael Taekman sputtered. "He's in a state of semi-arousal. That has to be a positive."

A male voice from the bed interrupted them.

"Believe me, Doctors, it's a positive."

"How are you feeling?" Dr. Taekman asked.

"Good," Stanley said. "And I need a favor. When you look at the wound..."

He paused momentarily when Dr. Taekman shook his head and then continued.

"Don't give me that! As I was saying, when you look at the wound, please let Aleta's hand stay where it is."

"Which hand?" Dr. Cook asked.

"The one on the leg, of course. When she wakes up the other one will be gone."

"We could just remove it now," Dr. Taekman said.

"Don't," Dr. Cook advised. "She tightens her grip."

"Really?" Dr. Taekman questioned. "It looks loose enough. See. I can stick my finger ...Whoa!"

"I told you," Dr. Cook exclaimed. "Now we'll need ice packs."

"She won't let go," Dr. Taekman exclaimed as he tried to extract his finger.

"Aleta can't be forced," Stanley said.

Chief Lyle West walked in, took one look at the situation and closed the door.

"Michael, why do you have your finger there?"

"Because he didn't believe me!" Dr. Cook spat out.

Lyle reopened the door a crack and spoke to one of the guards. "Tell the nurse we need a couple of ice packs. Don't let her in."

"Don't you have something you can say to make her let go," Dr. Taekman asked. "That's a forefinger I use a lot."

"It's your own fault," Stanley growled. "And I'm not going to tell her she's hurting me because that might break the spell."

"What spell?" the doctors chorused.

"I think she's healing my leg."

"My finger's numb," Dr. Taekman complained.

"Translate that into a man's most sensitive part," Stanley responded.

"Aleta," Dr. Cook said softly. "You're hurting Dr. Taekman."

Aleta jumped back and her head hit Dr. Taekman's chin.

"Ow!" she yelped. "Who hit me?"

She focused on Stanley.

"Someone hit me in the head."

"Dr. Taekman owes you a free operation."

"We don't want any more operations," Aleta declared. "Why is everyone laughing? That hurt."

"Ice packs," Lyle announced from the doorway.

Aleta blushed.

"Why didn't you wake me?"

"Dr. Taekman thought he could ease your hand away," Stanley said.

"Didn't you tell him that doesn't work?"

"He didn't listen."

"I hope Michael doesn't pick up that trait," Aleta worried aloud.

"They won't be related," Dr. Cook mentioned.

"He's a namesake. That's enough relationship for a child," Aleta stated. "Now, how is Stanley today?"

"Better," Stanley said, "except for my new doctor-induced injury."

Michael shook his finger in his step-grandson's face.

"This goes nowhere, Wayne," he charged.

"Not on the chart?"

Aleta jumped in. "You aren't going to clean his wound until after breakfast, are you?"

"No, they aren't," Lyle declared. "Bertha made a new breakfast dish. You guys are lucky I made it all the way here without stopping and eating half of it."

"Smells great," Stanley said. "Serve Aleta's first. I will feed her."

Aleta looked at her husband quizzically.'

"Give me your hand," Stanley said quietly.

Aleta put her hand in his. He placed it on top of the sheet covering his thigh. Her fingertips could feel the cold of the ice packs.

Lyle gave Stanley a plate of food and the first forkful went into Aleta's mouth.

She leaned over and set her other hand closer to the knee. He smiled at her and she knew that somehow she was helping him.

"You've got to taste this warm, Stanley," Aleta said. I want her to make this again."

Stanley put the next morsel into his own mouth.

"This is really good," he said, forking in another mouthful.

"That's two for you," Aleta complained. "There are two in this body. You don't want to starve little Michael, do you?"

"You've got a point," Stanley said eating another mouthful.

"Hey, that was mine."

"You were talking."

After breakfast, Dr. Cook said, "Try to be discreet for a couple hours. The staff had housekeeping chores and baths to do."

"Not me!" Aleta exclaimed.

"You can take a shower while Stanley gets pampered."

"Do I get clothes?" Aleta asked.

"No!" Stanley said.

"Okay, no clothes," Aleta said. "But I'm not a patient, am I?"

Dr. Cook grinned. "You've got a chart and everything."

As soon as he left, Aleta jumped out of bed and looked at her chart. "I'm Mrs. Stanley and I'm suffering from exhaustion."

"That buys you a day in bed," Stanley said. "I want you longer than a day."

"You want me to have a relapse?"

"If you can manage one."

Aleta switched to a new topic.

"What's behind the request that I give up the Fouts case? I was appointed by the judge. If you want me to withdraw, I need to tell him."

"Your choice," Stanley said. "How long did you prepare for the school board case?"

"All afternoon."

"What would you have done if I had had Lyle tell you what happened during the operation when you left the court at noon?"

"Come here and stayed with you, of course."

"Did we win?"

"Tim was super. He'd studied my arguments and he didn't just read them, he delivered them. And he stayed so close to my typing, it was as if I were speaking."

"But did we win?"

Brittany doesn't have to go to the continuation school. The argument about her being an outstanding scholar tipped the scales."

"And Sophia?"

"Her religion worked in her favor."

"And Carlton Brockbank?"

"He goes to the continuation school until graduation."

"His parents will get that rescinded."

"Not until the next board meeting," Aleta said. "Meanwhile I'm filing suit to demand that he pay half the medical expenses for each girl."

"You're going back to work, aren't you?"

"By me, I mean our firm. One of our associates can argue that case as well as the paternity suit. Chin, I think."

Stanley nodded.

Aleta glanced at her husband and frowned.

"You're upset."

"I'm not doing well, Aleta," Stanley murmured.

"Can I do anything?"

"I need to be alone."

"Now?"

"Yes."

"How long a shower should I take?"

"A really long one."

Aleta hopped out of bed and closed the bathroom door. She turned on the water immediately. Through the door she could hear him sobbing.

I'm going to be a prune, she thought as she stepped into the shower and began singing. First she sang all the songs the two of them had danced to. She couldn't think of the words to any others.

To Stanley those songs were a reminder that it would be a long time before they danced again. His tears flowed even faster. He put his pillow over his face so he could yell.

"Why God? Why me? What did I do?"

The tears gushed out as he thought about his leg.

"I want my leg back, God," he yelled. "I want it back. I want to be whole again. You perform miracles. Perform that one."

His rage mounted as he slid into despair.

"This isn't a little thing, God. This is major. I'm not sure I want to live through this. Death might have been an easier sentence."

Aleta hit a high note and Stanley paused to listen.

"She's happy, isn't she?" he murmured. "She's glad I'm alive even with half a leg missing, isn't she?"

He removed the pillow from his face and pressed the button to raise his bed so he could look at his leg. He stared at it for a long time. Then he scooted across both beds to the far edge of the Aleta's bed and dropped his right leg over the edge. He moved his left leg beside it. The bandaging kept his left knee rigid.

My baby can still sit in my lap, he thought, and then wondered where that thought came from. His mind took the next step and he smiled wanly. I still have a lap. I'm not paralyzed. I can still stand. And hop. And kick. And even swim. I bet I can still ride Minx. I don't even need legs to ride her. She never pays any attention to any direction I give anyway, especially, if I want to hurry her. Life won't be all that different. I have automatic shift. I can drive."

Then he sobered.

"Whom am I trying to fool?" he asked himself aloud. "Life will never be the same again."

The tears came again as he looked at the bandaged end of his left leg.

"My God," he murmured. "It's really gone."

The water stopped. Aleta poked her head out the door.

"Can I stop now? I'm a five-foot-six prune."

"Come here," he said, surprised that his voice wasn't shaking.

"Suppose someone comes?" she asked, hesitating behind the bathroom door.

"The guards talk to everyone," Stanley said. "Toss me your towel."

His words masked the sound of the door being opened behind him.

Aleta threw him the towel. It draped over his right foot, which he had extended to catch it.

"I'm set," he said.

He watched her walk toward him.

"Better my leg than one of hers," he mused softly. "Thank you, God."

Aleta saw Dr. Cook standing in the doorway, but she chose to ignore him. Stanley's eyes, still glistening with tears, were alive with desire.

When she reached him, she bent over and kissed him. His hands drew her closer and she moved so that their bodies touched.

Dr. Cook eased himself out of the room.

Stanley started at the slight click.

"I can see the door," Aleta reminded him. "We're alone."

"I wish I could make love to you," he whispered.

"You are," she said softly. "I will do whatever you want."

"You still love me even…"

She kissed him passionately and her hands undid the ties that held his gown on and she removed it.

He touched her as if he had never touched her before, hesitantly, almost with fear. Her hand fell to his wounded leg and he felt the peculiar warmth of her touch.

Her other hand visited a different part of his body and he felt it responding without even a smidgen of pain. The skin was still cool from the ice packs. The swelling had not gone down and yet her touch was pleasant.

God is healing me though her, he thought.

"Is it ready?" Aleta queried.

Bewildered, he asked, "Is what ready?"

"To enter me?"

Suddenly he knew.

"Oh, yes! But my leg may not be."

"Lay back," she suggested. "I will go very slowly and you can stop me anytime."

But he didn't stop her.

When they were done, she lay on his chest and kissed him.

"In my eyes, you are a whole man," she said.

"That can't be," he argued. "I have only half a leg."

"So there's a nick in your outer covering."

"A nick!" Stanley exploded, inexplicably upset. "You call losing a leg a nick?"

"So it's a big nick."

"I'm like a car with a wheel missing."

"That would be Scooby if he lost a leg," Aleta corrected. "You're more like a bicycle."

"Okay then," Stanley said, still upset. "Bicycles need two wheels to be whole."

"Get used to being a unicycle," Aleta said. "Some people like riding unicycles."

"That's all I am? A ride?"

Aleta giggled. "Don't knock it.'"

Stanley broke down and laughed.

Stanley heard the door behind him open and he reached back, grabbed his hospital gown and quickly shoved his arms into the sleeves. Aleta ran into the bathroom.

"Dangling, are we?" the nurse asked cheerfully. "That's real progress."

Stanley nodded.

"Who put the beds together?" she asked.

"Dr. Cook and Dr. Taekman."

"Doctors! I should have known. They have no idea how impossible it is to make up a bed in this position," the nurse grumbled and then added. "Why did they think you needed two beds?"

"My wife was in the other one."

"Where is she?"

"Taking a shower."

"After I get someone to help me separate the beds, we'll do your bath and I will change your sheets."

Twenty minutes later, Stanley and Aleta were neatly tucked in beds several feet apart.

As soon as the nurse left, Aleta jumped out of bed and pushed her bed next to Stanley's.

"The ties are gone," she wailed.

"We'll be careful," Stanley said.

Aleta climbed back into bed and crawled over close to Stanley.

"This is a single bed," he said.

"Yes, it is pretty narrow."

"Single beds are meant for single people."

"You are so right. We'll just have to make do, I guess. Scoot over."

"If I scoot any more, I will be on the floor."

"You want me back in my bed?"

"Yes. We're going to have a visitor," Stanley replied.

"How come I don't know that?" Aleta questioned, perturbed.

"Because I'm here to see Stanley," said the rough female voice of Aleta's grandmother. She walked around the two beds to Aleta's side and held out her arms.

"Oh, Grams!" Aleta exclaimed as they hugged. "I'm so glad to see you. So much has happened. They found one more bomb and it's safe for me to talk here. It was in the computer that I was carrying everywhere. There's one more bomb, so I won't talk after I leave here ... Oh, yes, and the doctors cut off Stanley's leg."

"All that was in order of importance?" Stanley joshed.

"No!" Aleta exclaimed. "But she needed to know not to be afraid. So, Grams, what did you want to talk about with Stanley?"

"It's private," Harriet said. "I want you to lay down, close your eyes and sleep."

"He'll only tell me later," Aleta insisted.

"Are your eyes closed?"

"I can't just drop off to sleep like that," Aleta protested.

"Pleasant dreams," her grandmother said stroking her brow.

In seconds both could tell that Aleta was asleep.

Harriet then moved the beds apart so she would be on the left side of Stanley's bed.

"Show me the leg," she requested softly.

Stanley gingerly pulled back the sheet.

"God told me the knee was important to you."

"The oncologist wanted the surgeons to cut above the knee. In fact he wanted them to take the whole leg," Stanley revealed. "Are you here to tell me I made a mistake?"

"No, I'm here to answer your questions," Harriet said. "And to give you these."

"What questions?" he asked, taking the two books she handed him.

"The ones you can't ask anyone else."

"Is it possible Aleta could be healing me?"

"It's possible."

"When she first touched my let it felt so good I discontinued the morphine drip," Stanley said.

"Tell me everything," the old woman ordered.

And Stanley did.

"What's Aleta's explanation?" she asked when he was finished.

"When I mentioned she might have healing powers, it bothered her. You know how Aleta gets whenever she's gifted with a new ability."

"Nothing you have told me thus far is convincing. Tell me, what convinced you enough to ask the question?"

"It's very personal," Stanley hedged.

Harriet notice he blushed and guessed.

"You had sex."

Stanley nodded. No sense holding back now.

"I was told that I wouldn't be able to have normal sex for quite a while," he said. "But we did. We catered to my leg, but we've done that before. It still falls in the parameters of normal."

"Now God's message makes sense," Harriet said.

"What message?"

"Let Aleta work," Harriet said with a ring of authority.

"So, she is healing me."

"It would seem so."

"It could also mean that I should let her handle the Fouts' case," Stanley suggested.

"I think He would direct her on that," Harriet remarked.

"But I asked her not to," Stanley elaborated.

"And she agreed?"

"Yes."

"I still believe my message has to do with you personally," Harriet said. "Oh, and I'm to tell you He's heard every word you've spoken."

"Great!" Stanley groaned. "I yelled at Him."

"Like a child."

"He took away my leg!" Stanley burst out.

"Cancer took your leg."

"It's still there, isn't it--the cancer?"

"He was very pleased that you asked Him what to do."

"He told me to let it go or it would kill me."

"You know that's true."

Stanley nodded reluctantly.

"One more thing, Stanley," Harriet said. "No prosthesis."

"Because I'm going to lose the rest of my leg?" Stanley queried.

"There's another reason," Harriet said. I don't know what it is. I'm sorry."

Chief West walked into the room.

"Harriet!" he exclaimed. "Why am I not surprised? I knew you were back. I brought lunch. Are you joining us? What happened to Aleta? And why are the beds pushed apart? You two didn't have a fight, did you?"

"I won't be staying," Harriet said. "I have a luncheon date. Let me wake our sleeping beauty."

She kissed Aleta lightly on her forehead.

Aleta opened her eyes.

"I told you couldn't sleep at the drop of a hat."

She looked around.

"When did Lyle get here?"

When lunch was over, Dr. Cook said to Stanley, "Your dressing needs changing. How's three for you two?"

Dr. Taekman picked up the chart.

"Why didn't you do it before lunch?" he snapped.

"They were busy."

"Busy? Doing what?"

"I am not a voyeur."

"He's barely twenty-four hours out of surgery," Michael protested.

"He's healing fast. How's your finger?"

"Sore."

"He doesn't need ice anymore," Dr. Cook said.

"I don't believe you."

Stanley glared at Dr. Taekman.   "You are not checking."

Michael frowned and muttered, "See you at three."

When they left, Aleta asked, "What did Grams tell you?"

"That God wants me to let you work," Stanley said.

"You mean stay on the Fouts' case?"

"That could be one of the meanings."

"That's a strange message for Grams to bring."

"It had levels," Stanley said.

"Like what?"

"As in I don't know yet."

"You're shutting me out again," Aleta charged.

"No, I'm not.   I think obeying God is an ongoing process."

"Are you obeying Him?"

"It appears that I have been," Stanley said. "May I answer a few of the questions you are afraid to ask?"

"Oh, please do," Aleta said.

"You have to move closer and let me hold you."

"So I can't look in your face and tell if you're lying."

"Aleta, I may not always tell you everything, but I don't lie to you."

She crept closer and kissed him.   Her hand rested on his leg, and his hand covered hers.

"You like my hand there, don't you?"

"I think I told you that I did," Stanley said.

"I guess I... Nevermind ... I like it too," she said. "Now answer my questions, please."

"First my grandfather died of secondary bone cancer. That means he had cancer elsewhere and it migrated to his bones."

"And your isn't?'

"Mine is primary bone cancer. It's rare. It rarely happens to people my age, but it happened to me."

"No cancer anywhere else?"

"No. I also won't pass it on to our sons."

"No possibility?"

"Some of the cancers are inheritable; however, I don't have the inherited abnormalities that accompany those cancers."

Aleta nodded. He hugged her.

"That's the good news."

"She looked at him questioningly.

"It's cancer, Aleta. The doctors think they got it all, but only time will tell. I chose the surgery after considering all the other options."

"When did you have time to study them?"

"I didn't, but I already knew most of the alternatives available. I was so curious about bone cancer after Grandpa died that I researched it. I was young. I needed answers. I wound up on mailing lists, so I was already up to speed when this cancer hit."

Aleta was silent.

"You don't want to second guess me, so let me tell you that I considered a less radical surgery where just the tumor would be removed and a permanent artificial prosthesis or a bone graft would leave my leg intact."

Aleta remained silent, her hand lightly stroking the surgically shortened leg. She was glad she wasn't facing Stanley because tears were streaming down her face. They were being caught by the shoulder of the cotton hospital gown.

"I considered a combination of chemotherapy and radiation, even though in some cases radiation causes bone cancer. The chemo might have killed most of the new growth and possibly reduced the size of the tumor, but my cancer was a fast growing malignancy. It called for a radical procedure to stop it cold. That's when I asked God if I was overlooking anything. And the thought that came to me when I asked that question was that I had a choice. Lose my limb or lose my life."

"I'm glad you were decisive," Aleta said. "I will miss your leg. I imagine you will too, but…"

Stanley's laughter interrupted her.

"Oh, Aleta, you do say the oddest things at times."

"I wasn't being funny," she returned, irked.

"That's why you were," he said. "Did I answer all your questions?"

She shook her head.

"You want to know what's next?"

"Yes, please."

"What's next is for me to get well," Stanley said. "I'm going to put off getting an artificial leg for a bit."

"But you'll have only one leg," Aleta proclaimed. "You'll have to use crutches."

"And get all my trousers fixed."

"Oh, Stanley," she cried. "No!"

"Aleta, the leg is gone," he stated evenly. "I won't have my trousers just hanging empty."

She turned and buried her head in his shoulder and cried as she had done at the beginning. Somehow it comforted him to have her cry. It was as if she was giving a voice to his feelings.

He could feel her hand on his leg. The warmth it brought was comforting as were her tears.

He remembered the words, "Let Aleta work."

"I'm sorry I snapped at you," he said.

Her reply came in hiccupy gasps. "The reality is hitting me from everywhere. I can't help myself."

"Your tears are helping me," Stanley murmured.

Aleta's head came up. "Are they really?"

"You're crying for me too."

"Sort of a surrogate weeper?"

Stanley chuckled. Only Aleta would use those terms.

CHAPTER 19

At three o'clock sharp, both doctors appeared. Stanley was sitting up reading aloud. Aleta's head was in his lap

"That doesn't hurt?" Dr. Taekman asked.

"You're less testy," Stanley observed.

"I was testy?" Michael asked, surprised.

Dr, Cook nodded and then told Stanley, "Grams was mad at him."

"You mean angry," Aleta corrected.

"I mean mad. She was irate, almost crazy with grief and full of recriminations. I'm surprised Michael held up as well as he did."

"It was Martha that Grams had a lunch date with," Aleta guessed.

Dr. Taekman nodded and said, "Martha served her usual luncheon fare--peanut butter sandwiches."

"That's all I ever wanted for lunch when I was growing up."

"So you're the one who programmed her."

She's not a good cook. You can't burn peanut butter sandwiches," Wayne said.

"If you don't ask for them on toast."

"Grams burns toast," Wayne observed.

"So I found out," Michael responded. "It's a good thing she has so many other sterling qualities."

"Like what?" Wayne asked smiling.

"She loves me."

"That's it?" Wayne jibed.

"Yep," Michael said. "Now let's see how the leg looks today."

Dr. Cook called for a nurse and the beds were moved apart and the drape shut off Aleta's view of the procedure.

"Remarkable," Dr. Taekman commented. "It's only been a day."

"No wonder he's so mobile," Dr. Cook observed. "No swelling."

Then Aleta heard Stanley say, "Are you checking my leg?"

She giggled.

On the other side of the curtain, Stanley winked at Dr. Taekman who responded, "I'm surprised you didn't mark it. You marked everything else."

"It doesn't have a knee."

"Oh, yes. We weren't to touch the knee. I do remember that. You do know they have excellent artificial knees that can be inserted during surgery."

"Up and down stuff," Stanley sneered.

"True, they aren't as versatile as a real knee, but they work pretty well."

"I'm a perfectionist," Stanley said.

"From the way you're healing, I'd say you can get fitted for an artificial leg pretty soon."

"I don't think I will go that route just yet," Stanley said.

"Your upper leg needs exercise," Dr. Taekman said.

"Horseback riding? Swimming? Weight lifting?"

"Any of those would be fine," Dr. Taekman said. "Except I'm not sure you can ride a horse."

"I have my knee. I can ride. Minx never pays any attention to my kicks as it is. She goes at whatever speed Aleta's horse is going."

"Bertha rides," Aleta called out. "He can go riding every day."

"You may not feel much like riding once you start chemo," Dr. Taekman cautioned.

"Is radiation therapy as bad?" Stanley asked calmly.

"It saps the strength. You won't get your energy back for a year," Dr. Cook said. "But it usually doesn't have many side effects."

"The body doesn't like either one, does it?" Stanley asked/

"Both radiation and chemotherapy are serious assaults on the body," Dr. Cook said. "You kill good cells along with the bad. There are casualties in any major battle. Cancer is a superior force. You need to hit it hard."

"I do believe that's what I just did," Stanley returned with a seriousness the doctors hadn't heard before.

"Yes, you did," Dr. Taekman said. "I will just tell you what you need and let you figure out how to fill that need."

Stanley nodded. "I'm listening."

"The leg you have left must do work for its own health."

"Got that." Stanley said.

"Cancer feeds on stress. It's fertilizer to a growing plant. You need to work on reducing your stress."

"Makes sense."

"Don't take up smoking."

"I wasn't planning to."

"Good, because if you did, I'd have to tell you to quit."

"Consider me told."

"We aren't certain how much diet weighs in on cancer. The researchers just finished four major long-term studies that apparently indicate that a low fat diet didn't help stave off cancer; however, the studies were begun before the awareness that certain fats were healthier than others. One of the studies did find a connection between a low fat diet and a low incidence of breast cancer, so I recommend a healthy diet with reduced saturated fat."

"Aleta will love that one." Stanley quipped.

The voice from the other side of the curtain said, "I like all the recommendations."

"Finally, since you can afford it," Dr. Taekman said, "I recommend regular bone scanning—every three months for the first year and then every six months. If your oncologist won't order them, I will."

"Do you have an oncologist?" Dr. Cook asked.

"I had one. I didn't like him. I won't be going back."

"Find an orthopedic oncologist," Dr. Cook suggested. "Meanwhile, Dr. Taekman and I will fill in as we are both officially your doctors."

Dr. Taekman looked askance at his fellow doctor.

"Where did that come from?" Dr. Taekman asked.

"Stanley has some weird notions about doctors."

Dr. Taekman raised an eyebrow as he looked at Stanley.

Stanley felt compelled to offer some sort of explanation.

"I just didn't consider Wayne my doctor because he'd never given me a physical," he said, and then added hastily, "You don't have to give me one. I learned my lesson."

"You need to tell me that story, Wayne," Dr. Taekman smiled.

Dr. Cook pushed back the dividing drape,

"Aleta, Chief West wants you to stay one more day. They have a line on Stuart Fouts. He managed to slip out of the tracking bracelet."

"Then we both go home, right?" Aleta said. "Jamara can change Stanley's bandage."

"I'm going wherever Aleta goes," Stanley said.

"There go all those great meals," Dr. Taekman groaned.

"We'll sign you both out tomorrow," Dr. Cook said. "But I want you in a wheelchair for another week."

"Deal," Aleta said before Stanley could utter his affirmation.

"Stanley, I want your word. No crutches for a week."

"You've got it."

"Why do I feel as if you found a loophole?" Dr. Cook asked.

Stanley smiled long after the doctors left.

"What loophole?" Aleta asked.

"Come. Let me read you another chapter."

"No more silk scarf nights, huh?" Aleta said as she scooted over and turned her back to straighten her gown.

The scarf was slipped on so smoothly, it took her a minute to realize it was there.

He guided her head into his lap.

'Your grandmother brought the scarf with the books. Bertha told her I might want it."

Aleta smiled as she settled down.

Stanley felt her relax. He hadn't realized she was tense.

He began to read.

Supper arrived at five thirty, carried in by the smiling Arborville Chief of Police.

"Compliments of Alfredo," Lyle said. "He made enough for six."

"Who else is coming?" Aleta asked.

"Michael, Wayne and Bernard," Lyle responded.

"Bernard?"

"He's got two women in labor," Lyle explained. "All four of your parents are coming later tonight."

"We're going home tomorrow," Stanley said. "There's no need."

"Don't fuss, Stanley," Aleta said. "I will take care of it."

"Take care of what?" Lyle asked.

"Grams insisted on seeing the leg," Aleta said.

Lyle nodded knowingly.

"So what's your plan?" he asked.

"I thought I'd cut off a pair of scrubs a bit shorter than knee length," Aleta said. "Stanley wants to be prepared.

After Gram's visit, he's more convinced than ever that to be unprepared is to invite disaster."

"They won't ask," Lyle argued.

But Lyle was wrong.

"Let's see the leg, Son," his father said the minute he arrived.

Stanley pulled aside the sheet. Aleta's hand, which she hand moved temporarily, came back and rested on his leg near the knee.

Lydia burst into tears. Hubert put his arm around her.

"Doesn't that hurt?" Bertha asked, more concerned about Aleta's hand than the absence of half a limb.

Stanley smiled when he answered. "It actually feels good. The doctors say I'm healing faster than normal. Dr. Taekman says I need to exercise the leg."

"It will get plenty of exercise when you're fitted," his father began. "Why are you shaking your head?"

"I am not going to be fitted for a while;"

"Why on earth not?" his mother blurted out.

"I am going to let the leg heal first," Stanley said, "which is why I plan to go riding with Bertha every morning. Aleta plans to work mornings until the Fouts trial. Oh, Mother, don't frown. Aleta's not neglecting me. She was afraid that you'd think that. She's planned my whole morning for me. Bertha and Jamara will be busy doing nurse things while she's off doing lawyer things."

"How do you plan to get up on the horse?" Bertha asked.

"Robert is going to rig a hoist to lift me."

"I can do that," Robert said. "I will get Jack to help me. He's been worried that you'd get rid of the horses and him too."

"Can't you do something less dangerous?" his mother probed.

"This is what I want to do."

Lydia turned to Bertha. "He can hold onto the saddle horn, can't he?"

"I am riding bareback," Stanley said.

"What a great idea!" Bertha exclaimed. "That will use those upper leg muscles."

"But, Stanley," his mother worried. "If you fall off, there will be nothing for you to grab on to."

Stanley smiled.

"Then I'd better stay glued to the horse."

"It's not humorous," his mother protested. "It's dangerous."

"You know, Lydia," Bertha interjected. "I'd agree with you if Stanley were planning to ride any horse but Minx. She's like the old plow horse I learned to ride on as a kid on the farm. He might slip off, but he won't be thrown."

"It's a foolish risk," Lydia insisted.

"I will be taking a lot of apparently foolish risks, Mother," Stanley said. "You will just have to trust in the fact that you raised a cautious son who weighs the risk of anything he undertakes."

"I want you to outlive me," Lydia declared.

"I will try," Stanley said. "I hope you're planning to live for a couple more months because I haven't finished grieving for my leg and I would want to give your demise my full attention."

"I will try to hang on for a little while longer," Lydia joked. "So what else are you planning to do besides ride a horse?"

The talk became general and soon the leg was forgotten as the five talked about the dog park case, which Lydia had just completed.

Bertha sat back watching the four engage Stanley in a review of the case and in guessing which way the judge would decide.

Bertha listened to the verbal exchanges, delighting in the energy in Stanley's voice. She noticed that Aleta was a bit more subdued than usual. She had been relatively quiet during the whole visit. She was still sitting curled up next to Stanley with her hand on his leg.

Curious, Bertha thought.

She studied the face of her stepdaughter and found contentment there and nothing else. Aleta was at peace.

And why not, Bertha mused. Her husband was alive and seemed to be handling this particular misfortune with surprising aplomb.

As she watched, Bertha began to wonder how much Aleta had to do with this unusual display of energy. He had obviously moved on from the denial phrase. He was talking about adjusting to his handicap. There was no apparent anger or grief, both of which Bertha knew came before acceptance. He couldn't have come to grips with his loss this quickly.

Aleta caught Bertha frowning. She pointed to her robe. Bertha brought it to her and Aleta slipped it on,

She kissed Stanley lightly and said, "Talk about man things. I'm taking my two mothers for a little walk."

Pleased at being included, Lydia joined Bertha and Aleta who suggested they talk in the visitors lounge. It was empty and the three sat down.

"You are both worried about different things," Aleta said. "When I leave the hospital, I will have to be silent again. Before that happens, I want to assure you that Stanley is doing well."

"He seems to be on a high," Bertha commented.

"Why would that worry you?"

"Because he's lost something precious—a part of himself."

Lydia nodded to indicate that she was wondering the same thing.

"Stanley is a very private person. I spent almost thirty minutes in the shower singing this morning so he could weep in private."

"Once isn't..."

"He had hours to grieve before I arrived last night. I've taken at least three long naps today and as many showers. I only mentioned the longest one. I'm a puckered wide-awake prune. There will be more anger, more grieving as he comes to different levels of his being."

"That's how it works," Bertha said. "It's a process. As long as he's grieved, he'll be okay."

"Mom," Aleta said addressing her mother-in-law, "Stanley is feeling his way. We've been dancing every evening . That's not going to happen again for a long time. For some reason, he latched onto horseback riding as an alternative. I want him to live, but I also want him to enjoy life. He has to pick and choose. I can't do it for him."

"You are right, dear," Lydia said. "I had ...it doesn't matter what I thought. Obviously, I have some adjusting to do."

"I believe your concern pleases him," Aleta said.

"I came off sounding like such a mother."

Aleta chuckled.

"That's what you are. It is what we all are. In fact, had that been Gerard twenty years from now, I would have been much worse."

"I am so proud of him," Lydia said.

"You should be. You reared a superb man."

"And you finished him," Lydia returned.

Suddenly she began to cry. Aleta burst into tears along with Bertha. Lydia pulled out a handkerchief from her purse. Bertha did the same. Aleta used the sleeve of her robe.

Meanwhile, back in the room, Hubert asked, "What did Aleta mean by 'man talk'?"

"She thinks all men ever talk about is sex," Stanley said. "She forgets little nuances such as men don't talk to their fathers about sex and they never even suggest to their wife's father that such a thing exists, children notwithstanding."

"So, did the doctors say you'd be affected sexually?" Robert asked.

"Yep."

"They said it would pass eventually, didn't they?" his father worried.

"They're no longer concerned."

The older men exchanged glances.

"You aren't saying what I think you are saying because it's way too..." Hubert stumbled.

"Don't worry. It was consensual," Stanley said wryly. Then he turned serious. "You have no idea how much Aleta's acceptance of this has meant to me. She makes me feel whole and yet she doesn't deny what happened to me."

"You know, Son, there are all kinds of advances in bone cancer treatment."

"Dad, I'm more of an expert than the oncologist I just fired," Stanley declared. "Just believe this if you can't trust me. Neither Dr. Cook nor Dr. Taekman would have taken my leg if there were another choice. Dr. Taekman has done far more difficult surgeries than would have been required to remove a malignant tumor and replace the bone removed with a prosthesis. My case called for the alternative I chose."

"I'm... I am sorry. I shouldn't have questioned you," Hubert stammered.

"Tell Mother, Dad," Stanley requested.

"I will," Hubert assured him.

"Stanley, would it be alright if I shared what you just told us with the staff?" Robert asked.

Hubert interjected a note. "It would help. I'm sure they've been researching bone cancer and will be concerned that you didn't get good advice."

"You can mention Grandpa," Stanley said. "That will explain my research."

"We will do it tomorrow before Aleta comes back." Robert said.

The four parents stayed less than an hour.

When they left, Stanley lay back on his bed and Aleta pulled the drapes, lowered her bed and dimmed the lights. Then she went into the bathroom and came out with a large towel.

"Your crying towel," she said. "I'm going to take a long shower. I won't be singing as loudly as this morning, but you'll be alone."

"I can't cry on cue!" he protested."

"Seems to me I said that about sleep this morning," she responded. "Somehow you'll manage. Just look at your leg."

"I don't want to cry," he snapped.

"And I don't want you biting my head off," she said, shoving the towel in his hand with a stern admonition, "Cry!"

She spun around and walked toward the bathroom untying her gown as she did so.

His reaction was immediate. He couldn't follow her. He couldn't shower with her.

He used the towel to yell into. Frustration and wrath were given words of which Stanley had a plethora. They flowed from his mouth as tears of rage cascaded down his cheeks. He finally gave in to howling, thus letting his grief take over his body. H wanted his leg back.

Cancerous or not, it was better than none.

A short time later he was done. He wiped his eyes and took a deep breath. He finally believed that he had shed his last tear for his lost leg.

He would again be saddened by the loss of it, but he wouldn't cry again. He wouldn't need to. He'd turned his soul inside out in that outpouring.

He heard the shower stop and he scooted to the edge of the bed to let Aleta know he was finished.

Four stories below, he heard an ambulance siren approaching the Emergency Entrance.

CHAPTER 20

He only noticed the siren because other sirens started up seconds later.

Multiple care accident, he concluded.

He wondered if their parents were all right. Then he remembered that Aleta was a prophet. And she had sensed no danger when they left.

Aleta emerged from the bathroom tentatively. He whispered to her to come. The moonlight coming in the windows caught the droplets of water on her bare skin.

She held out a towel.

"I thought you'd want to dry me."

She approached him and he took the towel and began to dry her. He scooted back on the bed and told her to climb up on the bed so he could finish.

"Where do you want me?" she asked.

"Guess," he whispered.

He felt her touch him gingerly. Then she slowly straddled him. She was almost fully down when she stopped.

"Don't move," she hissed as the door behind the curtain opened. The light from the hall streamed in.

Aleta put her hands on Stanley's chest to keep him in place.

"Lyle, don't come around the curtain," she said.

"Don't tell me," he joshed. "I..."

His radio crackled.

"Listen to me!" Aleta ordered.

The urgency in her voice made Lyle pause, but only for a moment.

"Not now!" he said. "I've got an officer down."

"It's a ruse," Aleta shouted. "Come around the curtain and you'll see."

"See what?" Lyle said pulling back the curtain.

He fully expected to see Aleta's vision, possibly displayed on an imaginary television set. He wasn't expecting what he did see.

Stanley threw the towel over his head.

"It's Fouts," Aleta said without moving. "I need you to do what I say so no one dies."

"Go on," Lyle said. "You have my full attention."

Stanley groaned beneath the towel, but Aleta charged on.

"Fouts is waiting at the elevator door. He has a gun. He plans to take you hostage. He figures it will get him through the swarm of police gathering outside."

"What do I do?"

"Nothing," Aleta stated flatly.

"Nothing?" Lyle gasped.

"He's got a police radio. Any plans you make he will hear."

"He will take someone else hostage," Lyle concluded.

"They will survive. You won't," she predicted.

"I won't be branded a coward," Lyle declared.

"You would rather be a dead hero?" Aleta asked, upset at his determination to walk toward certain death.

"Yes," he said as he turned to leave.

"I have an idea," Aleta cried, hopping off Stanley. "I will be back, dear. Wait for me."

Stanley tore the towel from his face and reached for her.

"You aren't going anywhere," Lyle said grabbing for her arm.

"Try and stop me," Aleta challenged, running out of the room.

"Lyle, for God's sake, stop her!" Stanley cried.

West didn't need to be told. He sprinted after Aleta and squeezed into the elevator as the doors were closing.

"Give me your gun," she hissed. "And make sure you're in front of Fouts."

"You are going right back upstairs," Lyle declared, punching the fourth floor button.

When it continued descending, he unsnapped his holster and took out his gun.

"You wanted to be a hostage," Aleta barked as she grabbed the gun.

They wrestled for a few seconds.

"Do it my way and I live," Aleta said.

Lyle let go.

Aleta fell to the floor and tucked the gun behind her just as the elevator door opened.

"What took you so long?" Fouts charged, sticking a gun in West's face.

"I was busy," Lyle said, pushing the stop button.

Fouts saw the naked woman on the floor and grunted.

"You lead the way, Chief," Fouts ordered. "To your car."

West quickly moved in front of Fouts. He inched his way forward.

"Move!" Fouts demanded.

"Duck!" Aleta yelled.

West dropped instantly. Fouts, shocked by the voice, didn't turn. He couldn't believe the naked woman lying on the elevator floor would pose a threat. He yanked the lightweight police chief back to his feet with one swift motion. As he did so, he swung his gun hand to one side to keep his balance. His reaction was lightning fast. So was Aleta's. Her bullet plowed into the back of Fouts' skull.

His finger reflexively tightened on the trigger of the gun he was holding. The round from his gun hit the glass window in the examination room where several nurses were sitting on the floor, their hands behind their heads. They screamed.

Fouts fell on top of West. Lyle shoved Fouts' body off his back onto the floor. He grabbed his gun.

Aleta shot up and pushed the elevator button. The doors closed and the elevator doors closed and it ascended to the fourth floor. She ran as fast as she could to Stanley's room, put the safety on the gun, stuck it in the drawer in the nightstand and then crawled in bed next to Stanley who was too shocked by her flurry of activity to say anything. She buried her head in his shoulder and he embraced her as he always did.

"I shot his head off," she said, her voice quivering.

"Fouts?"

She reared back.

"Of course Fouts! I wouldn't shoot Lyle. He's our best friend."

He drew her close and said, "Well, you never know. You don't like being disobeyed."

"I can't go back to what we were doing," she confessed.

"That's okay. I took a cold shower."

Again Aleta pulled back.

"You did not!"

"No, I didn't," Stanley admitted. "Embarrassment took the starch right out of me."

"Embarrassment!" she exclaimed, pulling away again. "You had a towel over your head. I was fully exposed," Aleta charged.

"You called him in," Stanley contended.

"He was going to go die."

Stanley took her head in his hands and kissed her. It was a sweet kiss, albeit short.

"Thank you for saving my best friend," he said.

Then he bent over and whispered, "And this is for coming back alive."

That kiss was also sweet but much longer.

When he finished, Aleta said, "I shot to kill."

"Did you have a choice?"

"There's always a choice," Aleta said.

Lyle rushed in as she was uttering those words.

"You had no choice. His gun was loaded and the barrel was jammed against my skull. Thanks for yelling duck."

Stanley hurriedly draped a towel over his wife's shoulders. Lyle grabbed her robe from the nearby chair and handed it to Stanley who helped Aleta slip into it.

"I came for the gun," Lyle said calmly. "I told my men you were in hospital garb."

"Fouts knows," Aleta said.

"He'll be taking that knowledge to the grave."

"I guess that's one way to clear a case," Stanley observed.

"I don't know how Fouts managed to get the upper hand," Lyle commented. "My guess is some big money changed hands because the only one left in the room with the prisoner was one of my guys."

"You came up here earlier with some news," Stanley reminded him, tactically agreeing to change the subject from a discussion of Aleta's action.

"Lennie did more than give us his suitcase with his share of the ransom, he agreed to testify against Fouts to keep Butch out of jail. I came to tell you we had Fouts cold on all the bomb charges."

"What about the deal?" Stanley asked.

"My father was very persuasive," Lyle said.

"Lennie wasn't reacting to the fact that Fouts tried to poison him?"

"He slept through that whole incident," Lyle said. "Dad didn't tell him about it because at the time we didn't know who had hired Rosie Reed."

"So is Lennie going to listen to Butch?" Stanley asked.

"According to Dad, the fact that Vannella listens to Chief Peets and Peets listens to me and, supposedly, I listen to you made Lennie come to the conclusion that you were the really big boss."

"Me?"

"Well, it was you or me," Lyle quipped. "And a rumor like that would ruin my reputation."

"What about mine?"

"Who would believe such a rumor about you?"

"You father did straighten them out, didn't he?"

"He told Lennie and Butch that he didn't know why but it appears that both Frank Catalano and Sergio Vannella had put the word out that neither you nor your wife are to be touched."

Stanley groaned.

"They'll jump to the wrong conclusions," he griped.

"Probably," Lyle said. "But that's not my father's fault."

"He didn't straighten them out."

"Come on, Stanley. Both Frank Catalano and Sergio Vannella have made no secret that Aleta has saved their lives more than once."

"You're right," Stanley said, a bit dispiritedly.

"And you did tell my father to tell them they weren't to make Vannella or you angry," Lyle went on. "You brought this on yourself."

"I did that so that Butch and Lennie would know that they weren't to break the law anymore."

"It was a smart move," Lyle said. "Butch understands about not making people mad. You put a face on what the law demands. It won't be what's right or wrong. It'll be what would make Vannella or you mad."

"But I'm not connected to the mob."

"Everyone knows that. You're a children's lawyer," Lyle responded. "To most people that means you aren't smart enough to deal with adult problems."

"Lyle!" Stanley barked.

"It's a perfect cover for a very clever crime boss."

"Cut it out!"

"I will when you accept the fact that you are connected to the mob. Aleta saved the lives of two of Chicago's crime bosses. They feel they owe her. You are under their protection. The whole world knows the truth and everyone processes the truth differently."

"So what is your father going to tell Vannella?"

"That Aleta told him that when you were robbed, Butch persuaded Lennie not to kidnap Aleta. And then my father plans to tell Sergio Vannella that he is following your advice on how best to protect Butch because you feel you owe him for protecting Aleta when the chips were down."

"That's what happened, Stanley," Aleta interjected. " I know you traded the gun for me, but Butch was the one yelling at Lennie not to be stupid."

"I forgot about that part," Stanley admitted. "But Aleta's right. Butch doesn't really want to be a criminal."

"Your plan has a good chance of working," Lyle said. "Dad said that Butch liked it. When he left, they were talking about what Butch wanted to learn."

"What happened to the nurse Peets arrested?" Stanley asked.

"Peets put Williams in a room with Rosie Reed who tried to poison Lennie and told him she would be an easy one for him to practice on. Williams was angry as hell about being ordered to practice on a perp that supposedly knew nothing. His anger scared Rosie Reed because she told him about another place where Fouts made his bombs. That took us by surprise."

"Fouts could have directed someone from prison," Stanley remarked. "It would only have been a matter of time."

"Williams didn't like the task, however," West reported. "He said he'd never do that again."

"Why?" Stanley asked. "He was successful."

"He believes it was a fluke."

"Can Peets turn him around?"

"Peets says he needs to wait until Williams wants to nail someone really bad, and then maybe he can persuade him to try again."

"Peets is right," Stanley said.

Lyle turned to Aleta and asked, "You're going to tell Lauren, aren't you?'

Stanley realized then that Lyle couldn't shake the remembrance of Aleta naked.

Aleta answered him, "No, I'm not. But you are. Not because someone might have seen your chasing me down the hall, but because we're all friends."

"I wouldn't know where to start," Lyle said flushing.

"Start with Stanley putting the towel over his head," Aleta said. "She'll be able to relate to that."

Lyle laughed.

"You're right. That was rare."

After Lyle left, Stanley was unusually quiet for a long time.

Aleta finally asked him what was troubling him. She figured he was still upset about Lyle seeing them engaged in sexual intercourse. She was surprised to find that he had moved past that.

"I was looking forward to having someone to represent. I was all set to be the advocate for those women at Fouts' trial. Now there's nothing waiting for me to do."

Aleta was silent. She sensed the despair, but she couldn't conjure up a case. Besides a new case wouldn't work. He needed an old case.

Until that moment, she hadn't realized that Stanley wasn't ready to face strangers. Much of the bravado he had exhibited that evening was gone.

He had planned his re-entry into the legal community and now he had none. At least that's how he saw it.

Aleta curled up with her head resting on his leg. Stanley patted her on the head and laid back.

Both were spent.

Each had his own reason to regret Fouts' death. Each had private demons to wrestle with.

God granted each a peaceful night/s sleep. What dreams they had didn't waken them.

Lyle went home and woke up his wife.

"Aleta saved my life tonight. I need to tell you something. You may not like it."

Lauren woke up completely at his first sentence.

She threw her arms around her husband.

"I don't care what Aleta did to save your life. I gather you were going to be heroic and she stopped you."

"She said to start with the fact that Stanley had a towel over his head."

"No, Start from the beginning. Don't deliver the punch line first."

Lyle took a deep breath and began, "You know I was working late because Lennie Archer had regained consciousness, and I was checking on Stanley when my father arrived. It seems that Alan Peets had given him a pro bono case."

"No one does that." Lauren said, recognizing at once that this was going to be an unusual tale.

"I will tell you about that later. What's important is that Fouts had been caught and that he had sustained a minor injury in the gun battle. I wanted to tell Stanley and Aleta that we had caught Fouts and that was why I went into their room at the hospital so late at night."

The story unfolded from there.

When Lyle finished, Lauren hugged him.

"I am glad Aleta saved you. She is beautiful, isn't she?"

"Yes, she is," Lyle said, still caught up in the throes of honesty. "So are you. I like you better."

"Spoken like a husband who knows which side his bread is buttered on."

Lyle kissed her and thanked her. She laughed as she pulled off her gown. Lyle accepted her invitation.

CHAPTER 21

The nurse who entered Stanley's hospital room the next morning was new. She pulled the curtain all the way back, saw the young woman's head on the bandaged leg and shook her.

"You are hurting him," she scolded.

Aleta woke instantly, withdrew her hand from its usual place, scooted off the bed and ran into the bathroom and closed the door.

Stanley, who had been awakened by the same words, realized that the nurse was concerned with Aleta's head not her hand.

He heard his wife sobbing and he slid off the bed and hopped across the room, ignoring the nurse's vehement protests. He pushed open the door and leaned on the door jam, breathing hard.

"Aleta," he said, huffing. "You weren't hurting me."

"She said I was."

"She thought your head was too heavy for my leg. You know it's not. I've told you that."

Suddenly aware that Stanley was standing in the doorway, Aleta burst out, "How did you get here?"

"Hopped like Peter Rabbit," he quipped. "But I can't hop back."

"I'm on the toilet."

"I can wait until you wash your hands," Stanley said.

Aleta went to the sink quickly.

As she dried her hands, she asked, "Do you want to try?"

The nurse spoke up.

"Miss, I will help him back to bed," she stated with authority. "Then I will take care of that need."

Aleta ignored her.

"Lean on me, Stanley. Now is as good a time as any to try."

"Close the door," Stanley said.

"Shut the door, Nurse," Aleta ordered.

"I won't do that," the nurse said, standing stock still in the doorway.

"Ignore her, Stanley. You will have your back to her."

Stanley let go. When he finished, Aleta turned on the water in the basin and Stanley washed his hands.

It felt so normal. Stanley liked the feeling.

Aleta handed him a towel and then asked the nurse to help her assist Stanley to his bed.

After the nurse left, Aleta said, "You hopped after me."

"You were crying."

"I'm glad we're going home today."

"Do you think I really need to be wheelchair bound?"

"You promised you wouldn't use crutches," Aleta reminded him. "You aren't well enough yet."

"I will leave that up to you."

"Really?" Aleta queried surprised.

"I'm way ahead of the game now. I feel great. And I think it's you. You aren't holding me back one iota."

"Is now a good time to mention no horseback riding until Friday?"

"As good as any," Stanley smiled.

When the doctors showed up for breakfast, Dr. Taekman read the chart.

"You were hopping?" he blurted out.

Aleta inserted her comment first. "Only to the bathroom, and so he doesn't have to do that again, can he use crutches to get in and out of the wheelchair and in the bathroom."

"Yes," Dr. Cook said. "But nowhere else."

"To get in and out of the car?" Aleta persisted.

"He's not going anywhere," Dr. Cook said, eyeing Aleta suspiciously.

"No, definitely not, but I would like to be able to take him for rides. We have a van, you know, with room for the wheelchair."

"Yes, I know," Dr. Cook said. "Why is it I don't trust you?"

"Because I'm a lawyer and you've learned we're a sneaky lot," Aleta replied. "But I won't hurt him."

"You actually hopped and didn't fall down," Dr. Taekman reiterated.

"We're on a new page, Michael," Dr. Cook said. "Pay attention."

"Yes, Stanley can use crutches to make transitions," Dr. Taekman said. "I can't believe you had the balance."

"He was motivated." Aleta said.

"The nurse told her she hurt me," Stanley explained. "And she fell to pieces. I told you she would."

The doctors nodded knowingly.

Stanley hastened to add, "The nurse saw Aleta's head on my leg."

"What am I forgetting, Michael?" Dr. Cook asked.

Dr. Taekman shrugged and then added, "No swimming until the bandage comes off, but, isn't that a given?"

"I don't trust either of them. You'll see."

"But this time it's Stanley, not Aleta."

"She's changing him," Dr. Cook declared, then changed the subject. "I hear there was a lot of excitement here last night."

"Tell us," Aleta urged.

"You must know," Dr. Taekman said.

"We only know what really happened," Stanley said. "We want to hear the rumors."

"Where's breakfast?" Michael asked.

"He's still trying to persuade Grams that he can make his own toast," Wayne Cook said. "That's when I switched to cold cereal for breakfast."

"I don't like cold cereal."

Stanley spoke up. "I've come to the conclusion that prophets can't cook. I think that gene is missing and a prophecy receptor gene put in its place."

"I know how you handle breakfast," Michael said. "And Claude doesn't eat breakfast, but I need breakfast."

"Have you ever tried telling Martha that you don't like burnt toast?" Aleta asked.

"Don't do it!" Stanley put in. "Prophets are very sensitive people."

"You could always have breakfast delivered," Aleta said. "Alfredo would do it. Do it as a treat first. Martha loves pancakes."

"She never makes them," Michael mentioned.

"She doesn't like burnt pancakes," Aleta said. "She'll never let you cook, but she'll let you treat her to breakfast."

"Every day?"

"Why not?"

Just then breakfast arrived, carried in by a smiling police chief.

"I see someone had a good night," Stanley said.

"Yes, I did," Lyle said. "Thanks, Aleta."

"I'm missing something," Wayne Cook said suspiciously.

"Nothing important," Aleta said

The Praetzels left for home late that afternoon. Bertha brought the van and wheelchair. The family was all at the house to greet Stanley, but they left at five-thirty as usual.

When they had all gone, Stanley asked Aleta to kiss him. When she did, he slipped the scarf over her eyes. A protest rose to her lips.

"Wheel me to the kitchen. I'll direct you," he said.

She wanted to say, 'I have good clothes on', but she realized that while she couldn't see, he could.

As he directed her to strip, she wanted to point out that they couldn't dance, but then she realized he enjoyed their evening games as much as he did, so she relaxed. He wanted the rules to stay the same. She had no idea how he managed to get the casserole out of the oven, but he did.

He fed her as usual. She kept her hands folded in her lap until he told her he had buttered her roll. Everything was again the way it was before.

They cared for Gerard together with him carrying the baby in his lap while she pushed the wheelchair. Gerard gurgled and laughed as he rode on his daddy's lap. Later Aleta danced the two of them around the room in the wheelchair. Then Stanley read to her while she held Gerard who fell asleep cradled in her arms. They put him to bed and then went to bed themselves.

It was only then Stanley asked for something different. She didn't even have to think. She knew he loved her touch on his leg when he was sleeping and he knew she was more comfortable on her side of the bed, so he took his pillow and turned himself around. She lay down beside him as she had in the hospital and used his thigh as her pillow.

He was surprised during the night when she put one arm underneath his leg as if to hug her pillow. He wondered if she would try to fluff his leg. It didn't worry him. The arm underneath the leg brought new warmth with it.

When she woke early the next morning, she kissed him lightly on the lips and mounted him.

As she lowered herself, he whispered, "I remember where we were."

She laughed, but didn't speak.

When they finished, she lay on top of him for a long while. He wrapped his arms around her, not wanting to let go. She didn't move, but relaxed into his embrace.

"Are you going to work today?" he asked softly.

She patted his chest lightly.

He untied the scarf, saying, "Bertha is early."

She hopped off, went into the bathroom and turned on the shower. From his upside down position in the bed, he had a full view of the bathroom, so he didn't move.

Jamara arrived while Aleta was eating breakfast.

As the black hands reached for Gerard, Aleta began typing on her computer.

"He needs his bandage changed. He needs to be bathed in bed. He will say no, but I am in charge of his care. He can use the toilet, but please accompany him. He was very unsteady yesterday. Both of you dress him the first time. Afterward, he will be happy to see just one."

The two chuckled as they read the instructions.

"He can ride anywhere he wants in a wheelchair. I will only be working half a day today and tomorrow," Aleta typed.

"Fouts is dead," Bertha said. "Wasn't that the case you were working on?"

Aleta nodded.

When she didn't elaborate, Bertha fell silent. Jamara, however, couldn't resist knowing more. The shooting had been all over the news.

"Was you the unnamed prophet?" she asked.

Aleta nodded.

"You shot him?"

Again Aleta nodded.

"Chief West story be pretty wild," Jamara commented.

Aleta raised an eyebrow.

"That he walked into an ambush because then only he would be hurt."

"Hurt!!!" Aleta typed furiously. "I don't predict 'hurt'. He walked into the ambush knowing he was going to die."

"But he didn't die," Jamara said.

"Because I changed things," Aleta typed. "I shot Fouts in the head and killed him. Someone was going to die and, God forgive me, I chose Fouts."

"He was an evil man," Jamara said.

"The choice wasn't mine to make," Aleta typed.

"Sure it be yours," Jamara retorted. "What be wrong with that? You think God doesn't know you be ready to save a friend?"

"I didn't ask," Aleta proclaimed. "I acted."

"You done right," Jamara declared. "Sometimes God needs to win a battle."

"Stanley will be feeling low," Aleta typed.

"You could be staying home," Jamara suggested.

Aleta shook her head.

"But..." Jamara started.

Bertha stopped her. "Let it go, Jamara. "He needs nursing this morning. That's what we are good at. Aleta needs to make sure the office is running smoothly."

Aleta left as Jamara was arguing with Bertha that one more day wouldn't hurt.

CHAPTER 22

When she arrived at the office, Alice told her that Mr. and Mrs. Brockbank and their attorney had scheduled a nine o'clock appointment with her.

Aleta glanced at her watch and held up ten fingers.

"I will try," Alice said as she picked up the phone.

Aleta had barely made the few steps to the office when Alice buzzed her.

"Mr. Waldenstein is on his way. He will be here at nine-thirty. I told him he might have to wait."

Aleta opened her laptop and began typing. When she finished, she printed the instructions. She left her office and went to Alice's desk and handed her the instructions meant for her.

"When the Brockbanks and Mr. Waldenstein arrive, show them into Stanley's office," Alice read aloud, and then gasped, "He's coming to work?"

Aleta nodded as she gave Alice Tim's instructions and hurried off to her mother-in-law's office.

"They wanted you specifically," Alice called after her. "Mr. Waldenstein was very clear about that."

Aleta nodded.

Aleta handed her mother-in-law her written instructions. Then Aleta opened her cell and when she reached Stanley, she passed the phone to her mother-in-law who read the first line, "Are you bathed and such?"

"Just started. Please tell me you called to tell them not to," Stanley begged.

"Put Bertha on," his mother ordered.

"It's my mother," Stanley whispered. "For you."

"Yes, Mrs. Praetzel," Bertha said.

"Bertha, you and Jamara have to work wonders. Aleta has handed me instructions. I am reading her words. 'Stanley has a nine-thirty appointment with Jacob Waldenstein who is representing the Brockbanks. I need him here. He's the firm's chief child advocate. I know you have this on speaker, Stanley. Didn't it occur to you I might want to talk with Bertha privately?'"

"Yes, that's exactly what did occur to me," Stanley said. "You also have me on speaker, haven't you?"

"Is Jamara there?" Lydia asked when Aleta pointed to the next part of the written instructions.

"Yes, Ma'am," Jamara said.

"He's to be bathed, shaved and dressed for the office. He can skip breakfast. He's done it before," Lydia read. "And change the bandage."

She paused and let Jamara acknowledge her orders.

Then Lydia continued to read, "Bertha, Tim will meet you in the parking lot behind the office and help with getting Stanley into the chair. I won't start without him. Stanley, it's a trap. I don't know what kind, but this is your bailiwick. I think that's why they insisted on seeing me."

Stanley's voice was firm when he responded.

"Get as much financial data as you can on the Brockbanks, Mother. Use Ed Ornstein. Tell him what you know. Summarize everything you get for me. I will go over it before I meet with them."

"See you at nine-thirty," Lydia read. "Don't be early. I want him to wait a few minutes."

When he hung up, Stanley said lightly, "I am all yours, ladies. Get me to the office at nine-thirty."

"Hair's too dirty," Bertha announced. "We need to wash it."

"Basin's too small. A shower be just right," Jamara said. "Got any swim trunks?"

"Lots," Stanley offered enthusiastically.

"Paul be wearing them," Jamara informed him.

Stanley's smile drooped.

"Do we change the dressing before?" Bertha asked.

"After. I needs to get some stuff so he can shower," Jamara said. "You be getting Paul."

Stanley lay in bed and thought about Jacob Waldenstein. He was an expensive Chicago attorney, the head of his own firm. Prepared, Aleta was his match. Unprepared, she wasn't. And he never came alone. He always brought along several associates who passed suggestions on to him as the meeting went on. So quick was his mind that he could be speaking and not drop a vowel, and yet still slip in some variation of the idea passed to him. He was a formidable opponent.

Stanley guessed he had deigned to come to their office to get a feel for Aleta. You can tell a lot about a person from his office. No doubt Mrs. Brockbank considered Aleta a lightweight and a handicapped one at that. Mrs. Brockbank must have heard about his hospitalization. She would figure the office was struggling to fill in.

He was Aleta's surprise. He appreciated her boldness in calling him. His mother would never have done it.

In addition, he knew his mother was reading from a script. Someday he would ask his mother how that came about.

He couldn't believe how excited he was.

Paul appeared in a pair of his swim trunks, which Stanley realized would probably split if he bent over.

"Let's get to it," Paul said. "How about me walking you in from here?"

Stanley scooted to the end of the bed.

"Wait a minute," Jamara called. "Go turn on the water. I need to waterproof the bandage."

Aren't you going to change it?" Paul asked.

"Not the tape on the thigh," Jamara replied.

"You stay here," Bertha said. "I will fix the water temperature."

She passed them with armload of clean towels. Stanley smiled. A lot of people are going to get wet.

After Jamara had wrapped the bandage in plastic, she removed Stanley's shorts and Paul helped him to his feet. Together they entered the spacious two-person shower and with Paul holding him, Stanley washed and rinsed his hair and bathed his entire body.

"I appreciate this, Paul," Stanley said.

"I understand, believe me."

The women were waiting when the two men stepped out of the shower. With his hands on Paul's shoulder, Stanley submitted to being toweled dry.

"Brush your teeth," Jamara said, "while I take off this plastic wrap."

The Bertha lathered his face, and while Paul and she held him steady, he shaved.

By that time he had shoved his modesty in the bottom drawer.

When he finished, Paul suggested he buy an electric razor. Bertha, hearing this, opened a drawer under the counter. It was full of electric razors.

"You don't like electric razors?" Paul asked.

"Not for the first shave of the day," Stanley replied.

"I suggest you learn to like them for a couple of months."

Stanley just smiled.

By nine-thirty Stanley was not only fully dressed, he and his wheelchair were in the van on the way to his office in

Willow Glen. Paul had returned to his painting and Jamara had begun to clean up.

Tim met the van in the small parking lot reserved for the law offices of Praetzel, Locke and Praetzel.

"There's a whole crew," Tim reported. "We had to get half the chairs from the library. I put them in your office."

"Aleta isn't in there, is she?" Stanley asked.

"She's waiting for you."

"How many associates has Jacob got with him?"

"Three," Tim replied.

"After you take me to Aleta's office, tell Chin, Jackson and Oliver to join us in my office," Stanley said. "I want them to see Aleta at work. How is she handling the new computer?"

"Just like she did the other one at the school board meeting," Tim replied.

Stanley left the elevator and stopped at Alice's desk.

"I will have lunch with the staff. No interruptions until then."

Alice nodded.

Tim rolled Stanley into Aleta's office and shut the door. One of Waldenstein's associates stopped Tim as he was coming out.

"We're ready to start."

"We need more chairs," Tim said. "I will have our associates bring them."

Chin, Jackson and Oliver were surprised and pleased at the invitation. That it came from Stanley was an added bonus. That he was going to have lunch with them afterward energized them all. They each marched into Stanley's office, set their chairs alongside Stanley's desk and sat down.

"Where's Mrs. Praetzel?" Jacob Waldenstein asked.

"Coming," they chorused.

One of Waldenstein's associates noted that none of the associates from Praetzel, Locke and Praetzel had a notepad and whispered to another, "They can't even pass notes."

"How long have you been with Waldenstein?" Roland Chin asked the whisperer.

"Three years," the man responded proudly.

"How many cases have you tried?"

"Two."

"Mr. Jackson, how many months have you been with Praetzel, Locke and Praetzel?" Roland Chin asked.

"Same as you. Six months." Jackson replied, puzzled.

"How many cases have you tried?" Chin asked.

"By myself?"

"Or as lead attorney."

"Counting the small ones?"

"Yes."

"Sixteen."

"Gentlemen," Roland Chin concluded. "We aren't here to pass notes. We are here to observe. Mr. Waldenstein's reputation precedes him."

"This is not a classroom," the original whisperer huffed.

Jacob's warning glance told him he was out of line.

The door opened and Tim wheeled Stanley into the room.

Jacob rose and said, "Stanley, how good to see you. I thought you were in the hospital."

"Got home yesterday, Jacob. May I present my wife, Aleta."

Stanley introduced his staff while Tim brought in a small table and set a laptop on it.

Then Tim helped Stanley into his chair behind the desk.

Aleta handed a note to Tim who read it aloud explaining that Mr. Praetzel had found sitting upright painful before the surgery and she wanted him to be able to lean back if he needed to do so.

"The surgery was recent then?" Jacob Waldenstein asked politely.

Aleta typed and Tim read her words as she typed them, "Yes. This is his third day post-op. The surgeons removed the lower half of his left leg on Monday."

Stanley kept a straight face as he saw the shocked expressions on the faces of the Waldenstein group and Mr. Brockbank. Only Mrs. Brockbank seemed oblivious to the magnitude of that announcement.

She burst right in.

"Who gives a rat's ass? What you're doing to my son is unconscionable!"

Aleta remained expressionless as she typed.

"Mrs. Brockbank, do you know what happened Tuesday night?"

"You shot someone."

Tim again read Aleta's words as she typed them.

"As long as we all know my husband and I have had a rough few days, let's get down to business. You're here to talk about your son's responsibility to his two unborn children and to their mothers."

"He's a boy. He's a minor. He shouldn't be held accountable," Charlene Brockbank proclaimed.

"Mrs. Brockbank, you have one of the finest lawyers in Chicago representing you. You have no idea what you are saying. I suggest you let him speak for you."

"I will speak for myself!" Charlene Brockbank declared.

Aleta nodded at Tim who turned on the tape recorder.

"Mrs. Brockbank," Jacob Waldenstein said. "Perhaps you would be better served if we approached this in a more orderly fashion. If you will permit me…"

"I will repeat what I said. He's a child. She can't mortgage his future because some foolish girls went to bed with him. She can't make him pay for their children just because they refuse to get abortions. He's not of age. He didn't rape them. He fooled around. It was innocent fun. We'll offer them a nice one-time settlement and they'll take it or they will wish they had."

Jacob Waldenstein said, "May I have a moment with my client?"

"No," Tim said strongly, reading the two exclamation marks as evidence that Aleta felt strongly. Then he continued. This is not a court. Your client isn't under oath. That she is a foolish woman is apparent. I want to know how foolish. And I'll tell you this. If we ever go to court and you don't call her as a witness, I will. Now let me tell you where I am coming from."

The room stilled as Tim read Aleta's words. The quiet grew and Tim's voice added timbre to the words he read.

"I shot a man on Tuesday, an evil man with a self-centered mother. He had raped numerous very elderly women so enraged was he at his mother's manipulating of him. Your son, Mrs. Brockbank, is walking down the same path. My job is not to stop, help, defend or save him. My job is to help his victims."

Tim stopped for a minute and let Aleta get ahead of him.

"With that in mind, Mrs. Brockbank, you have the proverbial snowball's chance in hell of protecting him from me. I will see that he suffers the consequences of his actions. He may be seventeen, but that no longer protects teenage murderers from being tried as adults. Consider him unprotected."

Mrs. Brockbank tried to interrupt, but Tim wouldn't let her.

"You son deliberately tried to impregnate three young women. His was a diabolical scheme, meant to visit suffering and deprivation upon innocent women, innocent in the sense that they had done him no ill. He raped their future. He spoiled their dreams. When he poked a hole in the condom, he violated their right to choose not to be a parent.

He did that and now he thinks he can walk away free?

"Justice demands that the perpetrator of an act be called into account. Mr. and Mrs. Brockbank, you son will be called into account. Make no mistake about that. My husband is a child advocate. I am a victim's advocate. If you satisfy him, I will not crucify you along with your son. As you, Mrs. Brockbank, have said repeatedly, he is a child. He is not responsible. More and more the law is making the parents responsible for the acts of their children. His were deviant acts, unconscionable attacks visited upon three women whose only crime was that they found him extremely attractive. Two have suffered an irreplaceable loss of their girlhood and been forcibly thrust into the adult role of mother, and worse yet, single mother. I cannot restore what they have lost. No one can. But I can see that Carlton understands that what he does has consequences. That is a lesson, Mrs. Brockbank, which you have failed to teach him. We will do it for you."

Having typed that, Aleta stopped, shut her laptop, turned and smiled at Stanley.

She blew him a kiss and then walked out of the room, her laptop tucked under her arm.

For several long moments, the entire room stared at the closed door in disbelief. Stanley swallowed his laugh. What an exit!

Stanley broke the silence.

"You came here with an offer and a request, Jacob," he said. "Let's start with the request. The answer is no. As for the offer, don't bother. I know what Carlton is worth."

"His money is in a trust fund," Charlene Brockbank proclaimed,

"Your lawyer purposely avoided my mother for that very reason. She is an expert in trust law," Stanley responded.

"He avoided her because I told him to," Charlene Brockbank claimed.

"Then, that was a smart move," Stanley remarked, "however, futile."

"Tell him what we want," Charlene Brockbank insisted.

"I know what you want," Stanley said. "And I know what your offer is. Let me tell you what we might agree to."

Jacob Waldenstein turned to William Brockbank. "Tell your wife she has had her say."

"Shut up," William said bluntly.

"What terms do you want?" Jacob Waldenstein asked.

"Carlton stays in continuation school."

"Never!" Charlene Brockbank burst out. "We will send him to a private prep school."

"As long as he doesn't return to Tri-City High," Stanley said. "Second, he gives one of this trust funds to each of his unborn children."

"They're his!" Charlene sputtered. "You can't have them. They can't get them, can they?"

"Go on," Jacob said evenly, ignoring the outburst.

"All medical expenses related to the pregnancy. A college education for each of the mothers and regular child support payments until the child reaches eighteen."

Stanley stopped, glanced over at Roland Chin and raised a brow in inquiry.

"Mr. Praetzel," Roland said politely. "You forgot all legal expenses connected with the case."

The young Waldenstein associates drew in their breath collectively. They were stunned.

Stanley smiled at Chin.

"Must have lost a few brain cells with that half leg. Thanks."

He glanced at the newer of his two black associates who leaned forward in his chair.

"Nigel?" he asked.

Nigel Oliver plunged right in. "Child support payments shouldn't stop at eighteen. Remember the case where the birthdays of the children fell in the middle of their senior year in high school. Payments should go a couple months past high school graduation just in case he can't decide what he wants to do."

"Three months or six?" Stanley asked.

"Three will give him a vacation," Nigel said. "Six is too much of a vacation."

Stanley looked at his other black associate.

"Come on, Andrew, what else did I leave out?"

"Children's medical expenses, say anything over five hundred dollars a year."

"Mr. Waldenstein, did you get all that because my recorder did."

Nigel coughed and Stanley looked over at him.

"Mr. Praetzel, I just thought of another."

"Go ahead, Nigel,"

"Suppose one of the girls has twins?"

"Good point," Stanley said. "That will be in the contract."

"Any wiggle room?" Jacob asked looking directly at the three young men.

All three associates nodded.

Waldenstein's associates' mouths dropped open. Jacob Waldenstein smiled smugly.

"Okay, Gentlemen, where is there wiggle room?" Stanley asked calmly.

"We could ask for graduate school for Brittany," Roland Chin said first. "She's brilliant. And she won't have time for part time work to save money for graduate school with both college classes and a baby."

Waldenstein's eyes widened.

"And the kids should get lessons," Andrew Jackson suggested. "Music, dance, skiing, swimming, ice skating—if the child is talented. That would be too much for a single mother."

"Music lessons even if they aren't talented," Chin put in. "Everyone needs music lessons. That's basic."

"Horseback riding lessons," Nigel added. "All the kids in this area seem to get them."

"They're expensive," Chin said.

Mr. Waldenstein, do you want them to go on?" Stanley asked.

"No, I've heard enough," Jacob said coolly. He'd called the man's bluff and lost.

"We'll draw up the contract after we speak with our clients," Stanley said.

Mr. Waldenstein rose.

"We will wait to hear from you."

"That's it?" Charlene Brockbank spat out angrily. "That's not what we came for."

Jacob Waldenstein scowled at his outspoken client.

"We got exactly what we came for—a counter offer. As soon as we have it in writing, we will discuss it."

"Tim, escort the gentlemen out," Stanley said.

Tim rose and opened the door.

Jacob Waldenstein extended his hand across the desk.

"Sorry about your leg," he said.

"Thanks," Stanley said politely, shaking the famous lawyer's hand.

When the Brockbank group left, the associates crowded around Stanley's desk.

"Where did you come up with those demands?" Roland Chin asked. "You didn't know they were coming."

"He's an expert," Andrew declared. "That's what experience does for you."

"If you're smart enough," Nigel Oliver put in. "I thought Jacob Waldenstein was a top lawyer."

"He is in his area of law, not in mine," Stanley explained. "That's why he asked for Aleta. He figured she wasn't an expert either. You guys were great, by the way."

"Didn't we make too many demands?" Nigel asked.

"We'll wind up in court if we don't allow them to hack at our counter-offer a little bit. Jacob knows where the soft spots are, so some of your suggestions are toast," Stanley commented.

"I would hate for them to take away the lessons," Roland Chin said.

"If we get the trust fund we asked for, there will be enough money for lessons and medical contingencies," Stanley pointed out.

"So what good were our suggestions?" Chin asked.

"Your three brought our goal closer to reality. You literally overwhelmed Jacob Waldenstein. He had underestimated us all."

"I wish Mrs. Praetzel had been here," Chin said.

"Her leaving was well-programmed," Stanley said. "There is a time when one's leaving rattles one's opponent. And Gentlemen, that is always a good stratagem."

The three associates left and Stanley buzzed Alice and told her he was expecting a call from Jacob Waldenstein. Then he called his mother.

"My wife has wandered away. Is she there?"

"Yes. Do you want her back?"

"I am going to nap until lunch. She had better be back by then or I will banish her forever."

"I will pass along your message."

She turned to Aleta.

"It went well. He's napping now, but he's eating lunch here."

Aleta raised a brow in query.

"He sounded happy," her mother-in-law remarked.

"I took a terrible chance," Aleta typed. "With the Fouts' case gone, he'd lost his incentive. He had planned to be the victim's advocate on that one."

"Bertha told me that it was a Herculean effort on the part of everyone to get him dressed," Lydia said. "Paul held him up in the shower after Jamara wrapped his bandage in plastic. Bertha insisted he have clean hair. Paul persuaded him to use an electric razor for the next few months. He has one, hasn't he?"

"He has a drawer full," Aleta typed, chuckling. "He likes to start the day with a close shave."

She paused and then typed, "Can Carlton's trusts be accessed?"

"Probably not."

"Then he won't pay," Aleta typed.

"Stanley will find a way," Lydia assured her. "He's in his bailiwick."

"Waldenstein is used to winning," Aleta typed. "He has a presence that's hard to battle against. I had to focus on Mrs. Brockbank."

"That was smart," Lydia said. "Why don't you take tomorrow off? Go horseback riding with Stanley."

Suddenly, Aleta burst into tears. She began typing rapidly on her computer.

A light blinked on the phone on Lydia's desk.

"Stanley has a call," Lydia said. "Who knows he's here?"

Aleta turned the computer around so Lydia could read what she had typed.

"Remember how proud Stanley was when he could swing his leg over a horse's back like an expert?"

Lydia nodded.

Aleta closed her laptop, wiped her eyes and left Lydia's office. She eased herself into her husband's office and listened to his half of the conversation.

"Yes, I understand," Stanley was saying. "The answer is yes. If Carlton leaves and goes to military school that will be the end of that part."

He smiled at Aleta and went back to taking notes. Aleta couldn't make out his scribbles. Mostly they were numbers. Stanley finished by promising the contract would be ready the next afternoon.

When he hung up, he shouted, "We got it all!"

Aleta stared at him. She didn't know what that meant.

He buzzed Alice.

"I want the entire legal staff in my office," he said. "What a victory!"

Within seconds the firm's legal staff began to file into Stanley's office. They sat in the chairs not yet returned to the library and the various offices and waited, their curiosity held in check by the anticipation of good news.

Stanley didn't keep them waiting.

"We rarely get a victory such as we got today. We got everything we asked for. A million dollar trust fund for each unborn child, a college education for their mothers, medical bills paid for the pregnancy, catastrophic medical insurance for the two unborn, child support until eighteen and a half, special tutoring or coaching in any area the child is interested in and our fee paid up front if I will accept a lump sum payment of one million dollars, which I did."

The room was silent. It was an awesome victory. An impossible outcome from a simple meeting.

Lydia broke the silence.

"Who writes the contract?"

"We do," Stanley said. "It has to be ready by tomorrow afternoon, signed by the parents of both girls."

"What about Carlton?" Nigel asked.

"He's being shipped off to military prep school, something he has fought against for three years."

"He will hate it," Chin said. "It's the worst kind of punishment for a guy like that."

"How come?" Nigel asked.

"He'll be thrown in the midst of a whole bunch of Carlton Brockbanks. And there will be no girls."

"How come we won?" Nigel asked, accepting Chin's evaluation as valid.

"It appears that William Brockbank is interested in the welfare of his grandchildren," Stanley remarked.

"He has deep pockets," Hubert remarked. "He's afraid of a lawsuit."

"That goes no further than this room," Stanley ordered.

"Why did we get our fee up front?' Roland Chin asked.

"Aleta said that if I was satisfied, she would not take them to court. They came here to assess her commitment to the case.   What they found out was that unprepared and without a voice, she was too formidable an opponent. They don't dare not satisfy me. My demands were on the high side, but still within reason.   Thanks to all of those in the room with me, we got a lot of nice extras."

"Like music lessons," Chin noted.

Everyone laughed.

CHAPTER 23

Lydia received a phone call at lunch and immediately took Hubert aside. All anyone heard was Hubert saying, "I will handle it."

Hubert followed Stanley and Aleta into Stanley's office and closed the door.

"You put me in charge of dealing with the girls' parents. Negotiating contracts is not my forte. Too much is on the line here. You two know these people. You've been fighting for them from the start. They need your input, not mine."

Aleta looked at Stanley.

"We will do it," Stanley decided.

"Are you up to it?" Aleta typed.

"I believe I am," Stanley replied. "Aleta get the files for both cases and let's go over our arguments."

Aleta nodded and left.

Hubert picked up the phone and punched in his wife's number.

"Now," he said, and hung up.

Stanley looked at him.

"Let's get you out of your wheelchair and back into the chair behind your desk so you won't roll out of here when I tell you what's going on," Hubert said.

Stanley stood up on one leg, hopped to his office chair and sat down. "I'm more mobile than you think. Now talk."

His father sat down.

"You continue to amaze me," he said.

"Talk!"

"Your friends are throwing a surprise party for Aleta."

"Aleta?"

"Hawk, thanks to Paige, found the last bomb. It was in the collar Auggie was wearing when he left your house. Harriet had a new one made for the dog show circuit with her cell phone number on it. She threw the old one in the utility drawer in her house."

"My word!" Stanley exclaimed. "It could have been weeks or months before we found that one. And if the dogs got excited, we would think they were just glad to see Auggie. We might even have slacked off."

Lauren is arranging the celebration. They all want to be there when Paige presents the collar--minus the bomb of course--to Aleta and tells her she can speak again.

Stanley nodded in agreement.

"Well, of course Paige should have her moment," he said. "She deserves it."

"Lyle is presenting the three dogs with certificates," Hubert added. "I don't know what that means."

"I do," Stanley said. "But why are you telling me about all this?"

"Because if you saw a crowd of people and cars at your house, you'd have turned around and gone to a motel."

Stanley laughed.

"Oh, Dad, you do understand me."

"I am so sorry about your leg, Son. I am so proud of the way you have handled what for you has been a grievous loss."

"I am not fully adjusted yet, Dad, but I am getting there."

"Do the doctors suspect that the cancer has spread?"

"No, but that doesn't mean that it hasn't."

"Are you afraid that you're going to lose the rest of your leg? Is that why you aren't being fitted for a prosthesis?"

"No to both questions."

"I don't understand."

"I'm not ready for an artificial leg yet."

"I can handle that," his father said.

Shortly after his father left, Aleta returned.

"Sit," Stanley said pointing to the wheelchair.

Aleta obeyed.

"Now put your hand on my leg and let's talk."

Aleta opened her laptop and put it on the desk. She pointed at it.

"When I said, 'talk', I meant that I am going to talk and you are going to listen," Stanley said, taking her hand and placing it on his knee.

"I am not sitting in silent obeisance while you keep from me what is really going on," Aleta declared pulling her hand away.

"You know?" Stanley asked, stunned.

Aleta looked at him quizzically.

"You spoke," he said.

She shook her head vehemently.

"Yes, you did," he insisted. "Do you want to know what you said?"

She shook her head. Her bewilderment told him she didn't know that she had said anything.

"You told me to be open and honest with you," Stanley said knowing that was God's message to him.

Aleta chuckled and nodded acceptance that that was something she would say.

"It is safe for you to talk here in this room," Stanley declared. "You just did and we are still here."

"It is safe, period." Aleta announced. "I feel it."

"Please put your hand on my leg and let me be honest with why I am asking you to do that."

Aleta placed her hand on his knee.

"I believe God is healing me through your touch."

"I am not a healer!" Aleta protested.

His hand kept her from withdrawing hers.

"Aleta, I am a lawyer. I don't use words carelessly," Stanley scolded. "Now what exactly did I say?"

"That God was…"

Stanley interrupted. "Emphasis on that first part. God is healing me."

He watched Aleta relax.

"All I need for you to do is let it happen," Stanley said. "Will you do that for me?"

"But if it's an illusion?"

"Two doctors have verified that I am healing faster than normal," Stanley said. "It isn't an illusion."

"God doesn't need time," Aleta contended.

"God doesn't have a pattern," Stanley said. "But I think it has to do with my choice."

"What choice?"

"Whether I was willing to let go of my leg to save my life."

"I don't understand."

"That's my problem," Stanley confessed. "So He is teaching me. The choice was bigger than I ever dreamed."

"Now you have completely confused me," Aleta said. "Tell me you didn't say anything about my healing you."

"I did."

"To whom?"

"Dr. Cook and Dr. Taekman didn't believe me. Harriet said all my so-called signs of healing fell in the parameters or normal."

"See!" Aleta exulted. "No proof."

"You are right," Stanley said. "But I believe. I need you to trust my belief."

"I can't share it," Aleta declared. "I just can't."

Abruptly she withdrew her hand and rose to her feet.

"Do you still plan to obey me as you promised at our wedding?"

She turned, startled.

"Of course. What brought that up?"

"I understand the message now," Stanley said.

"What message?"

"The one your grandmother delivered."

"The one you told me had layers?"

"Yes."

"And you found another meaning?"

"I was to let you work."

"You let me come in to work today. You let me take any case I want now. What more is there?" Aleta asked confused.

"Harriet said the message was more personal than that," Stanley elaborated. "I believe God is telling me to let you do the work even though you don't believe."

"I won't do it!" Aleta declared. "I can't."

"Good," Stanley said. "Come sit beside me."

Aleta did as he asked because reluctance wasn't part of her gift to him.

"Put your hand on my leg," he ordered.

Again she obeyed.

"Thank you, God," he said as he felt the warmth infuse his whole body. He closed his eyes.

"God, you and I need to have a little talk," Aleta said.

"Aleta," Stanley cut in. "Do the work. Argue later."

"I guess I can do that," she said as she watched the lines etched by pain fade from his face. She hadn't even realized he'd been in pain until his face showed its absence.

"Maybe I won't argue with You after all, God." Aleta said softly. "You seem to know what You're doing."

Aleta swore she heard someone chuckle.

The Prophet Series